MÀGÒDIZ

MÀGÒDIZ

GABE CALDERÓN

ARSENAL PULP PRESS
VANCOUVER

MÀGÒDIZ
Copyright © 2022 by Gabe Calderón

ARSENAL PULP PRESS
Suite 202 – 211 East Georgia St.
Vancouver, BC V6A 1Z6
Canada
arsenalpulp.com

The publisher gratefully acknowledges the support of the Canada Council for the Arts and the British Columbia Arts Council for its publishing program, and the Government of Canada and the Government of British Columbia (through the Book Publishing Tax Credit Program) for its publishing activities.

Arsenal Pulp Press acknowledges the xʷməθkʷəy̓əm (Musqueam), Sḵwx̱wú7mesh (Squamish), and səl̓ilwətaʔɬ (Tsleil-Waututh) Nations, custodians of the traditional, ancestral, and unceded territories where our office is located. We pay respect to their histories, traditions, and continuous living cultures and commit to accountability, respectful relations, and friendship.

Text and cover design by Jazmin Welch
Cover illustration by Moe Butterfly
Edited by Andrew Wilmot
Copy edited by Catharine Chen
Proofread by Vicky Bell

Printed and bound in Canada

Library and Archives Canada Cataloguing in Publication:
Title: Màgòdiz : a novel / Gabe Calderón.
Names: Calderón, Gabe, author.
Identifiers: Canadiana (print) 2022022868X | Canadiana (ebook) 20220228752 |
    ISBN 9781551528991 (softcover) | ISBN 9781551529004 (HTML)
Subjects: LCGFT: Novels.
Classification: LCC PS8605.A4567 M34 2022 | DDC C813/.6—dc23

CHAPTER I

ANDWÀNIKÀDJIGAN

A'tugwewinu tossed and turned, unable to rest. Her breath came in short gasps, and sweat beaded her brow. She quietly got up from her pallet on the floor so as not to disturb the bed's other occupant.

In the adjacent room, A'tugwewinu perched inside a hole in the wall large enough to fit her comfortably. The air was stiff and hot—no wind from the opening to soothe her blistering skin. The sky outside glowed orange, a dull light emanating from the centre of her field of vision. The sky was always orange and grey, dim and grim. Sometimes the light was brighter, other times it vanished completely. Regardless, it was always hard to see. The landscape that greeted her was barren: rocks and burnt-out stumps, rotting bushes, rusted metal, and crumbling buildings, sand and ash and dust thickening the air.

She looked down at her arm, her skin bronzed and grimy, and softly rubbed the markings there. Fresh scratches—a pattern from a merchant who'd told her a story his grandfather had passed on to him.

She felt fingers gently touching the nape of her neck. Her lover, Bèl, murmured in her ear, "Nanichi, when did these markings happen?"

"This morning."

Bèl gripped A'tugwewinu with her strong hands and turned her around. A'tugwewinu looked into Bèl's warm, immeasurably deep eyes—effervescent hazel irises—and watched her soft, dark lips form a quiet smile.

"Do you want to hear the story?" A'tugwewinu asked.

A nod. Bèl held her hand, her fingers calloused from fighting. She tugged A'tugwewinu away from the harsh sky and arid air, back to the protection of their little pallet nest.

"You do it," A'tugwewinu whispered, holding out her arm.

Bèl looked at her solemnly, then turned her attention to the fresh markings. She pressed them, transmitting the need to listen and to learn. The markings triggered and sent a cold snap through A'tugwewinu's head. For a moment, everything was silent. Suddenly, she felt word after word barraging her senses—a flood preparing to burst forth. She took a deep breath and opened her mouth.

"It was a bright, cold day in April, and the clocks were striking thirteen."

She shared the story as she'd heard it, word for word. Afterward, she slipped into a peaceful slumber in her lover's arms.

■

A'tugwewinu sat under the metal overhang near the outskirts of the village. It was her own little place; only those closest to her knew about it. She fiddled with the hem of her ribbon shirt. The frayed edges tickled the nerve endings under her fingernails. Footsteps then. A'tugwewinu looked up and saw her mother approaching.

"Kwey, nmama," she said as her mother sat down next to her.

"Kwey."

They were silent for a moment, staring out at the calcified stumps and bushes smattering the dappled grey hills around them.

"The seconds made fun of Nokomis's shirt. They said I'm weird because I'm an eighth but I always make myself look like a first, so then why was I wearing second's clothes? They said something was wrong with me, and maybe they're right—maybe no matter how hard I try, I'll never be right." She bit out the words.

Her mother crooned as she gently held A'tugwewinu's face in her hands. "Before this world lost its way, people still carried their stories in objects and not on their bodies. When the Madjideye destroyed that world, Kichi Manido chose the Andwànikàdjigan nation to become the marked ones, so the stories of the people would never die. To be chosen by Kichi Manido to be a storyteller is a humbling honour, Winu. When you were born, not only were you a storyteller, but ayahkwew too. Kokomis held you in his arms, and he looked at me with tears running down his face. He had been waiting his whole life for another ayahkwew like him, and there you were. You are a gift, Winu. And people are often jealous of gifts that are not for them."

A'tugwewinu threw her arms around her mother and clutched her tightly. For a moment, all was calm. The wind gently caressed their tanned skin as grey ash kicked up around them, specks of it kissing their broad noses. They were warmed by the dull-orange orb in the darkening sky.

Then her mother began muttering in a strange language—something she did when visions consumed her. A'tugwewinu withdrew. She stared at her mother's eyes, which had turned pearl white, without pupils, and her mouth, which was moving constantly, strange sounds and gurgles bubbling forth. Suddenly, her mother shot out her hand and gripped A'tugwewinu by the bicep. In doing so, she projected images into A'tugwewinu, so the young storyteller saw exactly what her mother was seeing: fire, people *she knew screaming in agony, moving metal machines with weapons that could kill thousands and level entire cities.*

A'tugwewinu's mother let go. The second she did, the images vanished as quickly as they had come. A'tugwewinu gasped.

"Run," her mother demanded. "Run toward the south, as fast as you can. Hide if you hear anything. Run!"

The eighth looked at her mother, whose eyes had returned to their usual chestnut colour. Tears slid down A'tugwewinu's cheeks. Her mother nodded.

With a final salute, A'tugwewinu turned away from her mother and ran. She stopped and turned around after a few moments, looked just long enough to see her mother walking back toward their village, her gait slow, yet resolute.

"Nmama! Come with me!" A'tugwewinu begged.

But her mother didn't turn or stop. With a cry of frustration, the story-teller spun back around and kept running.

"Nmama will save Andwànikàdjigan," A'tugwewinu muttered to herself. "I would just be in the way. Everything will be all right. Just keep walking south. Nokomis and Nmama will save everyone and come get me."

But a few hours later, she saw massive flames rising to the sky, clouds of ash and heat billowing up from where her village once stood. She listened to the roar of hundreds of spirits rising from the earth.

Then she loosed cries of anguish, for all that she loved was gone.

■

While A'tugwewinu slept, Bèl planned the morning: a tender, warm awakening filled with lengthy kisses, the feeling of skin on skin. But something interrupted her thoughts. A sound off in the distance—a vehicle approaching. Bèl stiffened. Weeks on the run, never staying in any one area for too long, yet still the Enforcers had caught up to them.

Bèl shook A'tugwewinu awake. "Madjideye!" She quickly gathered the scant few items of clothing they owned, a handful of ration packs containing vitamin mush, and a half-empty flask of muddied water and tossed everything into their only duffel bag before grabbing A'tugwewinu by the wrist. They rushed out the back of the ramshackle dwelling.

Four Enforcers stood before them, guns at the ready. A'tugwewinu spun around to run in the other direction, but two more Enforcers stood there, cutting off their escape. A'tugwewinu's heart beat rapidly—it was all she could hear. The Madjideye had been hunting A'tugwewinu for years. Every time they got close, she felt her skin shake, her lungs freeze; it was as if time stopped, and she was powerless in the onslaught of sensations. The Enforcers had chased them out of their home in Zhōng yang and into the wilderness, and if not for Bèl's ability to calm A'tugwewinu and keep her breathing, they likely would have been captured before now.

A'tugwewinu's mouth went dry. She tried to inhale but couldn't. *Not now, not now!* she thought desperately, trying to simply breathe.

Beside her, Bèl sprang into action, reaching for the machete at her belt. Bèl relished the tension in her gut, the way her heartbeat slowed when she readied herself for a fight, how time itself seemed to bend backward for her. The thrill of the hunt, the frenzied need to survive—a seductive crescendo of bones snapping and muscles thrumming. She swung at one of the Enforcers.

Had the Enforcers wished to battle fairly, Bèl would have bested them all without breaking a sweat; however, a second Enforcer took advantage of the opportunity and fired their taser gun at her while she was poised midstrike. The wires connected on Bèl's arm and chest, and she went down, seizing. The first Enforcer slammed their fist into her face. Bèl's head snapped back, hitting the ground hard. Blood spilled from her split lip. The Enforcer kicked Bèl in the chest. The sound of her ribs cracking echoed in A'tugwewinu's ears.

"Bèl!" A'tugwewinu screamed. Her lungs burned.

One of the Enforcers spoke, their voice icy and robotic: "A'tugwewinu of the Andwànikàdjigan and Bèl of the Warrior Taino Nation, you are under arrest for treason against the Almighty. Any further resistance will result in your death."

A'tugwewinu reached for her knife. "You'll kill us regardless!" she shouted. She ran toward Bèl, but two Enforcers tackled her before she could reach her lover. A'tugwewinu grunted and shimmied valiantly, trying to get clear of their considerable bulk but not succeeding.

Bèl, still writhing on the ground, swung her legs to try and gain the upper hand against the now four Enforcers holding her down. "I'll find you!" she screamed to A'tugwewinu, knowing they would be separated, knowing the Enforcers would put them in prisons as far from one other as possible. She watched one Enforcer pin A'tugwewinu with a heavy boot to her neck, while the other harshly tied her hands. "I'll get you back, nanichi! I'll—"

A shot rang out. Silence.

"You were warned," stated the Enforcer who'd spoken earlier. They holstered their gun and motioned for the other Enforcers to follow.

A'tugwewinu craned her neck as much as she could. She saw the crumpled form of her lover, unmoving. Time stood still. Her throat was raw. A high-pitched roar filled her ears; her head felt like it was being split open. Disbelief clouded her thoughts as an invisible hand reached inside and clawed out a piece of her.

She stared at the blood pooling around Bèl's body. She stared even as the Enforcers dragged her through the gravel. They opened the rear doors of their large metal vehicle—its sides dented by harsh weather, the paint chipped and rusted—and threw her inside. It wasn't until her body hit the cold metal floor that she realized she had been screaming the whole time.

They drove for hours until they arrived at the nearest Enforcer compound. A'tugwewinu strained her neck and peered up through the slats between the metal coverings over the windows. She heard loud, grating clangs as gate after gate opened and then slammed shut again behind the vehicle. She could see a chain-link fence taller than several vehicles piled on top of each other. The top of the fence was fortified with coils of barbed wire that were covered in what looked like rust or blood.

The vehicle crawled deeper into the compound before coming to a stop. Moments later, Enforcers opened the rear door and roughly pulled A'tugwewinu from the vehicle. Rows upon rows of fences surrounded the innermost containment square. The Enforcers tossed her into a corner of the square, the darkened sky looming above them. Without even a backward glance, they left, locking the tall gates behind them.

Shackled in the centremost enclosure, A'tugwewinu looked around. There were small piles of garbage and shanty dwellings made from tarps tied to the chain-link fence and various broken objects— no substantial shelter to be found. In the distance, beyond the many layers of fences, a large square building loomed. Its walls were cracked grey concrete, its roof dilapidated and falling apart in places.

Other prisoners lurked nearby, observing the new arrival with fearful eyes. Most ignored her, though, content to make themselves as small as possible, to remain hidden from the Enforcers.

A deep sadness overtook A'tugwewinu. But it lasted only a moment before suddenly, an overwhelming fury took root and dug its hooks into her soul.

CHAPTER II

ZHŌNG YANG

The set-up was immaculate. Riordan needed only to execute xir devious plan and then xe could claim xir prize. After months of calculations and spying and prying information from questionable sources, xe had finally set upon a quest to intercept the largest resource shipment the Madjideye of Zhōng yang had ever received. This central city, with its concrete buildings and slipshod metal overhangs, smelled acrid and sour. It was a desert filled with detritus; glass shards and sharp stones were weaponized by the harsh winds, causing harm to unprotected merchants or travellers trapped outside the city limits. Within the city milled thousands of denizens, huddled in layers of torn and frayed blankets, hiding under tarps or within holes in walls. Some preferred the darkness of the underground. Zhōng yang was a difficult city at the best of times, and those left to scramble for themselves—the masterminds and the orphans, the backward and the disturbed—were its life force.

As far back as xe could remember, Riordan had been alone. Born without a name or parents or even feet, xe scoured the streets, making legs from small, thick wheels suited for rough city terrain and attaching them to an old pair of heavy-duty boots. Xe removed the sole of each boot and inserted wires and tech that whispered to the inventor exactly how to tinker with it in order for the gadget to work. Fitting the boots to handle xir weight without adding unnecessary pressure to the stumps above xir ankles was a feat accomplished only after years of trial and error. Unsure of xir age but certain xe must be grown by now, what with the amount of *hair* xe had everywhere, Riordan's only concern was providing for those littler than xir—those starving and forgotten, despised by everyone.

Stealing was the best way to ensure people ate, and the best people to steal from were the Madjideye. Those bastards took everything for granted, leaving the people to claw out an existence in all the muck and misery that surrounded them.

So here lay the largest caravan of resources Riordan had ever seen: containers, each bigger than any single dwelling in Zhōng yang, filled with food, tech, materials, and weapons. They needed only one—then they would be set for months.

Riordan tilted xir head to xir second in command, motioning for the distraction group to move forward, out from behind the enormous pillar of rubble they were using as shelter. The distraction group scuttled forward like insects, then, with a flash and a bang, they dropped their noisemakers—cans filled with chemicals that Riordan xirself had fashioned. Enforcers appeared suddenly from all sides, large, clambering beings covered in ridiculous layers of dark leather and metal armour descending upon the scene, appearing every bit as inhuman as the people of Zhōng yang believed them to be. They were heavy and slow. Riordan's small, wiry street kids scattered and disappeared before their oppressors could track them. An Enforcer tank rumbled its way into the mess, using a makeshift forklift to grasp one of the large containers.

Riordan blew a whistle twice. The street kids materialized again, tossed more noisemakers and gas bombs. Enforcers took out their guns and started shooting blindly into the fog. Riordan inhaled the chaos, the Enforcers' grunts of frustration, and the giggles of the children, who treated this mission like a game. The wildness of the situation was like electricity in xir veins. Minutes went by. By the time the smoke had cleared, the children, with their knives and wrenches and handmade tools, had removed from the tank whatever bolts and wires they could detach and emptied the container of food rations, tech, gear, boots, and anything else they could get their hands on. Riordan blew the whistle again, long and clear. The street kids dispersed in just seconds, the Enforcers chasing the few they could spot back into the maze of the city. But Riordan's street kids were wise—the city was their playground. The Enforcers were chasing ghosts.

Riordan leaned forward and sped home, as usual taking a roundabout route in case xe was followed.

Xir arrival was met with celebration. The children were full of food, their stolen goods haphazardly strewn about the compound. The outer walls of the compound were taller than several people standing on each other's shoulders, with dents in the discoloured stone. Mismatched openings in the roof allowed a view of the murky sky. Several half-height walls twisted through the large space, sectioning off areas for sleeping and inventing, as well as a small kitchen.

Tomorrow, xe would bark at the children to sort everything out. Tonight, though, they had won. Xe let out a roar of a laugh. The city was cruel, but for now, they had bested it.

■

Elite Enforcer H-09761 touched the concrete wall in front of them. An image appeared there, of a second with pale skin and fiery red hair and metal wheels for feet. The Enforcer had never before witnessed a smile like the one on the second's face.

Elite Enforcer H-09761 shuddered and turned left. The scent was in them now. It wouldn't be long before Riordan Streetking was in their custody.

CHAPTER III

PASAKAMATE

Nitàwesì was dressing a wound on one of the village warriors, who lay in bed. They rinsed fresh blood out of the cloth scraps in the bucket at their feet and returned to cleaning the jagged scars that extended down the warrior's breast. They didn't think the warrior would survive, but there was nowhere else to go for help—village healers were scarce, and Nitàwesì was all the Pasakamate had left.

In the dwelling's entrance stood Shkitagen, a tall second with two long braids tied at the nape of his dark-ochre neck and ending at his lower back. He pushed aside the tattered curtain. "Ishkode, my odey?" he asked.

Nitàwesì nodded and smiled at Shkitagen with an affectionate, albeit exhausted smile. They did, in fact, need fire.

Their ears were filled with the competing sounds of chemical charcoal being chopped to pieces with a rock and the warrior's ragged breathing. By the time Nitàwesì had sewn the last of the stitches and cleaned all the splattered blood, Shkitagen had started a roaring fire.

Nitàwesì placed their hands on the warrior's chest and closed their eyes, sharing a prayer. Then Nitàwesì got up and grabbed the bucket of dirty water, exiting the dwelling with Shkitagen in tow.

"How was your day?" Nitàwesì signed after handing the bucket to Shkitagen. Their hands were slow and sluggish after hours spent healing.

"Long," Shkitagen replied. "My father wants everything perfect for the wedding." He reached out a dark hand and grasped his lover's, rubbing the smooth, pale skin there with his thumb. Nitàwesì rested their head on Shkitagen's tall, broad shoulder and sighed.

"I'm glad your father is taking care of everything," Nitàwesì signed. They smiled contentedly.

"How many is that in the past month?" Shkitagen pointed with his chin at the warrior's dwelling.

"Six," the healer signed, grimacing.

Shkitagen growled. "Those damn hunters!"

Nitàwesì faced Shkitagen and ran a soothing hand up and down the side of their lover's thigh. "Shh," they murmured.

Shkitagen held Nitàwesì's chin between his palms and kissed them. He pulled back before things got too heated and rested his forehead against Nitàwesì's. "I won't let them take you, my odey," he whispered.

The hunters wouldn't take me anyway, Nitàwesì thought.

"Let me at least pretend I'm a warrior, so I can try to protect you," Shkitagen said, as though he were a mind reader.

"You're a firekeeper," Nitàwesì signed. "That's much more important." Amusement pulled at their cheeks.

Shkitagen raised his index finger, and a small flame spiralled into existence, dancing lightly on his fingertip. "I won't let them take me either," he said firmly.

"Come on, let's go see what your father has planned."

Hand in hand, the two of them strolled toward the heart of the village.

CHAPTER IV

FIRE IN THE SKY

A'tugwewinu walked away from her village—for how many days, she didn't know. Her feet were crusted with blisters and cuts, her shoes keeping more dirt in than out. When she first arrived at the concrete city, she thought maybe someone would have a pair of shoes for her, but she soon learned that these people, in their countless numbers, were very different from those she'd known back in her village. No one cared that she was filthy and hungry. No one cared that she felt like she was on the verge of death.

She tried at first to find someone to tell about her village, but no one had time for a hungry child pestering them for information or food.

She grew over time—how much, she didn't know. The days and weeks blurred together. The ribbon shirt began lifting over her hip bones where before it had carefully nestled atop them. She stole and lied, and with every passing day felt farther away from her people, her village, her core. The connection was waning.

Except for the ever-looming shadow of Death. Its gangly form hid in the dark corners of the city. She saw it everywhere, around every corner and *down every unwelcoming alleyway. It mocked her as she shivered herself to sleep, taunted her as she struggled to swallow when no spit remained in her mouth. She grew increasingly lonely in a city filled with more people than she'd previously thought existed. Death was her only companion.*

One night, a shadow fell over her. A'tugwewinu ignored the presence, thinking it was only Death come to claim her. But she felt fingers softly pulling at the tattered remains of her once-glorious shirt. She opened her eyes and found herself peering into the most beautiful face she had ever seen.

The angel crouched down before her. "I'm Bèl," she said, a melodious tenor.

A'tugwewinu sat up straight. "A'tugwewinu," she said. Bèl nodded, then stood back up. She looked down at A'tugwewinu and beckoned her forward.

A'tugwewinu struggled to rise. On her feet, she followed close behind Bèl, who seemed familiar in a way that confused A'tugwewinu. Had they met before? Had she dreamed of those eyes like gemstones? Of that voice?

She pondered the tether she felt between herself and this stranger as they skulked through the shadowy maze of streets. Finally, they slipped under a large metal box precariously poised on mismatched bricks, lifting it just enough for them to get under and shimmy through a hidden crack in a wall to enter a small room filled with cushions and random objects.

Bèl opened her arms wide. "Welcome home."

Tears welled in A'tugwewinu's eyes. Bèl had spoken with the same tone Nokomis used to speak in when she visited him. Her legs buckled then. Bèl's strong hands caught her and caressed her skin. Gradually, by Bèl's whispered song and her own sobs, A'tugwewinu was lulled to sleep.

∎

Hours passed, but ever so slowly, the ties on A'tugwewinu's wrists loosened, her warm blood lubricating the way. Finally freed of their bindings, her hands fell limp at her sides. She was wary of her surroundings. Eyes stared back at her. The stench of stale sweat and blood permeated the air. She lay down on her back and inhaled deeply, letting the acrid smells overwhelm her senses. She closed her eyes and prayed, remembering a conversation with her grandmother years ago.

"There was a time when the ayahkwewak were honoured. Every village had ayahkwewak—they were needed to act as the in-between for the spirits and the rest of us here in the physical world. Without ayahkwewak as the bridge, we would be in the dark about so much happening around us. We would be out of balance with the world."

"How do ayahkwewak talk to spirits, Nokomis?"

The elder smiled, his dark, wrinkled face lighting up. "You need to be very still and very silent, oshis, then send your intent. Kindly ask them for a message, offer them a gift for their aid, and they will come."

The old grandmother picked up his grandchild and gently sat her on his knee.

"I am ayahkwew, just like you, oshis. In a few years, when you receive your first marks, you will come to me and learn how to carry your role for our village."

Grandchild held grandmother, the smell of sage and asema and the feeling of safety and kindred souls cloistered around them.

"I can't wait, Nokomis."

A'tugwewinu sat up and looked at her wrist. Dried blood circled it like a bracelet. Her skin was rubbed raw from the restraints. She swiped at the blood, dragging as much of it as she could onto her fingertips.

Three deep breaths. Eyes closed. Focus on intent. She sat up, slammed her hand down on the ground next to her, and called for them.

"Giibi," she whispered, "I have nothing to offer you but this. Please accept my blood as offering and aid me."

It took a moment, but the soil whispered back. A'tugwewinu grimaced and opened her eyes. The veins in her forearm turned black, and blood poured from her wrists as if they'd been cut anew; it saturated the dirt beneath and around her. She felt an ache deep in her veins as portals opened beneath her body—dark circles appeared inside the bright, shimmering opening, and tendrils of blue light slowly slithered through. She gasped, her extremities tingling from blood loss. Pain formed behind her eyes like a needle in her brain—a telltale sign of the approaching drop. The experience was different every time. Maybe because the smell of her lover's blood still lingered, or perhaps because fear reverberated through the very marrow of this prison, the spirits showed themselves quickly. Her bleeding stopped. The earth heaved and sighed and shook slightly. Wisps of smoke rose around her in shapes that wound themselves around her body and tickled her soul.

Upside-down and backward faces greeted her, with antler and horn, hoof and claw. They spoke to her. The rocks under her warmed as the dirt cooled. Her ancestors whispered encouragement in ancient tongues. They reminded her: they were always there. Six-fingered hands that felt like mist and ash caressed her wounds, wove through her hair, and lovingly embraced her.

Time passed in a haze. Eventually, the smoke receded, the shapes dissipated, and the pungent smells and intermittent screaming returned.

A'tugwewinu opened her eyes. All around her, beings—physical ones—approached her corner of the compound with trepidation. The call of the spirits was bringing them closer.

An old one crouched near her and inched closer. "Wh-who are you?" he muttered feebly.

"I am A'tugwewinu, last of the Andwànikàdjigan," she responded softly.

"Sachit, from the travelling camps," the old one said in return. A'tugwewinu nodded, acknowledging her.

For a long minute, no one spoke.

"Is it true?" someone finally asked. "Are you really one of the marked ones?"

A'tugwewinu nodded. She stood up and removed her long soil-crusted cloak, baring her arms and torso, neck and back. Every inch of her skin was covered in little red symbols, shapes that would be foreign to everyone else there. She sat back down; the others followed her example. She surveyed the dozen or so prisoners who had cautiously approached her.

"How do you mark yourselves?" Sachit asked.

"We don't," A'tugwewinu responded. "When someone shares a story, we listen, and the marks appear. When we press them, we can share that story again, word for word."

The strangers appeared dumbfounded.

"Would you like to see?" she asked.

Several nodded. A'tugwewinu took a deep breath and reached for the markings near her right shoulder. She pressed them, and words poured out of her.

"In the beginning," she said, "God created the heaven and the earth ..."

CHAPTER V

LOVE IN CEREMONY

Nitàwesì carefully wrapped the pouch in crinkly paper they had traded for with some passing merchants. For days they had been carefully sewing together pieces of leather to form a solid pouch and used precious, beautiful beads of coloured plastic to adorn the strap, which—if he accepted this gift—would fit across Shkitagen's broad shoulders. Into every stitch, Nitàwesì imparted their prayers for love and a long and healthy relationship. This last gift would complete the courtship process.

Months ago, mustering every ounce of bravery they possessed, Nitàwesì had placed burn medicine on the doorstep of Shkitagen's dwelling, along with a piece of red fabric that symbolized their love. Known for being courteous and kind, Shkitagen had received dozens of such proposals every year since completing his coming-of-age ceremony, though he had never yet returned the gesture. But not a day later, Nitàwesì had awoken to find enough food for a week on their doorstep, as well as the piece of red fabric. They felt their heart lift, and all of that day, they had giggled like a child. People came to them with cuts and sprains, a few with morning sickness, *and some children with a cough, yet still Nitàwesì smiled. The old ones had looked at them with glee in their eyes, the young ones with jealousy.*

Months went by, and more gifts were exchanged. Today, if this gift was accepted, Nitàwesì and Shkitagen would be able to announce their wedding date.

Nitàwesì stood up, tightly clutching the gift, and offered the spirits a prayer for success. They pulled open the curtain, and there stood Shkitagen, a thick handmade blanket folded in his arms. Both stood speechless for a moment.

"Uh, well, uh, this is for you. It's going to get colder soon. I hope you like it." Shkitagen thrust the blanket out in front of him.

Nitàwesì nodded. "I love it! Green is my favourite colour," they signed.

"It, um, reminded me of your eyes," Shkitagen whispered.

Nitàwesì laughed. The sound was clear and melodic. Shkitagen looked at them, mesmerized, as if a miracle had just occurred.

"This is for you," Nitàwesì signed, their hands trembling slightly, a giddy feeling in the pit of their stomach.

Shkitagen carefully unwrapped his gift. "Oh! Did you make this?" he asked excitedly.

Nitàwesì nodded.

"I love it! It's perfect! I didn't have one, and I've just been using my pockets. You have no idea how annoying they are to clean. Thank you," Shkitagen gushed.

Both fell silent again.

"Do you want to come in?" Nitàwesì signed.

"Uh, yeah, that would be great, sure."

Shkitagen followed them inside. They sat together on the bed in the corner. Nitàwesì shivered slightly as a cold breeze pushed through the dwelling.

"Can I make a fire for you?" Shkitagen asked. "We're engaged now, so it's fine, right?"

Nitàwesì blushed and nodded. "The coals are in the box in the corner," they signed.

Shkitagen got up and went over to the small dug-out pit in the corner. He took out a few coals and stacked them in a pyramid. Then, eyes closed, he muttered a few words with his hand outstretched over the coals. Flames burst from his fingertips. They grew in size until they engulfed the coals. Once he was sure they'd ignited, he made a fist and muttered a prayer for the flame's longevity.

"For as long as we're together," Shkitagen promised, returning to the bed, "I will never let you get cold."

■

Nitàwesì lay in bed with Shkitagen gently snoring in their arms. Their wedding day had been spectacular—the entire village had come out to celebrate them. Both had promised in front of the spirits to honour and work alongside each other. Throughout the ceremony, they had gotten lost staring into each other's eyes, their love for one another consuming them. After the ceremony, Shkitagen had gone to his dwelling and grabbed his things to bring over to Nitàwesì's, and minutes later, they'd tumbled into bed, their clothes strewn about, giggling and kissing and gasping for air.

Looking at Shkitagen now, Nitàwesì still couldn't believe that this incredible, beautiful second was their life partner and that they were living together in their own dwelling. Nothing could tear this happiness away from them.

A cough—from outside their home. Someone pulled the entrance curtain back, and a village warrior entered. With him was another warrior, who was clutching their stomach.

Nitàwesì tapped Shkitagen's bare chest a few times. He woke, groggy and confused. "Wha—" he muttered, before his eyes focused on the wounded warrior before him. He gasped and jumped out of bed, naked, and dove for his pants. Nitàwesì tossed a gown on. Normally they would bind their breasts, but there was no time for that now.

The warriors looked everywhere but at the two inhabitants quickly dressing themselves. With some difficulty, the wounded one managed to heave themselves onto the medical table in the corner. Nitàwesì rushed over.

"What happened?" they signed rapidly. Their eyes narrowed to slits.

"A rogue band of hunters tried to infiltrate the eastern point of the village, but our warriors pushed them back. My sibling is the only one injured—a rigged explosive detonated as the hunters retreated."

"Help me take their shirt off," Nitàwesì signed.

It was rare for hunters to use projectile weapons. Enforcers had sophisticated weapons, but they didn't come out as far as this little shantytown. The Madjideye based themselves in the cities, although every few years or so, they would visit, ask questions, and then leave. Nitàwesì had heard that they sometimes took children with them, but never from Pasakamate. The elders would never let them take a single person, no matter how high the resources offered in trade.

With the warrior's shirt removed, Nitàwesì was able to observe the wound before them. *Right side of the stomach—the liver has possibly been hit.* "This is going to hurt. Hold them down," they signed.

Shkitagen was off in the corner of the room, making fire and boiling putrid water in hopes of purifying it. He rushed over at Nitàwesì's command and pinned the warrior's shoulders to the table. The other warrior grasped his sibling's wrists firmly.

"There is no exit wound. This will take time," Nitàwesì signed, looking grim.

Time was of the essence if the warrior was to survive. Nitàwesì had learned their healing gift from their parents: one was Anishinabeg, from Andwànikàdjigan, a village a week or two's journey to the northwest; the other was Mexica, from Mexico-Tenochtitlan, an enormous city many months to the south and ten times the size of Zhōng yang. The two had fallen in love while sharing their unique talents, the different techniques and spirits they called upon to heal the wounded and sick. Feeling a calling to travel, the couple had visited other Anishinabeg villages. When they stumbled across Pasakamate, they were concerned by the severity of attacks the village faced by both hunters and, at the time, Enforcers. Pasakamate had no healers, and so the couple decided to stay and help. Not much later, Nitàwesì was born, though that wasn't the name their birth parents had given them.

"They're seizing!" yelled Shkitagen.

Nitàwesì returned their focus to the wound. Holding their palm over the gaping hole in the warrior's side, they searched for the shrapnel. Deeper and deeper went their spirit into the wounded warrior, until at last, they discovered the distorted metal. They surveyed the damage. The liver had been nicked, but it was not irreparable. They took a deep breath and asked the metal to come to them, to come to rest in their palm.

The shrapnel didn't budge. Nitàwesì screamed in frustration. The other warrior startled—he had never before heard the healer make so much as a sound.

"Keep holding them down!" Shkitagen barked at him.

The warrior nodded and returned to his task.

Nitàwesì bit the thumb on their other hand until it bled. They squeezed their blood into the open wound. Then they looked up at Shkitagen and glanced quickly at the coals in the corner of their dwelling.

Shkitagen retrieved a piece of coal and placed it near Nitàwesì, who picked up the coal and pinched their thumb again, dripping blood onto the coal before placing it against their forehead.

Please, help me get this shrapnel out. I offer my blood in trade through this prayer. They pleaded with the healer spirits, knowing their prayers were as loud as if they had been screamed. Then they placed the piece of coal on top of the hand that was positioned over the wound, palm down.

They took a deep breath and looked up. Shkitagen nodded and returned to his task of keeping the warrior pinned. Nitàwesì placed their mouth directly over the piece of coal. A small, shimmering portal opened in it; the coal acted as a conduit between the healer and their helpers and between the healer's hand and the wound. Nitàwesì began to suck the piece of coal, letting the force of the small portal between realms do most of the work; the healer's breath simply guided things. The warrior on the table began to scream and convulse. Nitàwesì inhaled and let their spirit tug the shrapnel up from where it was lodged. Slowly, bit by bit, inhale by inhale, the metal moved.

Almost a dozen minutes later, Nitàwesì felt the shrapnel surfacing. They tossed the coal into the fire and lifted their palm from the warrior's body. Resting there at the wound's surface was the offending piece of metal. With their thumb and forefinger, Nitàwesì carefully pulled it out from the warrior's flesh. A gush of black blood flowed freely as they did so.

"Poison!" Nitàwesì signed. They swayed and buckled slightly.

Shkitagen was beside them in an instant, supporting their weight. "What do you need?" he asked. He pulled over one of the chairs and helped them onto it.

"Hot water and some of the mashkiki." Nitàwesì signed sluggishly with their blood-covered hands. They put their face in their palms, leaving red smears on it.

This gift is to be used for the people, Nmama had once told them. *You will get tired, you will feel sick, you will feel faint, but you can transfer it from you to Ahkigowin aki and then you will be better again.*

With an exhalation, a gust of resolution, Nitàwesì dipped one of their hands into the steaming hot water in the bucket Shkitagen had just placed on the table. The water smelled bitter and sharp—the mashkiki was already mixed in and ready to do its work. Placing one hand in the liquid and the other on the warrior's wound, Nitàwesì focused their intent. The water and mashkiki slipped into their body through the pores of their hand, then entered their bloodstream. It coursed through them until it exited out the other palm, directly into the wound and the warrior's bloodstream—drop after drop, until the warrior's ancestors and guides and spirits rushed into Nitàwesì's head and told them it was enough.

Nitàwesì removed their hand from the bucket and thanked their ancestors and those of the warrior for their help. They nodded to Shkitagen, who picked up the bucket and poured the remaining water over the warrior's wound. Nitàwesì then reversed the process: they removed their hand from the wound, then sealed their lips over their palm and sucked out the poison, spitting it into the bucket.

After repeating the process for an hour, the same amount of water that had entered the warrior's body had been returned to the bucket. This time, however, it was black and grey and filthy. The warrior's wound had sealed, colour had returned to their face, and they were breathing normally, asleep now after everything they had endured.

Their work done and their spirit returned inside of them, Nitàwesì took some deep breaths.

"Are you blood related?" they signed to the warrior standing by.
"Enh," he muttered.

Nitàwesì looked at Shkitagen and motioned toward their medic kit.

"They lost a lot of blood. Can you give them some of yours?" Nitàwesì asked the warrior.

He nodded. "Yes, of course. And kichi miigwech—we lost our sister a few months ago to hunters. I can't tell you what this means to me. Miigwech!" he repeated breathlessly, tears in his eyes.

Nitàwesì nodded. Shkitagen set up the needles and the transfusion bags—the last ones they had. More would have to be made or traded for, and soon. Once everything was in order, he returned to Nitàwesì's side. They looked paler than usual, sweat beading their brow, their skin slightly green.

Here it begins, he thought.

Sure enough, Nitàwesì grabbed the bucket full of black water and vomited more into it, over and over, until all that came out was ordinary stomach bile. Hands trembling, they handed the bucket to Shkitagen, who carried it over to the fire and dumped out its contents. The flames— his fires never went out unless he asked them to—burned momentarily brighter as the poisonous liquid drenched the coals beneath them. Smoke filled the room. Shkitagen summoned the spirits in his breath and took a powerful inhale, then bellowed a gust from deep inside his body, pushing all the smoke in their dwelling out through a small opening in the wall.

He snapped his fingers, and blue flame emerged from his palm. He pushed the flame into the empty bucket to burn away any traces of poison. The task complete, the flame extinguished itself.

Over by the table, Nitàwesì let out a small gasp right before crumpling to the ground. Shkitagen ran over and placed his hands over his love's face. He picked them up and gently laid them on the bed.

"Are they all right?" the warrior asked, worried.

Shkitagen nodded. "You haven't been here for healing much, eh?"

The warrior shook his head.

"This is normal—well, for shrapnel, that is. Takes a lot out of them."

The warrior nodded. "Earlier, they let out a sound. I thought they couldn't talk at all—that's why we call them Nitàwesì. Why don't they—"

"That's enough," Shkitagen barked. The warrior closed his mouth with a click. "It's none of your damn business."

"I'm sorry. I didn't mean anything by it. I was just wondering."

"It's not my story to tell." Shkitagen sighed. "Anyway, you need to keep giving blood until that bag fills up."

The warrior nodded. He turned his gaze to his sibling, still sleeping peacefully on the table.

Shkitagen poured some freshly boiled water into a new bucket and, using scraps of fabric, began to wash the dried blood from Nitàwesì's face and hands. He combed through their curly hair with his fingers, gently rubbing the tension spots around their eyes and neck. He kissed them tenderly.

Someday, I hope you'll tell me that story.

CHAPTER VI

CAUGHT

Like a bug crawling on one's neck, Riordan sensed something creeping closer to xir compound. Something out to get xir. In the corner of the compound that doubled as Riordan's workshop, lined with meticulously organized shelves, and small sleeping space, xe lay on the ground, restless, unable to sleep, when suddenly xe was possessed by an overwhelming urge to *run, escape, flee.* Xe flopped onto xir hands and knees and, using xir wheels, thrust xir body vertical. Xe scanned the compound—nothing seemed out of place. Everything was quiet, still. But the feeling grew. Like a shadow, xe slipped outside, onto the street.

There was no opening or a doorway into the compound—Riordan and xir band of misfits had carved cracks in the walls, dug tunnels underneath, created small dents in surfaces to help them climb up and over. Nothing an adult would ever think of, with their lack of imagination.

In xir peripheral vision, Riordan spotted a figure hovering just behind xir. Xe rolled xir eyes and quickly wheeled to the next intersection to wait behind the corner of a building. Xe listened to the figure getting closer, until they were just inches away. Quick as a bullet, Riordan rolled out to meet them head on, fists high. Xe struck at their face, but met empty air. Before xe could wonder what the hell was going on, xe felt the air shift behind xir. Xe had just enough time to duck before a leg swept through the air where Riordan's face had been seconds earlier. Xe swiftly raised xir fists again and punched. This time xir fist connected with an armour-plated stomach. The figure materialized in front of xir, standing a few feet away.

"Who'da hell are ya?" Riordan screamed.

The figure shrugged off their dark cloak to reveal an armour-clad Elite Enforcer.

"Elite Enforcer H-09761," they answered in a robotic monotone. "Riordan Streetking, you are charged with treason against the Almighty."

Riordan scoffed. "Nob'dy calls 'em that down 'ere." With a one-handed salute, xe sped off at breakneck speed. It was too close to the compound—xe needed to get the Enforcer away from xir home. Xe grabbed xir whistle and sounded four quick, short blasts, waking up the entire neighbourhood. Xe dodged left and right, weaving between wires and collapsed buildings. Xe peered behind xir to see the Elite Enforcer still hot on xir heels. Their fists were balls of concentrated flame. Riordan tilted left just before the blast struck xir dead-on; it hit xir arm instead. Xe toppled over from the sheer force of the impact, clutching xir arm as pain shot through xir and the stench of burnt flesh hit xir nostrils. Xe looked at the damage: the entire right side of xir body radiated pain from a charred hole in xir arm, where the skin and muscle had been sheared away. Xe screamed.

Riordan pulled out a gun xe had retrofitted with stolen Enforcer tech to cause more damage. Struggling to use xir wounded arm, the sixth managed to switch off the weapon's safety. Elite Enforcer H-09761 closed in, their steps measured. Reflected on the smooth surface of their helmet was the light of the small fires the city's occupants used to mark their dwellings. Riordan aimed at it.

The shot rang out. The Enforcer whipped their body to the right—the bullet struck the wall where they'd been standing. Riordan fired again, shot after shot, but the Enforcer continued to dodge and weave with impossible speed. The Enforcer's hands began to glow again as a ball of energy formed in their left palm. But suddenly, they froze, grunted in pain, and collapsed to the ground, their body lightly spasming.

A small child emerged from the shadows between the walls like a ghost. She was wielding a taser that Riordan had built. The device's wires were connected to the flesh at the back of Elite Enforcer H-09761's neck.

Riordan felt a wash of pride for xir little one, even as pain caused xir breath to come in quick gasps. Xe felt suddenly faint.

Slipping out from beneath piles of garbage and through sewer grates, a dozen older children assembled, all gangly limbs and coordinated strikes. They tackled the Enforcer to the ground and effortlessly stripped away their armour, then wrapped the Enforcer's hands with fabric and zip ties and taped their mouth to prevent them from speaking or calling for help. Before long, Riordan was looking at a half-naked Enforcer with scars adorning their torso, arms, and legs—the most prominent of these being two lengthwise scars under each pectoral and a jagged mesh of burnt flesh, now healed, on their left cheekbone. A few of the warrior street kids rushed over to Riordan and helped xir back up. Xe grunted with the effort. A dangerous smile pulled at xir lips.

Xe wheeled over to the Enforcer and gripped their short black hair with xir good hand. "This is fer my arm," xe snarled.

The Enforcer remained expressionless. Riordan let go of their hair and, with every fibre of xir strength, pulled back and smashed xir fist into the Enforcer's face. Riordan watched with glee as the Enforcer bent backward and hit the pavement with a sickening crack.

Xe nodded once, and the warriors grabbed the Enforcer and started dragging them back down the streets toward their compound. Riordan grasped xir bleeding arm as xe wheeled alongside them, glaring down any neighbour nosy enough to peek out of their dwelling to see what all the commotion was about.

No one would dare speak up—not for Enforcers, not in Zhōng yang. Any civilian who worked alongside them would be cast out; this was not a city for traitors.

Back home, the children strapped the Enforcer to an old pipe in the back of the massive compound. Here, the walls were high enough on all sides that the captive wouldn't be able to see anything beyond the small space. The only entrance was a crack at one end large enough to fit one person sideways. The Enforcer's hands were kept separated and encased in mesh bags that Riordan had traded for ages ago from merchants from another city. They were a Madjideye invention made with fibres the likes of which Riordan had never before encountered—made to prevent gifts from being used, the merchants had promised. Riordan had paid more for them than xir legs had cost, but now xe was grateful for the gloves.

One of xir street kids, Cassiopeia, a sarcastic fifth with plump hands and jagged hair that she cut whenever she was bored, was a gifted medic. She immediately set to the task of patching up Riordan's arm, her large eyes grim as she surveyed the damage.

"Just do what ya can, Cass," Riordan said gruffly.

Cassiopeia grimaced as she worked. She succeeded in stopping the bleeding after a few minutes. Then she doused Riordan's wound in a potion that smelled worse than xir charred flesh and bandaged it tightly. Riordan thanked Cass, who went off shaking her head.

The street kids piled everything the Enforcer had been wearing into a designated pile of garbage in the northernmost corner of the compound, where they salvaged the important tech. Riordan told xir inventor kids to take the armour and the weapons and figure out how they worked. All that remained was a small device that made strange sounds, a pouch of rations, and another container filled with odd-looking pills. Riordan gave the rations to another kid and kept the strange device and the pills. Xe had never seen the likes of these before. Was this Enforcer sick? Were they simply vitamins? They had never stripped an Enforcer before; usually they simply captured or killed them. This time, though, Riordan had ascertained that to better know their enemy, they needed to look into their eyes.

Intrigued, xe placed the pills in xir pocket and went off to find an open patch of dirt where xe could attempt to fall asleep again, instead of sleeping in xir usual space—xe didn't want to get blood in xir bed.

CHAPTER VII

STORIES BENT INTO BONE

Time seemed endless, yet patience reigned inside A'tugwewinu. Most days followed the same listless pattern: She would wake up, and people would gather to listen as she shared stories. Some of the prisoners stayed simply to listen, having nothing else to do; others felt a calling and dedicated themselves to memorizing every word of what she said. Then evening would fall, and the Enforcers would come and toss rancid food to them over the wall of the gate, sending most prisoners diving for whatever they could get their hands on. Each night, A'tugwewinu would wait until the desperate had taken their share, then she would approach and grab whatever was left.

This particular morning, she heard the clang of the innermost gates being opened—a rarity that happened only when another prisoner was being admitted or when the Enforcers wanted to toy with them. Those who'd gathered to hear A'tugwewinu's stories scattered immediately, hiding in corners, making themselves as small as possible.

For some reason, they moved as far away from the storyteller as they could.

A'tugwewinu stared at her trembling hands while taking deep breaths to try and calm her rapidly beating heart. When she was a child, shape-shifting had been a game, something that came as naturally to her as breathing. After the destruction of Andwànikàdjigan, though, something about it changed. She often fell into fits where her lungs froze and she couldn't inhale; her heart would beat so quickly that her head would spin. When this happened, the shift would manifest, revealing to anyone watching that she was an eighth. She tried to steady her breathing, allowing small tremors to travel across her skin as it shifted. Her marks disappeared one by one, her jawline lengthened, her nose bent, and her eyes shrank in her skull. It never hurt, but it ached like stretching a muscle for too long. She breathed a sigh of relief, knowing she was better hidden now than any of the other prisoners concealed under piles of garbage.

She heard clang after clang as gates slid sharply along walls taller than any dwelling she had ever seen. The rattle of the barbed wire continued long after the gates were locked again behind the group of armed Enforcers marching into the prison. A'tugwewinu brought her thighs to her chest and wrapped her arms around her knees. She tucked her chin down and rocked against the chain-link fence at her back.

The thud of Enforcer boots echoed on patches of concrete. They drew nearer with every step.

The footsteps stopped. A'tugwewinu opened her eyes and slowly peered up and into a black visor in front of her. The Enforcers were clad in armour from head to toe. It stripped them of their humanity, made them seem that much more spiteful.

The Enforcer crouched down, brought a gloved hand to the last storyteller's face, and gently brushed her cheek. A'tugwewinu sucked in a breath and held it, one solitary tear slipping down her cheek—and with it, fear slowly leached from her body. She crinkled her eyebrows, enraged, as the Enforcer tucked a strand of her long hair behind her ear.

"You forgot one," the Enforcer whispered. Their voice was metallic. They traced a symbol on the side of A'tugwewinu's neck, below her ear.

The storyteller's hands stopped shaking. She roared violently and sprang to her feet, throwing her whole body at the Enforcer. She headbutted the black visor, cracking it.

She felt warmth then—blood streamed down her face from the point of impact.

Don't stop your assault until your opponent is down for good. Bèl's training rang in the back of her mind.

A'tugwewinu swung out one of her legs in a swift kick and punched with both arms. She struck leather and metal, though the impact of her swings was significantly less powerful than what Bèl could have managed. The Enforcer wheezed a slow chuckle in response.

The sound infuriated A'tugwewinu. She swung out again, but this time was interrupted by a swift fist to her midsection. The impact knocked the breath from her lungs and sent her careening forward. She spat blood.

The Enforcer let out a deep, maniacal laugh. A'tugwewinu's blood ran cold—this was a sound she had never heard an Enforcer make before. Enforcers were machines, or so most people surmised. There couldn't possibly be flesh and a beating heart behind those masked helmets. They killed without remorse, burned down homes, poisoned water sources, and destroyed whatever they touched without care for the survival of the sparse population of people left alive on this land. But that laugh, the hand that had touched her face ... they were both so ... human.

A'tugwewinu looked up through the red haze clouding her vision as the Enforcer ripped off their cracked helmet. Before her was a third with flesh and skin and eyes and everything that humans possessed.

Those eyes, though—piercing blue, with a feral glimmer in them.

"There you are, storyteller," the Enforcer sneered. Sure enough, A'tugwewinu looked down at her arms and saw them once again covered in marks. She quickly touched her face—her nose had widened and flattened to its original shape, and her cheekbones were more pronounced. She sighed deeply. She was done for. Now they would execute her, or worse.

Two other Enforcers, who had been watching at the sidelines, marched toward A'tugwewinu and picked her up by the arms. She writhed, twisting her body in an attempt to break free from their grasp. She screamed curses at the top of her lungs.

"The Madjideye's reign will end! Your fucking empire will crumble to ash and dust, just like the rest of this world. I swear it upon my ancestors! The fucking Madjideye will die!"

Ahkigowin aki trembled with her words, whispers in smoke reverberating in the empty spaces of the prison. The Enforcers were oblivious to it. They dragged her along the concrete, causing an endless stream of pain; her threadbare pants barely protected her legs from sharp rocks and detritus. Her voice cracked, her throat raw from overuse.

Finally, they entered the building she'd seen looming over the prison's entrance when she'd arrived.

Bright lights on the walls illuminated their tread. A'tugwewinu stared in awe—she'd never seen bright light from anything but fire. It burned her eyes if she stared too long at it. The long hallway was lined with small cells, some of which contained people groaning or screaming or standing to greet her when she passed close by the bars. Some stared defiantly, as if to give her strength, while the most defeated looking offered only pity.

At the end of the hallway was a closed door. The helmetless Enforcer pushed it open. In the middle of the room sat a long slab of metal with a pair of leather restraints at each end.

The Enforcers dragged her inside and threw her onto the table. They worked quickly, strapping down her wrists and ankles.

"No no no no—please no!" A'tugwewinu begged. She sobbed as the helmetless Enforcer, whose leering smile made her want to vomit, grabbed her hair in an iron grip and pulled her head back.

"We have so many questions about your kind," they sneered.

A'tugwewinu panted, her breath exiting her clenched teeth in quick, short bursts. Her scalp ached as some of her hair was ripped out from the roots.

The Enforcer produced a knife from their belt and pointed it at the storyteller's upper arm. "For example, what happens if I do this?" they whispered.

A'tugwewinu watched in horror as the Enforcer pierced her skin with the knife and sawed its serrated edge back and forth, flaying her upper arm. Her flesh burned with pain as the Enforcer cut and ripped away her skin, finally dangling a piece of flesh the size of her palm over her face. Blood dripped onto her cheeks.

Pain lanced her entire body. It seared her. "Kichi Manido, nìdòkàzowin!" she screamed through sobs, her voice high pitched. It was a prayer to any ancestors who would listen—she would not let this sacrifice, this flesh offering, go to waste.

A gentle warmth materialized at her feet. She opened her eyes. Nokomis was there.

"Enàbigis, Nokomis ... please, please ... nìdòkàzowin," A'tugwewinu pleaded.

Her grandmother looked at her, tears in his eyes. "This is but nikineshkà, oshis," he whispered—a promise that it would soon feel better.

A'tugwewinu cried out again. Nokomis gently shushed her and placed his hands on her ankle. She felt warmth sweep through her body, all the way up to her head. Her eyes felt heavy. The pain weighed her down, sleep pulled at her. "Miigwech," she sighed.

The Enforcer peered down at her, confused. They ordered the others to wake her, slapped her face and doused her in cold water, but nothing worked.

A'tugwewinu's spirit floated above herself, suspended, protected, as her body fell into a deep, blissful sleep. She dreamed.

■

"When Ahkigowin, aki or Ah-ki', was young, she had a family: Tibik-kizis, her grandmother, and Kizis, her grandfather. The Creator of this family was Kichi Manido, who placed the four directions on Ah-ki', and each direction was sacred. Then Kichi Manido filled Ah-ki' with water and sent the singers and the flyers to Ah-ki' to fill the sky, then the swimmers to fill the water, and it was a beautiful place. So beautiful that Kìjìgong Ikwe up in the Sky World was mesmerized as she stared at all that Kichi Manido had placed on Ah-ki'. She leaned from Sky World down below to Ah-ki'—she leaned so far forward that she fell. The flyers and singers that Kichi Manido had placed saw that Kìjìgong Ikwe was in trouble. They flew to her and caught her, but they could not carry her for long. Below, in the water, was Mikinàk. The flyers gently put her down upon its back.

"But the swimmers and the flyers were worried, because Kìjìgong Ikwe would not be able to live on the back of Mikinàk as it was. In her hand,

Kìjìgong Ikwe had some seeds. 'If only I had some soil, I could plant these seeds and live here,' she said to all the animals gathered around her. So Wajashk, the humblest of the swimmers, dove deep, deep down to the bottom of the water that surrounded them all over Ah-ki'. There, they grasped some soil, holding it in their tiny paw. Wajashk floated back up to the surface, but the journey had been too much for the little creature. It gave its life to bring this soil to Kìjìgong Ikwe, who took the offering with gratitude. She spread that tiny piece of soil all over Mikinàk's back and planted the seeds in her hand, and from it sprang all life that we once had here in this land."

Sitting with the other youths, A'tugwewinu was listening intently to the elder, but also staring at her own breast, desperate to witness the appearance of her first markings once the story was completed. She had just celebrated her day count, marking thirteen years since she was born, and finally she was able to join the others who had already begun their adulthood rites of passage. The passing of the Anishinabeg creation story was a moment they collectively waited for to finally join the ranks of the storytellers in their village, earning marks that would define their life's role within the community. Nokomis had told A'tugwewinu she needed to get her marks in order to begin training with him in ayahkwew work. Her knees bounced up and down with untethered energy.

Hours later, the elder completed the story, smiling. A'tugwewinu gasped as a sudden warmth pooled above her left breast. A cold snap locked into her mind, making her eyes roll to the back of her head. When she could look again, she saw small red markings no larger than the length of her shortest finger rising from the skin over her breast. She moved her fingers over them, felt the thump of her own heartbeat. She jumped up and ran toward her mother and Nokomis, embracing them both as they congratulated her on her first mark.

The trio quietly removed themselves from the throng of celebrating families. They approached a withered stump on the outskirts of the village, one of the last remaining things that occasionally turned green. Nokomis rested his hand upon it and muttered a prayer. With his other hand, which was weathered and calloused, he grasped A'tugwewinu's small brown fingers and placed her hand atop his.

Feeling the stump pulse, A'tugwewinu gasped. The beat was unlike the one in her chest but resounding nonetheless. Whispers filled her mind, stories and poems from ancestors who looked through her eyes onto this discarded landscape. They wept for Ahkigowin aki, who had perished, turning the beautiful environment of the elder's story into this desolate and forlorn place.

Nokomis removed his hand, and A'tugwewinu's fell limp at her side. Nokomis reached over and wiped the tears from her face.

"Remember," he whispered, "the spirits will always be there, and they will share with you the most sacred of stories."

■

A'tugwewinu woke with a dry throat. She ran her tongue over her teeth and tried to generate enough saliva to swallow, but to no avail.

"Here."

The voice was familiar. Kind, warm hands of deep brown lifted her head and held a tin cup filled with muddy water to her parched lips.

A'tugwewinu took careful sips. The liquid soothed her aching throat.

"Sachit?" she asked, when she could speak. The elder returned to his task of wiping down her body, rinsing off the blood and grime.

"They wanted to keep you alive," Sachit said. "They brought me here to tend to your wounds."

"Why you?" A'tugwewinu asked.

"I was born here in this prison. I have been doing this for others since I was a child."

"But you said you were from the travelling camps."

"When I close my eyes, I imagine that I am from a travelling village. I can only hope that one day I will be freed, and on that day, I will join the nearest travelling camp and see the world." Sachit's tone was wistful, her eyes seeing a faraway place, one he could only imagine.

A'tugwewinu smiled. *What a beautiful dream*, she thought.

Sachit proceeded to bandage her knees, which were bloodied and raw. "What do your spirits say about it?"

A'tugwewinu's eyes widened. "You can see them?" she said, surprised.

Sachit shook his head. "No, but you can, and that's all I need." She spoke with reverence.

A'tugwewinu smiled tenderly. "Your belief is mighty."

"It is my only possession." Sachit took a few steps back and surveyed A'tugwewinu's body, looking for any injuries he might have missed. "If I let you escape, they will kill me and everyone you've shared stories with," he whispered. There was pain in her voice.

"I know." A'tugwewinu swallowed.

"Your wounds are superficial, except for your arm. I did the best I could, but I don't know if you will be able to use it before it's healed. Did they take that story?"

A'tugwewinu looked down at her left arm to see that it was swaddled in blood-soaked cloth. "Can I tell you a secret?" she asked. Sachit nodded, placing his palm over his heart. "The markings are engraved into our bones. Our skin is but a reflection of them. My people's very blood whispers stories; they could flay my entire body, and still I would know every symbol and word."

Sachit smiled. "For that, you give me hope, storyteller." He wiped a tear from his eye. "Thank you. I have to leave now, before the Enforcers return."

"Can I ask you for one last favour?" A'tugwewinu said, as the first turned to leave.

Sachit nodded, hesitant.

A'tugwewinu spat out the words. "Cut my hair. Shave it so there's nothing left."

"I have but a dull blade."

"Nothing you do could hurt worse than what has already been done to me."

"I have met first peoples before, is it not ... Is this not forbidden? I was told your hair is sacred."

A'tugwewinu nodded. "Once you've cut it, I ask that you bury it where it will never be found."

With that, Sachit pulled out the shank he carried. He gently grasped chunks of A'tugwewinu's hair and hacked at them. With every strand ripped from her scalp, A'tugwewinu felt lighter.

Never again will filthy Enforcer hands touch sacred hair. She closed her eyes and sighed. The frigid, gangly form of Death appeared over her. She smiled. *Soon, I will join you, Bèl.*

■

"Why Nmama cryin'?" asked A'tugwewinu.

Nokomis carefully picked up the toddler and held her in his arms. "Because your papa died, and she is sad he's gone," he replied.

"No! Npapa's right 'der!" A'tugwewinu pointed at the shadow embracing her mother.

Nokomis sighed. "That is your papa's spirit. Only you and I can see him, oshis. No one else. Your papa's body died, but his spirit stayed to say one last goodbye to you both."

"Npapa's sayin' bye-bye?"

"Yes, he can't stay here. He has to return to Kichi Manido."

"No! He can't! Npapa!" the little one cried. She wriggled free of her grandmother's arms and ran toward the shadow.

"Npapa, don't leave!"

With a watery smile, the spirit crouched down and kissed the top of A'tugwewinu's forehead before vanishing. She was inconsolable. Beside her, her mother took up the machete she always carried as one of the village warriors. She held out her long braid and, with a single sharp tug, cut it off.

A'tugwewinu's mother picked her up and held her tightly in her arms. A'tugwewinu grabbed at the back of her mother's neck, for the first time feeling the tiny prickles of short hair there.

Her mother never grew out her hair again.

CHAPTER VIII

FACE TO FACE

Enforcer H-09761 couldn't remember ever being this sick. In fact, they couldn't remember much from before. It confused them a great deal. *Where has my memory gone?* They threw up the contents of their stomach, noting how little there was. They looked around. Their hands were chained to a rusty pipe in the wall and had been concealed inside a pair of gift-cancelling gloves, the likes of which the Enforcer had seen before. They'd been stripped of their armour and wore only a pair of tight leggings that were soaked in what they assumed was their own urine. They rolled their eyes and shuddered in disgust.

"Sorry it's not up to yer standards," Riordan drawled.

Seeing xir in the corner of the room, H-09761 felt anger boiling in their gut. This was supposed to be their target, their *prey*, and yet here they were, captured by this filth of a human being.

"You are a fugitive of the Almighty!" they yelled.

Riordan smirked, amused. "I'd love to see da Almighty get ya outta this mess." Xe spat the word "Almighty" with disgust.

The Enforcer rolled their eyes.

"But they won't," Riordan resumed. "A failed mission means death, don't it? So why don't ya co-operate with me, den?"

"Is that why you have me chained, at your mercy?" H-09761 sneered.

Riordan laughed. Xe gripped the chain above the Enforcer and pulled their face close until they were mere inches apart. The sadistic twinkle in Riordan's eye and xir taunting smirk transformed xir pale features menacingly. H-09761 took note.

"Ya should beg for my mercy. But right now, the only thing ya have is my pity. I'll make sure every second yer here is agony. Ya'll pay for every life ya've taken, every family ya've desecrated, and only when I've extracted every piece of information from ya will I show ya mercy and sever yer life from this world." Riordan slowly emphasized every word, then shoved the chain—and H-09761—away.

The back of their head hit the wall hard. Nausea rippled through their insides. H-09761 looked up as Riordan turned and calmly wheeled away, tension lines visible across xir back and shoulders.

Riordan spat on the ground just outside the small enclosure at the back of the compound that was serving as their guest's makeshift cell. Xir hands trembled. It took every ounce of xir willpower not to kill this machine. And yet, Riordan had never seen an Enforcer without their armour before. Had never looked into their eyes, which were dark brown and appeared so human. Had never smelled their fear. Xe had never seen the humanity of their lightly dusted skin, the scarred ridges of molten flesh on their face.

Were those scars from people who'd fought back, or were they training wounds? Riordan had evaluated xir captive's fearful eyes and short black hair, the serial number tattooed on the back of their neck.

Their muscle mass was lean, and they were short in stature. Though their scent clearly projected a third—stronger and faster than any other gender—without their gift, this Enforcer wasn't a threat, not at all.

In every situation where Riordan had fought against armoured Enforcers, xe had feared for xir life and done what was necessary, because Zhōng yang had no room for the weak. Xe began to regret xir plan to keep this Enforcer captive for information. Xe should have killed them like the rest.

Riordan tossed and turned that night. Xir enclosure was safe—no one had ever reported it, and besides, at street level no one could tell what was inside, for the walls were too high. And yet, this Enforcer had found xir so easily.

Xe turned over and accidentally grazed the wound on xir arm. Xe bolted upright with a hiss and pulled the bandage down. The wound was raw, red, and inflamed with a green crust that was hot to the touch.

Damn, xe thought, *this isn't good at all.*

■

"Yun-seo! Yun-seo!" A melodious voice rang through the dwelling. Little hands reached up toward the smiling face above. Were these their hands? Who was this smiling face? The figure reached down and picked them up, swinging them around and around. Laughter resounded in their ears. They were suddenly released in mid-air. They felt fear for a second before realizing they were gently floating, twirling around without a care for gravity—

Elite Enforcer H-09761 startled.

"Kwey," gasped a weak voice from the corner. "Turns out I can't sleep 'cuz of this hole ya made in my arm. My medic doesn't know what to do with it either. So why don't ya tell me how ta fix it, eh?" Riordan barked.

Xe trudged forward unevenly, xir breath coming in rapid bursts. Xe was weak from infection and fever. H-09761 noticed all this and said nothing, unsure how this brute would take their medical advice. Riordan dropped down in front of them, xir hands at the Enforcer's throat.

"Shit," xe muttered before promptly losing consciousness. Xir body teetered forward and collapsed onto H-09761, both arms outstretched, xir face mashed against the Enforcer's thigh.

Well, how very fortunate, H-09761 thought, smiling as they wiggled free of the lumbering giant. They swept their leg out and dropped their heel onto Riordan's nose. Riordan grunted but otherwise didn't move.

"That's for not killing me," H-09761 muttered grimly.

For the rest of the night, H-09761 watched as blood from Riordan's nose pooled under xir face, as xir breath got shallower, as xe started to gurgle. Nausea rolled through H-09761 again, started to overwhelm their senses. They needed their pills. They figured it hadn't been more than two days since their capture. They would die soon if they didn't take their pills.

Riordan woke with a grunt. Xir face hurt. Dried and flaking blood coated xir mouth and chin. Xe noticed right away how weak and dizzy xe felt. Trembling, xe pushed xirself up to a seated position, xir arm protesting painfully. The flesh was red, inflamed, with green pus seeping from the wound. Riordan looked up then and saw xir captive shivering with fever. The stench of sweat and urine filled the space. The Enforcer's taupe skin had turned pale and jaundiced, and their eyes were clouded and bloodshot.

Riordan swore. "Whatta sight we are, eh?" xe muttered grimly.

H-09761 stared at xir. They opened and closed their mouth a few times, releasing no words. They swallowed. Riordan was taller than anyone they had laid eyes upon before. The shoes with wheels xe wore gave xir a solid six inches of extra height. Flaming red locks of untameable hair, scarred ivory skin that was terrifyingly pale, thin lips almost always pulled in a grimace. And xir eyes—they were the same grey colour of the clouds during the rare lightning storms that happened but a few days a year, and they assessed H-09761 constantly.

Xe was not to be underestimated. Those born in the streets were made from something the Enforcers could never hope to brainwash into their soldiers.

Riordan grunted again and yelled for xir medic. Cassiopeia stormed in a moment later with a heavy satchel full of supplies she had gathered.

"Please, kill me," H-09761 whispered feebly.

"Well, you've changed yer tune, haven't you? Where did tha' asshole from yesterday go?"

H-09761 began to shake and cry. Riordan spat at their feet.

"Have you never seen your victims cry?" H-09761 screamed, enraged.

Riordan tsked. "Actually, you're the first."

Xe grunted as Cassiopeia swabbed xir wound with alcohol. "Some we found dead and some refused ta co-operate, so we killed 'em. Either way, none survived more'n two days. Why do ya suppose that is, eh?"

H-09761 ceased their crying. "It's the pills, they make us forget. If we don't take them, we die."

Riordan's maniacal smile returned. "I figured. Well congrats, ya made it past day three. So, let me ask ya: How many of yer victims have *you* seen cry?"

Memories assaulted H-09761's mind: countless victims begging, pleading for their lives, their families. And in every case, the Enforcer had looked on passively, using their gift to end lives. Orders were orders.

H-09761 screamed. *These memories—it has to stop!* Frantically, they scanned their surroundings for some way to stop seeing the images, stop seeing those faces. They fought against their chains, rocking back and forth, smacking their back and shoulders against the rough stone on the wall as they desperately tried to inflict damage on themselves. They felt a stabbing pain at the base of their neck and turned in time to see the medic withdrawing, an empty syringe in hand.

"Wha—" H-09761 muttered. They suddenly felt very tired. Their muscles went lax.

"That will keep you calm for a few days," Cassiopeia said.

"Can't have ya dyin' by any means other than my own two hands, got it?" Riordan smirked as if xe would enjoy nothing more.

H-09761 stared at the gnarled flesh on xir pale arm. The wound was far more infected than xir medic would be able to deal with—it required surgical intervention.

"What if I healed you?" H-09761 let slip without thinking. They were feeling blissfully calm as the drug worked its way through their body.

Riordan laughed. "Now that's a new one. I won't fall fer it, though."

"I'm weak right now, I couldn't escape if I wanted to. And if I tried anything, you could just kill me, right?"

Riordan cocked xir head. "Why?"

"I don't know," H-09761 responded honestly. It was the first thought that came to them, birthed from somewhere inside—a *feeling,* something they hadn't even known existed until only moments ago. They looked up as the medic, holding a taser in one hand, started untying one of their arms. Cassiopeia unlocked the glove covering the

Enforcer's left hand. H-09761 flexed their sore muscles. Their fingers trembled. It took tremendous effort just to lift up their arm.

"Come closer," they whispered. Still uncertain, Riordan shuffled closer, along their side. Xir expression was incredulous, as if xe couldn't believe xe was going along with this. But what choice did xe really have? Riordan had over a hundred kids who needed xir to survive until tomorrow. If this Enforcer had a way to keep xir alive, then maybe information wasn't the only thing they were good for.

H-09761 felt the heat of this giant looming over them. With a shuddering breath, they raised their hand until it touched the crusted flesh on Riordan's arm. They focused on that feeling deep within them and watched, astonished, as their hand gently pulsed and glowed with soft, licking flames. They could feel heat seeping from their palm and entering Riordan's body. They looked up. Riordan inhaled sharply, gritting xir teeth at the dull pain, the burning heat. Xir eyes bore into H-09761, who couldn't hold that gaze. They returned their attention to Riordan's flesh, watching as the flames burned away the infection, as old blood dried and peeled off.

Minutes later, Riordan's wound was free of pus. The skin was still red, but that was much better than green.

H-09761 removed their hand as rolling waves of nausea cascaded into them. They turned to the side and vomited, hearing only a sneer of disgust before everything went black.

The Enforcer's head lolled back, held in place by the rusted pipe at their back. Riordan looked from their scarred face to xir own arm and the slightly burnt flesh left behind, shaking xir head in disbelief. Xe put xir wheels in front to try and propel xirself forward, but no sooner did xe try than xe was hit by a wave of vertigo. The world darkened as xe pitched forward.

"Fucking gifts," xe cursed before xe, too, slipped into unconsciousness.

Cassiopeia scoffed. "You're way too heavy to move anywhere," she muttered at Riordan. She replaced the glove on the Enforcer's hand and tied it to the chain again. Wrinkling her nose at the smell, she packed up her medic's kit and left them both behind.

■

Elite Enforcer H-09761, you are ordered to execute rebels in the eastern district of the central city. You will carry out your mission at 0600.

"Please! Please! You have to let me live! I have a child!" screamed the human before them.

But they did not hesitate. They called upon an empty place within themselves. Watched, detached, as flames engulfed their fingertips. In rapid succession, small spheres of fire burst forth, directed at their human target. The fire spun and arched, leaving behind a sizzling crater of melted flesh where their target's face had once been.

In the distance, a child screamed for their father.

More screams. Pleas for mercy. Orders. Eat vitamin mush. Sleep. Take the pills every day. Take the pills. Every. Single. Day.

■

H-09761 was startled awake. Riordan was brusquely shaking their arm. They jumped, scrambled to a seated position. Their muscles ached again, which meant the drug they'd been injected with had worn off. They had been unconscious for days, possibly. It must have been an effect of the unfamiliar gift they had used. H-09761 was still befuddled, unsure how they had known the flames from within could help their captor. The filth around them had been cleansed. Their soiled clothes remained, however. An ancient-looking intravenous fluid system had been inserted into the crook of their elbow, the bag and needle raised far above their head, so they wouldn't be able to fidget with or remove it, no matter how much they struggled.

Riordan sat next to them, cross-legged. Any semblance of sickness or infection was gone; xir skin was still frighteningly pale, but no longer tinged green. Xir shocking red hair stuck up all over the place, the piercings along xir eyebrow, lip, nose, and ears glinting in the dull morning light. No more blood from xir broken nose either, which was already starting to heal.

Riordan stared pointedly at the Enforcer. "Now, let's try this again, eh? Don't make me drug ya this time. Do ya remember who y'are? What you've done?"

H-09761 nodded. They started to sweat, fear and trepidation running through them. Their throat felt like they had swallowed razor blades.

"Good. Gimme the answers I need and I'll give ya a sip of water. Refuse and I'll leave ya parched." Riordan spoke grimly, as if xe could read the Enforcer's mind. "How do I get ridda the bounty on my head?"

H-09761 sucked in a breath. "I don't—I don't know. We receive orders and carry them out, or they dispose of us." There was fear in their voice.

Riordan swore. Xe used xir wheels to push xirself upright. "I think I'll come back tomorrow, when more of yer memories have returned." Xe grabbed the water bottle at xir side and poured it out next to H-09761. The liquid seeped into their leggings, soaking their side. They swallowed reflexively.

"I deserve it," they said, full of remorse. "For all the things I've done."

"I need ya to remember everything about 'em!" Riordan bellowed. There was no compassion in xir hard gaze. Xe wanted this Enforcer to *suffer*, to be riddled with guilt for the atrocities they had committed. "Remember all the people ya've killed and every order ya've carried out, and somehow, somewhere, in all that, remember anythin' tha' might be useful for me to help keep my kids safe."

H-09761 shuddered. "That's impossible. There're thousands like me, and their gifts are stronger. Another Elite Enforcer will come once they realize I've failed. The Almighty—"

"Don't call 'em that!" Riordan barked. With that, xe turned and sped away, wheels propelling xir at an inhuman speed.

CHAPTER IX

ACID RAIN

Shkitagen woke to something cold and wet on his face. He opened his eyes to discover droplets of water falling from a leak in the ceiling. He wiped his brow and listened to the thundering rain outside. It hadn't rained in weeks. He hoped it was the good kind of rain and not the poisonous kind that fell every so often, making everyone sick and unable to leave their dwellings. He rose from bed, taking a moment to stare at Nitàwesì's beautiful sleeping face. Their dusted tan skin, broad nose and cheekbones, strong jawline—facial features that so many of their people shared. The soft rolls on their belly as their chest rose and fell in a peaceful rhythm. They were at least two heads shorter than him and about half his muscle mass. Shkitagen's build spoke to his father's nurturing care and the intense firekeeping training the elders had put him through.

The past few months since their union had been a whirlwind. Both had been busy with work; their shared home was regularly filled with people who were sick, who needed the warmth of a fire and the hands of a healer.

Shkitagen put on some warm, thick clothes, grabbed some tools, and went out to fix the roof. Having been patched countless times with mismatched materials over the years, the roof of the dwelling was shoddy at best, just like every other roof in the village. The elders claimed their village was ancient, that the ancestors had lived here since time immemorial. Once, dwellings had been made out of animal hide and wood, but then came stone and metal, and here it remained, in the crumbling detritus of that time. No one knew how to make new dwellings anymore. The wood and stone and metal necessary to build, the tools and the knowledge—it had all been lost. They made do, though, repairing things as best they could, just as Shkitagen's father and grandparent had before him.

Shkitagen spread paste on some of the shingles before nailing new pieces of metal to them to ensure everything was sealed tight. His vision was getting hazy, his breath coming in quick. *Damn. The poisonous kind of rain, then.*

He shuffled off the roof just as Nitàwesì rushed outside, holding a stick attached to a rounded piece of plastic over their head. Their expression was frantic.

"You need to cover yourself completely!" they signed, eyes wide.

Shkitagen chuckled. "You worry about me like an old grandparent," he teased as they went back inside together.

"You should be more worried about yourself." Nitàwesì raised an eyebrow, not at all amused.

Shkitagen couldn't help but laugh. He loved the way his odey cared for him, fussed over him, ensured he was always at his best health. He removed his soaked clothes and placed them by the fire to dry, so the rainwater wouldn't hurt either of them.

"Let me take a look at you." Nitàwesì marched over and placed one hand over Shkitagen's heart, the other on his head. Behind his forehead, Nitàwesì could feel the poison from the rain. They moved their hand to the back of Shkitagen's head. A deep inhale, exhale—their breath moved in quick pulses over the hand pressed to Shkitagen's forehead. Nitàwesì felt the poison slowly leaving their love's head, moving farther and farther back until it lay in their other hand. They stood and went over to the fire, shaking grey specks from their palm— trace amounts of poison.

"Miigwech," Shkitagen whispered. His head felt fine now, and his vision had returned to normal. "Now come back to bed. I won't be the only one stupid enough to go outside today."

Nitàwesì rolled their eyes. "You most certainly won't be," they signed, exasperated.

Using their gift came naturally now, after years of practice, but it was still taxing. They closed their eyes and rubbed their smooth cheek back and forth over Shkitagen's chest.

It didn't stop raining for weeks.

CHAPTER X

MEMORIZERS

A'tugwewinu stared at her bloodied fingers. Her nails were gone, and the bandages around them were mostly red. She had spent days in that room, though once Nokomis showed her how to let her spirit leave her body, the pain couldn't reach her anymore. It wasn't long before the Enforcers grew tired of her silence. They asked her if there were others like her. They wanted information about the marks, about her village. They were grasping at air, looking for any answers they could find. The storyteller remained silent the entire time, save for her whispered prayers in Anishinabemowin, which none of the Enforcers could discern.

Once the Enforcers understood that no amount of physical pain they caused her would quench their thirst for answers, they released her back into the main prison. This suited A'tugwewinu just fine; she had her life's role to accomplish, and so she returned to her work. The prisoners who gathered around her every day had dedicated themselves to memorizing the stories she told. A new nation—not of her village, not of marked ones, but of memorizers—arose within the confines of the prison. As she told stories, they sat before her, repeating the words over and over again. An informal resistance was growing, one of whispered words from ancestors and spirits, of listening ears and watery eyes.

Death took on corporeal form, its spindly limbs tickling her as she attempted to sleep. Not long now ... Soon, very soon, she would join her beloved.

The flesh of her arm ached. Using her arm at all sent tendrils of pain into her core. Worse than that was the missing weight on her scalp, her once waist-length hair now ragged, shorn patches. She hated to touch the prickly remains, hated remembering why she'd had Sachit cut it in the first place. And yet, every time she put her head down, weary after a day of sharing stories, the first thing she recalled was not sweet memories of Bèl, but the sneer of the Enforcer's yellowed teeth and the stench of his breath. A'tugwewinu recoiled and reached her arms up to the sky. The dull orb in the dark-grey clouds was beginning to descend. She embraced her old friend, Death, who inched closer, tendrils and wisps of smoke from beneath their cloak tickling the eighth's skin. Their skeletal form enveloped her.

Suddenly, Death jerked away and, with a sad smile, they vanished.

Confused, A'tugwewinu got up off the ground and looked out across the horizon, wondering why Death would leave her so suddenly. In the far-right corner of the prison she saw a crouched shape fiddling with the outer fence. The prison was eerily silent for once, and except for a few shuffling prisoners, no one save this figure seemed to be moving.

Something about them gave the storyteller pause. A'tugwewinu stared as the hooded figure deftly pried one metal link from the next with a large tool she had never seen before. Finally, after making a gap in the fence large enough to crawl through, the figure ducked and crawled over to the next one. A'tugwewinu looked around. The other prisoners were mostly huddled in their respective corners, some hiding under dilapidated tarps or rusted metal slats. The hooded figure seemingly went unnoticed, even as they crept closer to the centre of the prison. A'tugwewinu sniffed the air. She smelled a third, and something familiar, like a memory.

She stiffened. *It couldn't be.* She panicked.

The figure rolled over to the fence beside her and ducked down. Mere inches away, the figure pulled back their hood to reveal clear eyes with irises the colour of dark, polished amber.

A'tugwewinu held her breath. She stared at Bèl's beautiful, rich skin, her strong hands clasping the metal chain-link, and reached out with shaky fingers. Her index finger barely brushed Bèl's knuckles, but when their skin touched, they both released deep sighs that seemed to echo into the earth.

A'tugwewinu inhaled a sob. She started to withdraw her hand, but Bèl took hold of it with her fingers.

"How?" A'tugwewinu whispered, the first word spoken between them in months. "I saw you die. I watched the blood leave your body." She sobbed quietly, her forehead to the fence, as close as she could get to Bèl's warmth. As close as the prison would let her.

"I begged the spirits to allow me to be with you once again, nani-chi," Bèl whispered.

"And what was the price for that? Will you have to leave me again?" She was hesitant, afraid that this was a dream, or that Death had taken her after all.

"No, the sacrifice was solely mine to make," Bèl stated solemnly.

A'tugwewinu pressed her face to the chain-link. Her chapped lips met Bèl's soft ones. Bèl kissed her like it was their first and last kiss, like soothing water caressing a parched throat. They kissed without care of the Enforcers or of impending doom, they kissed like the world was ending. But really, hadn't it already ended?

They pulled away from each other, breath ragged, a haze of lust between them.

"Let me get you free," Bèl stated.

A'tugwewinu watched as the warrior wrangled her long metal cutters. In minutes, the fence was cut and loosened enough that A'tugwewinu could slip through.

She rushed through and tackled her love to the earth, feeling joy erupt within her. She trailed her fingers to the spot where Bèl had been shot, feeling gnarled skin and matted scar tissue instead of an open wound, and breathed a sigh of relief.

Bèl grasped her lover's chin. Her eyes moved to the bandages covering A'tugwewinu's body, the shorn hair, her gaunt appearance, her eyes, which had witnessed such horrors.

"What have they done to you?" There was anger in Bèl's voice. She delicately traced her lover's arms and shoulders, resting her fingers at the base of A'tugwewinu's neck. She brushed the short, bristled hairs there. The eighth gasped and flinched. They looked at each other, shocked. A'tugwewinu had never recoiled from her lover before.

"Oh, nanichi," Bèl crooned. "May I ..." She swallowed audibly, having never had to ask so explicitly before. "May I touch?" She waved her hand near Winu's scalp.

"Not ... today," A'tugwewinu responded, hands trembling. Her mind was fixated: gloved hands holding her immobile, a fist clenching her hair.

Bèl nodded, shaking off the disappointment.

"Your execution was announced," she said. "It's to take place in a few hours. The Madjideye rounded up their best Enforcers to witness the last storyteller die. I saw a caravan of vehicles on the way here. We need to go."

A'tugwewinu nodded. Softly, she clacked her hand against the chain-link in a rhythm—a code she had devised with her followers. Soon, the memorizers came. The younger ones slipped out through the hole, while the older ones stayed behind.

"We will only slow you down," one said.

"Besides, someone needs to stay to tell stories to the other prisoners," whispered another.

"Where's Sachit?" A'tugwewinu asked. From behind a pile of discarded objects whose names had long been forgotten—large, flat rectangles with shattered glass screens, tiny devices with broken buttons and faded markings—the first stepped out, eyes watering as she regarded the gaps in the fence.

"What kind of machine is capable of breaking this cage?" Sachit asked.

Bèl smirked. "My ancestors kept all kinds of tools. This one simply needs the strength of a third." She held up the rusted metal cutters in her hand.

A'tugwewinu took Bèl's small pointed dagger and addressed the old one in front of her. "Do you trust me?" Sachit nodded. A'tugwewinu lifted the dagger to the skin above his left breast and carved marking symbols, small scratches that bled. The old one hissed in pain, yet remained still. "This is the first marking we receive. Give it to those who dedicate themselves to this path," A'tugwewinu explained.

Sachit shed a tear. "This is the greatest gift anyone has ever given me. I swear I will carry it with great honour." They grasped each other's forearms and stared into each other's eyes. A'tugwewinu inhaled. All the gratitude and pain and terror the two of them had faced sucked deep into the earth as they embraced.

Sachit pulled away. A'tugwewinu gave him the dagger.

"There are no words to thank you for all you have done for me," she whispered.

"For the first time in my life," Sachit said, speaking with great respect, "I thank your spirits for allowing me to be born in this place so that I could meet you, storyteller."

A'tugwewinu and Bèl made a swift exit then, A'tugwewinu pausing to look behind her only once. She bore witness to the others carving symbols into each other's skin above their hearts, to the memorizers staring with awe at the small scratches on their skin.

She smiled. The marked ones were reborn.

■

"Since time immemorial, our people have told our stories orally. We have always listened when someone shared a story, and we have always shared the stories that we carry."

A'tugwewinu sat upright and listened attentively to what Nokomis was saying.

"But there were other people in the world who didn't share stories the same way. They would use tools to record their stories and put them in objects, and people would learn the stories from those objects."

"Wouldn't they just get markings?" A'tugwewinu asked.

"No, they wouldn't. If they didn't take the time to learn the stories from these objects, they never would. And they didn't listen to each other, so they never learned to share, either," Nokomis explained.

A'tugwewinu frowned. What strange people, *she thought.*

"Not so long ago, certain people rose to power, and they realized that if they destroyed these objects, no one would be able to learn anything, and they in turn could hold all the power. So they did just that, and without their objects, all those people forgot their stories."

A'tugwewinu was even more confused.

"Around the same time this happened, our people noticed markings appearing on our bodies. These markings had been the kind found on or in the objects that the people in power had destroyed."

"What does that mean, Nokomis?" A'tugwewinu asked, alarmed.

"We're not quite sure, but the spirits have told me that our way of sharing stories can't stay within only our people anymore. It's time to share this way of learning with others. Just as we have adapted a new way of learning, we are meant to adapt to a new way of sharing."

■

A'tugwewinu and Bèl walked away as fast as their legs could carry them from the compound. "I am no longer the last of the Andwànikàdjigan," A'tugwewinu whispered. She took Bèl's hand in her own, and their fingers intertwined.

A'tugwewinu spied the shadow of Nokomis off in the distance, raising his hand in salute. She nodded to him as he turned and vanished.

CHAPTER XI

YUN-SEO

The Madjideye's brainwashing hit H-09761 in waves. Frustrated by their circumstances, they considered how to escape, only to wonder where they would go. Back to the Enforcers? Some part of H-09761 shivered in fear at the thought. They would certainly be killed for failing this mission. For the time being, they complied with their captors. The strength and loyalty of the orphans led by Riordan Streetking made H-09761 want to demystify this stranger.

"Tell me wha' the damn Madjideye know 'bout me," Riordan ordered one day.

H-09761 snorted. "Your day count isn't known, but they have your biometrics and a recent image, and you're listed as a second on your arrest warrant."

"How da hell do the Madjideye know all that, eh? M'not registered anywhere."

H-09761 sneered. "Don't call the Almighty by anything less."

"Ya didn't answer my question." Riordan was tired of these antics, the Enforcer's constant mood swings—from pitiful and mournful to enraged and vindictive.

H-09761 calculated their leverage. They were tied up, and there was no backup coming. They were their own last resort. If they didn't return to their base, they would be assumed dead.

They sighed. "If I answer your questions, will you at least give me something to eat or drink?"

Riordan nodded. Xe grabbed a ration pack from one of xir pockets and approached the Enforcer. Xir nose wrinkled at the smell. Xe opened the pack and placed it on their lap, untying one of their hands and removing the glove so they could eat.

H-09761 grabbed the pieces of vitamin mush and took a few small bites. Riordan watched with interest.

"You were registered by your mother, that's how you're in the system," H-09761 said. "We've been watching you for years. The Almighty has better things to do than worry about a petty thief and xir band of misfits, but the murders you've committed recently, and your last stunt—those were in direct defiance of the Almighty and will not go unpunished. I am but the first of many to come. It's only a matter of time before an army tears down your walls!"

Riordan mulled over the words. "Sure," xe responded nonchalantly.

"You may not value your life, but what about the children around you?"

"Don't ya dare threaten them!" Riordan snarled, xir face suddenly inches from the Enforcer's. Xe put xir fist behind their head.

H-09761 didn't flinch. Riordan got up, untying the Enforcer's other hand—freeing them for the first time since their capture. Then Riordan got up on xir wheels and motioned for H-09761 to follow.

Together they went to the entrance of the room. In the open space of the compound, as far as the Enforcer could see, were a hundred or so children, ranging in age from toddlers to young adults. A few glared at H-09761. Some sparred with each other, while others were busy putting together weapons and machines from scraps and spare parts.

Escape wouldn't be so easy, H-09761 realized.

In the corner, a young person cleared their throat. The Enforcer snapped their gaze onto them. The young person nodded, beckoning to H-09761. Suspicious but curious, they followed.

They were led to a curtained-off corner of the dwelling. On the ground inside were a few buckets filled with dingy water and a bar of soap. On a bench to one side were some clothes.

"Ya stink," the young one muttered before pushing them inside and leaving.

H-09761 breathed a sigh of relief. Finally, a proper bath.

"Don't even try ta run, got it?" Riordan warned. Startled, H-09761 looked behind them as they undressed. Riordan's eyes roamed over their naked body. Blushing, the Enforcer turned their back to xir.

"It would be difficult without my armour and surrounded by your warriors," they muttered. They had underestimated these street kids, who had, after all, successfully taken them down, gift and all.

Riordan laughed. Xe looked at the small, naked enemy in front of xir, their muscle mass slowly dwindling after weeks of inactivity. "How old are ya, H-09761?"

"Is this really the time to question me?" the Enforcer's voice cracked.

"Ya look young. The Enforcers recruit children to fight their wars?"

"I'm not sure. I don't remember. I don't remember anything except my name."

"Oh? What is it?"

"Yun-seo."

"Well, that's much better," Riordan said. Something was hidden in xir tone that Yun-seo couldn't understand.

Yun-seo laughed, a bellowing sound from deep within. The fact that they were having a conversation with their captor was beyond logical.

Riordan smiled, looking slightly confused. Then, abruptly, coldness returned to xir eyes. "I don't trust ya at all. Yer my prisoner. Don't ya forget that."

"Why?" Yun-seo asked quietly. The emotional whiplash was sobering.

"Because it's time my kids had the upper hand over the Madjideye, and yer gonna help me get that."

The inventor kids were Riordan's favourites; they reminded xir of how xe had been as a child, finding wonder in scraps of rejected garbage and piecing them together like a puzzle only xe understood. That was how xe was able to make xir wheels. Xir most recent pair looked like an oversized pair of boots. The small wheels underneath were triggered by minute differences in how xe balanced xir weight. If xe pushed too far, too fast, xe would land flat on xir face. A stomp, and xe would brake; the slightest pressure forward, and xe would advance at a leisurely pace.

Riordan's earliest memories were of sitting in the street, able only to move by crawling around. Xe didn't know what had happened to xir feet, but guessed that xe'd never had any to begin with. Riordan didn't remember ever having an adult around, so xe assumed that one day, xe'd just materialized into this world, found a street corner, and sat there looking pitiful until people had given xir some food. A'tugwewinu and Bèl had taken xir in. They looked at Riordan fiercely, like nobody should ever feel sorry for xir. It was the two of them who taught Riordan how to steal and find tools and told xir where the good garbage was.

And now look at xir. The world feared Riordan—xir speed, xir genius, xir army of street kids. No one dared pity Riordan Streetking.

Xe looked at the strange device in xir hands. Xir inventor kids had finally figured out how to work it. There was a strange button on the side that, once pressed, opened a screen of sorts. When this was illuminated, it showed a picture of Riordan's face, with strange markings all around it. Xe had never seen symbols like these before. Xe tapped the bottom of the screen, and another picture popped up: it was a beautiful fourth with long, black, curly hair, skin the colour of warm khaki, and a weathered but still-hopeful face. Xe looked at that image for a long time, trying to find something there. Was he also being hunted? There was a diagonal red line across his picture.

Riordan took the device over to the cell where the Enforcer slept.

Yun-seo woke up and saw the device in xir hand. "My telecom."

"This ... telecom," Riordan said slowly, the word foreign to xir tongue, "why does it have my picture and next to it, a picture of this fourth?" Xe showed them the screen.

"He's your mother," Yun-seo said.

Riordan was confused. "How do ya know that?"

"That's what it says: he's your only known relative."

Riordan looked at the screen again. "It talks to you?"

Yun-seo let out a sigh. "Shit, I forgot none of you know how to read."

"What?" Riordan was getting angry.

Fearing the second's imposing presence, Yun-seo brought their legs closer to their body, trying to make themselves small. "The markings on the screen are characters. Each character makes a sound, and together the sounds make words—like us talking, but written down on the screen." Their teeth chattered, and they flinched whenever the inventor got close.

"Stop that," Riordan ordered. "I'm not going to hurt ya." Yun-seo nodded a few times, then rolled their shoulders back. They lifted their chin, but dared not look Riordan in the eye.

"Show me how to speak with the markings," Riordan demanded. "Can ya do that?"

Yun-seo stared blankly at the wall next to them as if lost in thought. Then their chest heaved and their lips parted, and out came encoded mutterings interspersed with curses—some in harsh whispers, others in panicked shouts. Riordan felt sorry for the way this Enforcer was unravelling before them. Xe quickly tamped the feeling down and wheeled away.

Riordan looked at the picture of the fourth. *I had a mother*, xe thought, staring intently at his face. Xe had no memories of him, and he looked nothing like xir—xir skin was far paler, and xir hair was red, not black. Riordan didn't understand how xe could be biologically related to this person. Perhaps Riordan's other parent looked just like xir? There were smatterings of people around with pale skin, one or two with red hair, but people's skin tones and hair colour in Zhōng yang varied in every possible way a human's could.

Xe was so confused. Just when xe had felt like xe finally had the upper hand, xe had discovered the Madjideye had some sort of secret marking code that only Enforcers could understand. Was that how they had subdued the remnants of humanity all this time? No one remembered a time without the Madjideye. No one remembered a time when the sky hadn't been grey with a dull-orange glow that periodically appeared and then went away. To everyone alive now, darkness had always been the norm. No one remembered the ramshackle buildings ever being new. No one even understood any-more how to build them in the first place.

But the Madjideye know all this. And I'm going to find out for myself, Riordan thought.

CHAPTER XII

HIGHER GROUND

The poison rains had not stopped since they began, nor had they ever lasted so long before. Many villagers succumbed to illness.

Nitàwesì became increasingly concerned as time went by. Pasakamate rested at the bottom of a basin. With each day, the puddles grew larger, gradually becoming small lakes. The water was now inches deep everywhere—in their dwelling, they had to move everything off the floor.

Shkitagen was the only person still capable of making fire with everything so wet. The other village firekeepers were all elders, and their gifts were waning. If the rain didn't let up, they would have to leave the village, but how, when it was dangerous to be out in the rain? Things were looking dire.

Shkitagen sat cross-legged on the bed, naked except for the pouch Nitàwesì had sewn for him, which was tied around his neck. Inside was the precious fire-starting kit he had carefully cultivated: a small chunk of the mushroom he was named after, which in its scarcity was passed down from generation to generation, and some fabric fluff. Every good firekeeper carried a kit such as this. Fearing the rain, Shkitagen never took his off. Beside the bed stood a pair of boots that protected his feet from the poison rainwater, enabling him to walk safely anywhere in the village.

The only good thing to come from all this rain was that the village remained safe from hunters, who feared the rain as much as they did.

"You think this will ever stop?" Shkitagen asked, rolling over in bed and facing Nitàwesì. He tenderly stroked their back.

Nitàwesì shook their head. "We need to talk about leaving," they signed.

Shkitagen sighed. "The elders are saying that we should stay, that there's a reason for the rains. That they'll go away when they're meant to."

"We can't stay here." Nitàwesì sat up. "We should pack up the essentials and leave before the hunters show up. We can try to find someplace safer where we don't have to worry about getting kidnapped every day, where we aren't scared of drowning in our sleep." They took Shkitagen's hand and placed it over their stomach. "I want to try," they signed, pausing for a moment to look Shkitagen in the eye. "I know it's rare for fourths to carry children, but—"

"We'll try," Shkitagen whispered.

"But only someplace where we're safe," Nitàwesì signed, eyebrows knit together with concern. "A baby would die in this rain."

"Sounds like a plan." Shkitagen leaned forward and kissed Nitàwesì tenderly, clutched their torso, bringing their bodies flush together. His kisses turned heated, his mouth moving south with chaste pecks on their shoulder, arm, chest, navel, thigh, calf, and finally their toes. Rising, Shkitagen brought his large hands to rest under his lover's thighs. Nitàwesì moaned, a deep guttural sound, as Shkitagen sucked them between their thighs. The healer gently placed their palms on the firekeeper's head, holding him to their core, feeling the motion of his tongue as it savoured them. In this moment, time suspended, the rain itself frozen in its mission to destroy their village. They *breathed*. Their two bodies spoke, created fire, dispelled myths.

Together, they quieted the raging storm.

Only a few others from the village wanted to come with them. The elders stubbornly refused to give up the land, and many sided with them. This village had resisted the Madjideye, they reasoned; the Enforcers rarely bothered them, and the only price they had to pay for this freedom was the occasional attack from hunters. The rain was there, the elders claimed, to keep them safe from the hunters, at least for a time.

Shkitagen regarded their belongings, which were carefully packaged in waterproof containers tied together with twine and plastic bags. He wore a plastic covering over his body. Another villager had fashioned them some wide hats out of plastic container lids—they protected the body from rain so long as the wearer hunched over. Shkitagen hoisted his belongings and secured them to his shoulders and waist.

Outside, Nitàwesì was waiting for him, along with two of the village warriors, Pejik and Amisk, a nurturer, Nodin, and her child, Ojiwan.

Shkitagen's father was there to say goodbye. A tall, heavy-set first with large hands and an ample bosom, he was one of the few in Pasakamate adept at mixing food rations with the last remaining creeping and crawling things found under rocks in order to nourish their small family. Shkitagen clutched his father, who had nurtured him his whole life. After one last embrace from both Shkitagen and

Nitàwesì, his father turned her back to them and returned to her dwelling.

It destroyed Shkitagen to leave his father. If only he could persuade the other villagers to join them. But perhaps the elders did know best; perhaps their cohort would return one day, begging forgiveness for having left.

With a nod, Shkitagen led the group away from Pasakamate.

It took two days of continuous uphill walking for them to exit the basin that Pasakamate sat nestled at the bottom of. On the third day, they passed an overhanging cliff that looked out over their village. The dwellings looked so small way down in the drainage basin. It was a sore sight for everyone—they quickly marched onward into the unexplored terrain. Only the warriors were familiar with the land that stretched out ahead of them, having taken this route on their patrols.

Shkitagen had seldom ventured out of the village. As a child, he'd often dreamed about going on adventures with his merchant father, who came to visit when their travelling village was nearby. But those desires vanished when Shkitagen turned seven and the elders came to his dwelling to explain that he was the sole firekeeper of his generation. The responsibility associated with that gift dominated his thoughts. As early as the days when they were courting one another, Nitàwesì quickly became a tether for him, calming him against the elders' overwhelming determination to pass on to him every song and ceremony regarding the importance of firekeeping. Shkitagen was grateful for his gift and couldn't imagine himself carrying any other role, but the peace he felt while wrapped in his lover's arms couldn't be surpassed. The thought of having a family, of raising children with Nitàwesì, of a home filled with warmth and small, laughing children, was Shkitagen's greatest wish. Throughout his life, he had seen people disappear and warriors killed at the hands of hunters. And though this land was gifted to them by Kichi Manido, and Pasakamate had existed in this exact place for thousands of years, that didn't mean there wasn't potentially someplace better and safer out in the world.

Shkitagen noticed Nodin was getting weary. Nitàwesì also took note and gently tugged on the firekeeper's sleeve until he motioned for everyone to stop and rest. After eating, Nodin and Ojiwan rested their heads on their packs while Pejik and Amisk toyed with the weapons they had brought with them—handmade spears, menacing with their serrated blades bound with wire.

A distant roar sounded then.

"Do you hear that?" Pejik asked.

The roar grew louder. "Pasakamate!" yelled Amisk.

Shkitagen gestured to Nitàwesì and Amisk to follow him. "Stay here with our belongings," he ordered the remaining three.

They ran toward the cliff as fast as they could. The cacophony intensified with each step until it was deafening. The earth trembled slightly—

And then silence.

They reached the cliff. Where previously a small valley between mountain ranges had protected their village for generations, the drainage basin was now completely filled with water. It rose to just a few feet below the cliff edge and stretched as far as the eye could see. In the distance, where once a giant wall had loomed over the village basin, there was now nothing but rubble. Water was rushing through and over the rocks, cascading into the basin, which was nearly full now. Debris floated on the water's surface: remnants of dwellings and personal belongings, as well as a few bodies.

The village of Pasakamate was no more.

Nitàwesì collapsed to their knees and broke the tense silence with a scream. Amisk, stunned, sat down on the ground and rested his head against his knees, hands trembling as he rocked back and forth, muttering, "No, no, no, no, no, no."

Shkitagen couldn't breathe. His home was gone. All the feeling left his body; he felt no cold or warmth, and what wind there was seemed to pass right through him. He felt his spirit floating through and above him. The wave of dread and pain that should have hooked into his gut was instead ravaging his spirit, just beyond his reach.

Now, finally, the rain stopped—for the first time in weeks. But Shkitagen was too full of rage to notice. Too numb to move. He let the other two mourn for a few minutes more.

"Let's go back. We need to keep moving."

Nitàwesì looked at him, frightened. They were inconsolable, shaking their head, unable to stand. Shkitagen picked his lover up and hoisted them onto his back. Shouldering the short shaking fourth, he started back toward the rest of their group, followed by Amisk. Nitàwesì's tears darkened his shoulder the entire way.

The others stood up when they arrived.

"The village is gone," Amisk stated sadly. "Water has filled the entire basin. The rain from all the past weeks must have overwhelmed the back wall."

Nitàwesì jumped down from Shkitagen's back. They rushed over to Nodin and wrapped her in their arms. Ojiwan was nestled between them, clutching his mother's coat and crying softly. The two warriors enveloped them and started to sob as well.

Shkitagen watched, still numb inside. Nitàwesì looked at him and opened their arms, inviting him in. Shkitagen's feet moved without his consent, and soon he was in the arms of his beloved, surrounded by their group. He felt safe, secluded in a cave of warmth and family and acceptance. Only then did his tears start to fall, did the names of the dead, of the family he had left behind, leave his lips.

■

The group stayed rooted to that spot for days, unable to bear travelling farther from the village but unable to get any closer. Together they took turns returning to the cliff, each time hoping to see that some-one, anyone, had survived. And each time, they returned dejected.

Nitàwesì refused to sign. They shook their head or nodded to com-municate, but that was it. Shkitagen noticed how Nitàwesì's hands trembled and how they stared, too, as if they couldn't understand what was happening to them.

Shkitagen made fire, but his flames were small, pathetic, a fraction of what he was capable of. The warriors couldn't throw their spears or loose their arrows with accuracy; the nurturer couldn't soothe her child. They were all broken by the loss of Pasakamate. Shkitagen thought he should have died along with the village. When he looked at the others, he saw the same thought etched in their otherwise empty gazes.

Shkitagen attempted to keep the group fed. They sat huddled together underneath a makeshift shelter. There was a small fire in the corner, and a pan with a broken handle rested above it, cooking tender pieces of food.

The warrior who'd been away at the cliff came running toward them at full speed. "Hunters!" he screamed at the top of his lungs.

Shkitagen put out the fire and quickly placed the child on his back. Nitàwesì and Nodin gathered up the group's belongings.

The other warrior grabbed her weapons and ran over to her coun-terpart. "Go! We'll defend you!" she yelled.

In the distance, Shkitagen spied an opening in the mountainside. Perhaps they could hide out there for a few days, until the hunters moved on, assuming everyone from the village to be dead.

"There!" he yelled. "Head toward the cave in the mountain!"

Nitàwesì kept pace with him, their short legs strong from so much labour. Nodin, however, faltered and could not keep up. Shkitagen grabbed her hand and spurred her forward. With his other hand at his back, he held Ojiwan close. Together, the three adults ran, tripping occasionally over stones and uneven terrain.

"Don't look back!" he yelled, and then he did exactly that—just in time to see the warriors locked in battle with over a dozen hunters swarming the path.

The villagers from Pasakamate had first encountered the hunters back when Shkitagen's father was a child. She'd told her son horrifying tales of this culture that covered their bodies in ash and kidnapped people to be sold in the big cities—or, worse, to the Madjideye. Many had gone to the cities to try and find their loved ones, yet none succeeded. Some returned years later, adamant that whoever they'd been searching for had died. They said that people in the cities had told them of the atrocities done to hunted humans. They were forced to do the worst things one could imagine, and often they disappeared. No one knew where they went or, even worse, where their bodies were.

Against this ongoing terror, a generation of warriors rose up. Pasakamate had once been a firekeepers' village, but in light of this crisis, the fire needed to go underground so the villagers could be protected. Shkitagen's father often mused that this was the reason her son was the only one in his generation born a firekeeper. Anyone else capable of making the flames was either an elder or had been taken.

Nodin was wheezing now, her pace sluggish. Nitàwesì's breath came in short, stuttering gasps. Shkitagen stopped short, and the others followed suit. He looked back and saw that Amisk and Pejik lay on the ground, unmoving—the hunters had succeeded in subduing the warriors and were now heading toward them. He began to shake. He knew the only course of action at their disposal.

"Take the child," he ordered. Nitàwesì lifted the infant from Shkitagen's back.

Shkitagen turned and faced his love, held their face in both hands. Tears streamed down Nitàwesì's face. They shook their head, Ojiwan clinging to their torso for dear life.

"I'm going to offer myself up to them. I might be worth enough to spare the three of you," Shkitagen whispered. "Get to the cave. You can hide there for a few days, wait this out. And when it's safe, head to the city and find me. I'll make it so you can find me. I know you will."

Nitàwesì sobbed openly. Nodin murmured to Ojiwan, who cried loudly. "I'm going with Shkitagen," she whispered, offering no further explanation. She nuzzled her mournful child. "Ojiwan, I'll watch over you." Then she kissed him and stepped away, turning to face the incoming hunters.

Shkitagen placed a kiss on his love's lips—one last promise, one last desperate plea to the universe for mercy for the both of them.

Nitàwesì wanted to sign something, *anything*, but they couldn't while holding the child. Ojiwan screamed for his mother, wriggling as if trying to free himself from the healer's hold. Nitàwesì gripped the thick bundle of blankets around Ojiwan tighter, their knuckles whitening. They let out a deep, echoing wail, their voice cracking from disuse. The sound startled the child into sudden stillness. Shkitagen gasped, his eyes wide. Nitàwesì's chest heaved.

The firekeeper shook his head and chuckled. "I love you, too, my odey."

Nitàwesì bit their lip and nodded stiffly. They took two steps back, turned away from their other half, and ran.

The farther they ran, the louder Ojiwan screamed for his mother. Finally, they reached the cave's entrance, and the child quieted, releasing only tearful hiccups.

Nitàwesì watched as, in the distance, Shkitagen and Nodin both raised their hands. Shkitagen snapped his fingers, and flames appeared in the palms of both his hands.

"You have your prize," Shkitagen sneered, pointing at himself. "Go after the others, and I will unleash hellfire and end all our lives."

The hunters nodded. They proceeded to bind his hands, also sheathing them in strange gloves that prevented him from directing his fire. The threat remained, however; if he had to, Shkitagen could use his entire body as a portal to send out fire in every direction, forfeiting his life and the lives of anyone in the vicinity.

He glanced back one last time and prayed to the Creator of all things living and nonliving. "Kichi Manido, let them find us," he said, feeling a deep pang in his chest as he marched behind one ash-covered hunter. Nodin trailing behind another. He took one more look at the warriors who had given their lives and offered a prayer that their souls would find peace.

Nitàwesì entered the cave ahead of them and skittered deep into the shadows. They leaned back against the cool, dry rock and slid down to the ground, extending their sore legs in front of them, the child resting on their knees. Nitàwesì covered their mouth with a hand to muffle their screams.

I'm not worth this sacrifice. I should have been captured with Shkitagen.

Ojiwan clutched them for comfort. Nitàwesì put an arm around him and rocked the both of them. Eventually, exhaustion overwhelmed them, and they fell asleep.

CHAPTER XIII

RETURN

After walking for days on end, Bèl and A'tugwewinu faced a familiar sight: Zhōng yang loomed over the horizon.

"We should hurry," A'tugwewinu stated.

Bèl shook her head fiercely. "Absolutely not. It's crawling with Enforcers. They probably have your face plastered all over those machines they walk around with. You'll go right back into the hellhole I just spent months trying to bust you out of." She was annoyed— they'd had this argument far too many times over the past few days.

A'tugwewinu looked at her imploringly.

I can't believe I'm agreeing to this, Bèl thought. She groaned and raised her eyes skyward, as if to plead with whatever spirits existed behind the haze. "We go straight to Riordan," she said.

A'tugwewinu smiled wide. She opened up her pack and took out an old can with a faded label. It contained some sort of edible mush. She sawed into it with a serrated knife, struggling until she was able to peel back the metal lid. Inside were small chunks of what was perhaps meat from some extinct animal.

A'tugwewinu and Bèl took turns diving in for pieces. The thick liquid in the can coated their hands.

Bèl looked her lover over. "How is it healing?" she asked, nodding to A'tugwewinu's bandaged arm.

The eighth slowly peeled back the bandage, hissing as she did. The wound was no longer bleeding; still raw flesh, it was in the very first stages of knitting itself back together.

"Huh," A'tugwewinu huffed. "I could have sworn it was getting infected."

Bèl grimaced, trying to hide her aversion to her lover's many wounds and bruises.

"One day, we'll go back there and put an end to those Enforcers and free everyone." Bèl clenched her fists, crushing the empty can in her iron grip.

A'tugwewinu placed her bloodied, bandaged fingertips on Bèl's arm. Bèl glanced up and saw concerned eyes staring at her. A'tugwewinu nodded once before scooting over and resting her head on her lover's shoulder, the prickles on her scalp tickling the warrior's skin.

"Tell me how you found me," A'tugwewinu said, as she wove her arm around Bèl's and snuggled as close as she could.

Bèl sighed. "I woke up alone, confused, like I had been dreaming for years." She closed her eyes, trying to remember every detail.

A'tugwewinu was the storyteller of the two; Bèl had a hard time speaking elaborately about past events, or any event, really. For her, words were sometimes difficult to formulate. Her body was her language—with it, she could lash out in anger or undulate in pleasure or shake with joy. And no matter what, A'tugwewinu always seemed to understand. Most days, Bèl wondered why she deserved something so *good* as A'tugwewinu. Why, in a world filled with struggle and torment, would the spirits grant her such a gift? It was a question she would ponder until her final breath.

"Then I saw someone. They were hazy, their face unclear. They were healing me." Bèl rubbed her forehead, trying to remember.

"A healer stumbled upon you?" A'tugwewinu said.

"No, I don't think they were living," Bèl clarified. "It felt like there were hands inside my body, like there was warmth in every part of me. And I prayed, Winu—every second of every day that I lay there, unable to move. I prayed, asking them to take my blood, my eyes, whatever they wanted, just so I could make it back to you. I pleaded with them—'It's too soon,' I told them. And I guess they agreed with me, because one morning I just woke up and sat upright. It hurt like a deep ache, but I did it. My hunger came back with a vengeance. I could feel my toes and fingers, and that was when I realized: I think I might have died, or been close to it. I know I'm not making too much sense, ita'. I just—I wanted to be with you so desperately that I didn't care what it cost me."

A'tugwewinu cried silently. "I prayed every day for Death to take me so I could be with you," she whispered.

"It looks like I prayed harder than you," Bèl teased. But deep down, the third was worried. It wasn't the first time that A'tugwewinu had wished for Death, called them friend and welcomed them.

"Am I—" The warrior paused, already regretting her question. "Am I the only thing you live for?"

A'tugwewinu was stunned by the question. "I don't—I think—" She broke down and started sobbing. Bèl heaved her body on top of A'tugwewinu's so she could wrap her arms around her lover properly and hold her close as she cried.

"Mo-most days, yes, it's just you," the storyteller said through her tears.

Bèl sighed, having figured as much. "Sometimes I think even the spirits are fearful of our love. They test it only to find it could shatter Atabey with its might."

A'tugwewinu nodded. "They're all gone—Nokomis, my parents, my village ... How am I supposed to live in this world without elders to guide me?"

Bèl held her tightly, mindful of her wounds. "I don't know. Perhaps we just need to live long enough to figure that out. A generation of children left without guides, save scant spirits who speak in riddles and leave more questions than answers."

A'tugwewinu wiped her face on Bèl's broad chest. "Tell me the rest," she said, trying to change the subject. She didn't want to think about having to function in a world where she was the last of her people. Though other memorizers now existed, they would never know the heat and rush that came from hearing a story for the first time, the feeling as it found its home within your body—a familiar, something that stayed with you and held you close. The memorizers who now existed would never know how it felt to trigger words, to have them flow out of you with the ease of breathing, would never know the words in Anishinabemowin that named the world around them. Words that weren't simply spoken, but felt as if they were the very life force within one's veins.

Bèl, too, knew this feeling, though her calling was that of warrior. Her blood pulsed with the thrum of battle; her heart beat for protection and peace.

"Well ..." Bèl started.

Realization dawned on A'tugwewinu. "Stories," she said suddenly. "Stories are my reason for living."

Bèl smiled. "Then that is what you must fight to protect."

A'tugwewinu nodded and motioned for Bèl to continue.

"There honestly isn't much else to it. I followed the Enforcers' tracks for a while, then I came upon a travelling village. They pointed me to a nearby camp. I was terrified I'd be searching camps endlessly and would never find the one they sent you to. But on my way, I spotted a caravan. I had a gut feeling: that many Enforcers wouldn't displace themselves for anything short of a special occasion. As I got closer to the prison, I heard Atabey whisper and smelled ghosts in the air. I knew you were there. Finally I saw you surrounded by a dozen people, sharing stories. I wanted to scream and run to you right then, but I knew I needed to wait. The rest you know."

"Chi miigwech," A'tugwewinu breathed, unable to utter anything more.

They rested there that night, comforted by the sounds of each other's breathing, holding each other close.

■

"You are a third—do you know what that means?" exalted her uncle. Bèl shook her head. "It means your gender is better than a first or a second. You will be stronger, able to carry three to four times your body weight. You'll be faster, too, than any other gender—perfect for a guazabara," he stated.

Bèl simply nodded, absorbing the information.

"I am only a mere second." He said the word as though it was acid on his tongue. "But I will do my best to train you in the art of fighting, so that one day you may join our family's generations-long legacy of guazabara. You know of this legacy, right?"

Bèl shook her head. She was only seven. But this seemed so important—why didn't she know?

Her uncle sighed again. "We are Taino. We have been guazabara for thousands of years. These ancient techniques have been passed down through the generations. You will learn them, understood?"

Bèl nodded. All the adults around her and some of the older kids were warriors. They were brave, and so she would be as well.

"Come, sit next to me. We will start by changing the way you breathe."

Bèl ran over and plopped herself down next to her uncle.

She did exactly as he did, moving when he told her to. He showed her the art of utilizing her environment to her advantage, predicting outcomes and making changes to suit her needs. It was gruelling work, day in and day out. But it was important to the survival of the ancient ways. Deep down, Bèl was sure her parents would have been proud of who she became.

One stormy day a few years later, her uncle and cousins were hired as mercenaries in another city. Bèl was tasked with ensuring that their home, which contained tools accumulated over hundreds of years, was kept safe and ready for their return.

Over a decade passed, and still she waited for her family to come back.

■

A'tugwewinu and Bèl lowered their hoods to cover their noses. This limited their view of what was above them, but Bèl didn't dwell on that. The city's buildings were mostly piles of rubble, anyway; the majority of people lived below the streets, in the sewers and gutters. The rest lived on the ground. In Zhōng yang, looking down was life preserving.

Inside the city's perimeter, they kept about twenty paces apart, staying in constant view of one another, but not so close that they seemed to be together. It was a practised dance. With a code of subtle hand gestures—brushing one's left or right shoulder, scratching the back of one's head, or pulling on the bottom of one's cloak—they let each other know how safe a new street corner was.

A few Enforcers looked their way but moved on; it seemed A'tugwewinu and Bèl passed as inconspicuous. They took a round-about and backward way to get to Riordan's home. It was one of xir rules: *Never get there the same way twice. Always make sure you aren't being followed—if you are, double back. Never bring anyone to xir home that xe hasn't vetted first.*

After a few hours of this, they arrived together at one of the hidden entrances to Riordan's compound. With a final glance around their periphery to make sure they hadn't been followed, they crawled into the small opening behind an old metal container and emerged on the other side in a large, open space filled with children and young adults of all shapes and sizes. Some of the children recognized them imme-diately while others glared warily.

Aware that all eyes were on them, A'tugwewinu and Bèl removed their cloaks and strolled to the other side of the compound, looking for Riordan. Xe pulled back the tattered tarp that served as a curtain and a door to xir sleeping space and beamed as soon as xe saw them. Xe wheeled over faster than either of them could run and threw xir arms around them both. A'tugwewinu barely reached xir shoulder, though Bèl was almost the same height as Riordan.

"Sibs!" xe yelled, holding them tightly. A'tugwewinu had tears in her eyes. It had been too long since she had seen her sibling.

Riordan pulled away, leaving a hand on each of their shoulders. "Ya both look like death warmed over," xe said disapprovingly, noting their gaunt faces. Xe raised the bottom of Bèl's shirt an inch to fully reveal the mottled skin on her abdomen. "And you were shot at close range." Riordan whistled softly, then turned to A'tugwewinu and took her hand. Xe noted the bandages on each fingertip, the bruises dotting her skin.

"The Madjideye caught ya, eh?" the inventor breathed.

A'tugwewinu nodded.

"Come get somethin' to eat and tell me everythin'." Riordan spoke softly, as if afraid any sudden movement or change in tone might scare them off.

In the distance, they heard screams coming from somewhere within the dwelling, in a language neither of them could comprehend. Sobs and wails followed, along with more shouting.

Riordan spoke up before A'tugwewinu or Bèl could utter a word. "Would ya like to meet Elite Enforcer H-09761?" xe asked.

Bèl reeled back. "You captured an Enforcer? And brought them here? What about the kids?" she shouted.

Riordan's grin was demonic. "I'm on their hit list. My choices were either ta capture an Enforcer and try ta get the bounty taken off my head, or ta keep killing 'em as they come fer me." Xe shrugged.

"But how did you capture them?" A'tugwewinu asked.

"Well, I have my warrior trainer to thank for that." Riordan nodded to Bèl. "Also, I think we got an easy one. You'll see, they're pretty unstable."

Together, they headed over to where the prisoner was being held.

A'tugwewinu and Bèl both gasped in horror at the sight of the human writhing on the floor of the makeshift cell. Their body was covered in sweat, their hair was tangled, and their clothes were dirty and twisted.

"Riordan! The hell you doin' to them?" A'tugwewinu cursed and rushed over to the Enforcer, a young third. She placed her hands over the Enforcer's, which were chained to the pipe above their head.

"Hey, don't blame me. I didn't do this to 'em. The Madjideye makes 'em take these pills. Most Enforcers die after two days without 'em, but this one's been at it for weeks now."

A'tugwewinu tsked harshly. "How many Enforcers have you captured and killed?"

"Really?" Riordan bit back angrily. "Ya watched yer entire village get obliterated by 'em, been hunted by 'em for years, and you seriously feel compassion for these machines? I thought you were delusional before, Winu, but fuck yer bleedin' heart!"

Riordan felt a firm hand slap down on xir arm where the flesh was still raw. Xe cringed.

"That had better be the end of that subject," Bèl threatened. She squeezed Riordan's flesh without mercy.

Trust Bèl to find the most vulnerable spot. Riordan grimaced in pain. Xe shrugged out of Bèl's grip, knowing full well xe was able to do so only because the warrior let xir. Otherwise, xe would still be in a world of pain.

A'tugwewinu ignored the two of them and wiped away some of the sweat from the Enforcer's brow. She gently lulled a song her mother had used to sing to help her sleep. After a few minutes, the Enforcer stilled and appeared to fall asleep. A'tugwewinu gently laid them down.

"You sure they're an Enforcer?" Bèl asked.

Riordan nodded. "Yup, blasted a hole through my arm and everythin'. Haven't left my house in weeks cuz of the Madjideye's bounty on me. This one here gives me info when they aren't being tortured by their own memories."

"Wait, blew a hole through your arm?" Bèl asked.

"Yeah, damn gifts. This Enforcer can make balls of fire with their hands. Melted a chunk off my arm, then used a soft fire to burn away the infection. Helped heal the wound." Riordan spoke nonchalantly.

"How can someone be both a warrior and a healer?" Bèl asked.

Riordan shrugged. "They don't know either. Must be something Enforcers are trained to do."

Bèl investigated Riordan's upper left arm. The scar was in the same place as A'tugwewinu's. Bèl's eyebrows rose. *Ri and Winu have always been connected in a strange way, like siblings who crossed lifetimes to be part of each other's families.*

"Why are their memories torturing them?" A'tugwewinu asked.

"Those pills made 'em forget—keeps 'em from questioning orders, they said. I always wondered if Enforcers were actually machines, but it's the Madjideye. They keep 'em all brainwashed and complacent." Riordan shrugged again and wheeled off toward the kitchen.

Bèl followed, looking behind her one last time at the person shivering on the floor. *Are all Enforcers just scared kids under all that armour?* This person looked younger than A'tugwewinu. How young were those the Madjideye was recruiting for their army?

A'tugwewinu rested her hand on the warrior's cheek, as if reading her thoughts. She shook her head, and they followed Riordan out.

CHAPTER XIV

FAMILIAR

Their father only ever smiled when his eyes rested on them or on their mother. His smiles were special, like a secret he shared with them. Whenever his eyes drifted outside the dwelling, his smile turned into a scowl, and his gaze became hard, like he was staring down an enemy.

On the day the Enforcers arrived at their village, he whispered, "Yun-seo, you need to hide! Run to our spot and stay there. I'll come get you when it's safe."

Yun-seo nodded. This was a game they played often, whenever the big armoured Enforcers visited their village. They ran out the side of the dwelling, toward the outcropping of rocks in the distance. Behind them, they heard shouting. They turned to see Enforcers dragging their parents from their home.

"Hide, Yun-seo!" their father screamed.

But they couldn't move. They watched as one of the Enforcers' hands glowed dark blue, as a ball of light snapped free of them and struck their mother's face. Her dark eyes, beautiful brown skin, and full lips were no more—in their place was only melted flesh and blood. They watched as her body crumpled to the ground.

Their father screamed again. He brought his palms together, hands radiating light—something Yun-seo had never seen before. His hands glowed red, growing brighter and brighter. Another Enforcer fired a gun at Yun-seo's father. The bullet went straight through his midsection. He faltered for a second, then looked Yun-seo in the eye and shouted something.

But Yun-seo heard nothing over the crackling of their father's hands. They turned and ran as fast as they could.

From behind them came a loud pop and a wave of heat that pushed them onto their knees.

They looked back to where their dwelling had been, but nothing of it remained. Their home, their parents, the Enforcers—all had been reduced to ashes.

■

Yun-seo bolted upright, screaming. They started sobbing anew, the memories freshly washing over them.

A shadow appeared overhead. They looked up to see the tall brute staring down at them.

"Feel up to some visitors?" Riordan teased. The Enforcer and the inventor were still mutually wary, but after seeing so much of each other every day for what felt like weeks, the two had become uncomfortably familiar.

Riordan bent down and handed Yun-seo a cup of cold water, which they gulped down greedily. Yun-seo looked down at themselves. They had lost track of time; they had no idea exactly how long they had been here, at the street kids' compound. It had been several weeks, at least. They were provided a bucket for their waste. The poor medic came in every few hours to discard its contents. Every few days, they were also given a bucket of water and a washcloth, and one of their arms was untied, so they could clean their own filth. Along the way, Yun-seo had inherited a warm shirt and a soft pair of pants, the material faded and worn.

"You want me to meet people looking like this?" Yun-seo responded, gesturing to their clothes, which were twisted and filthy. They were covered in sweat. After they'd been allowed to bathe, they'd figured that they had proven they could be trusted, but no—once they were dressed again, Riordan had dragged them back to their cell and tied them right back up.

"We've seen worse," said A'tugwewinu, as she entered the space.

Yun-seo assessed the visitors. The one on the left was a third, tall with broad shoulders, a wiry yet muscular frame, and deep, calculating eyes. A dozen thick braids neatly lined her scalp, tied at the nape of her neck and reaching to midback. Her fingertips and hands were calloused, a testament to decades of warrior training. Her gait was light, graceful, as if she could spring into action at a moment's notice. Weapons—knives, machetes, and other sharp objects Yun-seo didn't know the names of—were strapped to her arms, pants, belt, and chest. And those were only the weapons Yun-seo could see. Out of everyone in the room, they realized, this person was the most dangerous.

Next to her stood a first—or perhaps an eighth. Yun-seo was confused and having difficulty sensing this person's gender as it fluctuated before them. She was much shorter than the rest, with a shaved head of tiny black prickles and tawny bronze skin adorned with hundreds of tattoos. Yun-seo focused on the tattoos, a spark of recognition in their rattled mind.

"You're the survivor from Andwànikàdjigan!" they stated.

A'tugwewinu flinched. Bèl swept in front of A'tugwewinu, one hand poised above the machete at her belt.

"What do ya know about that, eh?" Riordan sneered.

"I don't know much. Just that we received a report a while back, when I had finished my, uh, training," they stuttered. Memories punched into their core: higher-ups beating them, mocking them as they wept from lack of food and the constant pain that lurked in every muscle. "The report," they resumed, shaking away the nightmares. "It stated that one of the villagers had survived. You were deemed one of the highest-level threats. They sent an entire team after you."

"They caught me," A'tugwewinu whispered. "They caught me and shot her." She swallowed and pointed at the tall third shielding her. "And then they took me to some prison and left me there for months."

Yun-seo swallowed. "The Almighty"—all three of the visitors' stares turned hard—"I mean, the Madjideye, they know you escaped. They must know. If you let me look at the telecom, I could tell you."

Riordan stalked off and returned moments later with the telecom. Xe handed it to Yun-seo.

Yun-seo checked the bottom of the screen for status updates. There were a few. They tapped various buttons, and a list appeared, with one entry marked "urgent." They tapped that, and A'tugwewinu's image flashed back at them, with an image of Bèl next to it. Yun-seo turned the screen to show them.

Bèl scowled. "We need to leave—what if they find out we're here?"

Riordan shook xir head. "Yer safest here with the kids. They give me eyes ta every square inch of this city. We'll know when they're coming. Out in the wild, ya have no one but yerselves."

"In the wild, our children aren't at risk!" A'tugwewinu protested.

Bèl ripped the telecom from Yun-seo's hands. "This needs to be destroyed."

"Wait!" Riordan said. "I need to figure out how it works. We could use it against the Madjideye."

"It's too risky—Winu's life is at stake!" Bèl shouted.

"I know what's at stake!" Riordan roared back.

Bèl's chest heaved. For a moment it looked like she might break the device. A'tugwewinu reached between them and placed a hand on Bèl's arm. Bèl deflated instantly. She turned and stormed off without a word.

"Typical day for the family," Riordan said before wheeling away.

A'tugwewinu stared a long time at Yun-seo, who appeared confused. Behind the cowering human, Nokomis's shadow had shifted into her periphery. A'tugwewinu gasped as he looked at her. He raised his palm and gently placed it on Yun-seo's head, then looked at A'tugwewinu and smiled. *Trust them,* Nokomis whispered to her ear alone.

Though she didn't understand exactly what he meant, A'tugwewinu approached Yun-seo anyway.

"I'm A'tugwewinu," she said.

"Yun-seo," they responded, stretching out a hand. A'tugwewinu stared at it. "Do the Andwànikàdjigan not shake hands?" the third asked.

"I don't know what that means."

Yun-seo dropped their arm. "Destroying the telecom won't do anything. The Madjideye will still be able to send out notices on every other Enforcer's device."

A'tugwewinu nodded and sat down in front of them. "I see. Where are you from, Yun-seo?"

"My mother and her family came from a land across the ocean, very far from this continent. But no one knows how to get back there, or if anyone there is still alive. I grew up in a merchant village that travelled west of here. My father was of the first peoples and knew how to navigate the land. That's as much as I remember," Yun-seo finished sadly.

A'tugwewinu stared, curious. "I don't carry many stories about other lands. Maybe one day you could tell me more about yours, and then I could hold on to it and tell others? What was your mother's land called?"

Yun-seo smiled softly. "She couldn't remember."

"Oh. I'm sorry," A'tugwewinu whispered.

"That's why the Andwànikàdjigan terrify the Madjideye so much. They control everyone, you know, not just Zhōng yang. Once everything had a name, not just us. The buildings, the nations, the clothing we wore—they all had names. And once books and the internet were destroyed, well, everyone forgot, except for you and the other storytellers."

A'tugwewinu was confused. "What are books and … internet?" She tried to digest these words, to commit them to memory.

"The markings that cover your body—the Madjideye identified them as an ancient syllabic system that first peoples developed thousands of years ago. The Madjideye use a different system for writing based on a holy language that also existed hundreds of years ago. When they take us, they force us to learn it by putting the markings down in objects that were once called 'books.' But now we use these telecoms."

A'tugwewinu nodded. *These are the objects Nokomis talked about!* She glanced at Nokomis for confirmation. He simply looked at her.

She pressed on with Yun-seo. "Are there other storyteller villages?"

"Not that I know of. Yours was unique. There are other first peoples' villages, though. My father was from one called Omamiwinini."

"Where is Omamiwinini? I've never heard of it," A'tugwewinu interrupted.

"Omamiwinini is gone. The bombs took it before I was born," Yun-seo stated sadly.

"Bombs?"

"Giant explosions with fire that rises into the sky."

"Oh. That's how the Madjideye destroyed Andwànikàdjigan."

"I know." Yun-seo looked at the brick wall next to them, unable to meet the storyteller's gaze.

A'tugwewinu wiped her eyes and cleared her throat. "You say first peoples, but we are Anishinabeg. That's our word. It means we are the people who are connected to Kichi Manido by our belly buttons. It's a sacred, spiritual connection. It ties into our creation story."

Yun-seo smiled at her. "I would really love to hear that story."

A'tugwewinu took another glance at Nokomis. Yun-seo turned their head to look to where she was staring but saw nothing. Nokomis nodded.

This is your purpose. His voice rang in A'tugwewinu's mind and then he dissipated.

A'tugwewinu hummed. Yun-seo looked at her expectantly, but she didn't offer any explanation. She shuffled closer. "Push these markings here." She pointed at a smattering of scratched markings on the skin above her heart.

Yun-seo swallowed, nervous for some reason. They reached out and touched the slightly raised skin, the marks like smooth scars. Then they watched, stunned, as A'tugwewinu's shoulders pulled taut and her eyes rolled back for a brief moment before her soft-brown irises reappeared.

Her mouth fell open, and Yun-seo listened in awe to a story about the creation of the world. As A'tugwewinu spoke, the nightmares that plagued Yun-seo's psyche were slowly pushed away by the strange, warm light that accompanied each word.

This must be what sunshine feels like, they thought.

CHAPTER XV

WALKING AWAY AND TOWARD

After hiding in the cave for days, eating various mosses and greedily sucking moisture from rocks, Nitàwesì knew it was time to move on. Ojiwan had reverted to quiet hiccupping and staring off at the horizon with far too much stillness and focus for one so young. Nitàwesì fashioned their overcoat to open in the front so the child could nuzzle inside. They cut a long, thin piece of fabric off the bottom of the cloak and tied it around themselves and Ojiwan so they could rest their hands.

Nitàwesì knew the way to the big city from stories that the villagers had told. Even though they had never been there, had never even left Pasakamate before, they were sure of the way. The rumour that hunters traded humans there spurred them forward. Ojiwan was heavy and clung to their shoulders like his life depended on it. On their back, Nitàwesì carried all that was left of their packs: some rations, a few tools, and a tarp. The precious little trinkets that Shkitagen had gifted them were tucked away. Nitàwesì couldn't think about their love, wouldn't even let the image of his smile into their head for fear they would cease to function. This kind of love, the kind that broke one down and destroyed all sense of self, wasn't healthy. They realized this, but now wasn't the time to ponder it. Every ounce of their focus remained on putting one foot in front of the other.

They walked in silence for days. Ojiwan slept, when he wasn't staring listlessly or looking out for his mother. The sharp, jagged rocks, chunks of concrete, and cold, sandy soil stung Nitàwesì's feet and ankles. They ripped strips off the bottoms of their pants to strap around their shoes, which were riddled with holes. This left them with bare legs subjected to the elements. A few hours of hiking produced yet more holes and filled their shoes with gravel regardless.

The wind whipped up dust, small rocks, plastic bags, and other detritus. Nitàwesì held one arm in front of their face as they walked, but that barely did anything to protect them from the scratches and bites that marred their skin.

They stopped when the sky was so dark they couldn't see their feet. Gently, they let Ojiwan roam free and then turned to their packs to find some food. They lit a small fire using two old charcoal bricks, some fabric, and wax. The flame was just big enough for the two of them to see one another.

"Do you know," Nitàwesì signed, "my parent taught me that the orb in the sky is called kizis?" They spelled out "kizis" and then showed the child the sign for it.

Ojiwan's eyes brightened. "Kizis?" he signed back, mimicking the gesture.

Nitàwesì nodded. "My parent would tell me all sorts of names for everything around us. But they died a long time ago, so I don't remember a lot of it." Their face fell.

Tears streaked Ojiwan's face. "Like my mother," he signed. His chubby little fingers trembled as he made the sign for "mother."

"We don't know that your mother is dead. Shkitagen and she will look after each other, keep each other safe. We'll find them in Zhōng yang." Nitàwesì reached out and pulled Ojiwan close, comforting him.

Zhōng yang was the closest city to their village. The elders had said that there were dozens of cities across the continent, each of them as confusing and densely populated as Zhōng yang. Merchants were the only travellers who frequented the cities, coming and going with goods and wares and that which was most precious of all: news. Information about the Madjideye and their Enforcers, which cities were most prosperous and which ones had been decimated by drought or earthquakes or soilstorms, and how the other small villages like Pasakamate were faring.

But, Nitàwesì thought, there is no guarantee that Shkitagen is in Zhōng yang. And if they spent ages getting there, only to discover that Shkitagen hadn't even been taken to that city in the first place, then all would be for naught and he would be lost to them—forever.

■

The warriors were patrolling Pasakamate. Their usual route was a circle around the outskirts of the village that ended up at the healers' hut. The two healers inside originated from the village of Andwànikàdjigan, one of the few cousin villages nearby. The healers had informed the Pasakamate warriors that the hunters they fought so hard to keep away hadn't yet ventured out to the storytellers' village. The warriors didn't know if that was still true, as communication between the villages was scarce. The merchants who travelled between these nomadic villages were their only connection. People tended to stay within the villages where they were born. The elders always said that Kichi Manido had placed them there for a reason, that each villager chose to be born to the family to which they'd been given, and that each person had lessons they needed to learn in this life in order to pass on peacefully back to Kichi Manido. The warriors' sole purpose was to protect their village.

Once it had been a role that only seconds could carry. Now, in such desperate times, any gender could become a warrior. The sole exception was firekeepers. Only one had been born in this generation. The elders surmised that because their people were under constant threat, fewer firekeepers had been born. But just when their situation had seemed most dire, two healers from Andwànikàdjigan had appeared, bringing with them the ability to heal almost any injury. One of the two had been carrying a child who, once born, the elders were grateful to welcome into the community. The family were adopted by the Pasakamate, and they were gifted one of the few remaining unoccupied dwellings in the community. A small single-room hut made of concrete, without closures for the windows or a door for the entrance, it was isolated from the rest of the village. Though the elders regretted that this shanty dwelling was all they had to offer, the two healers said it was more than adequate. They made it a livable space, with a table and medical tools to one side so they could work on patients as needed.

The warriors always paid close attention to the hut to ensure their healers remained safe. The village's survival depended on the two of them.

One day, two warriors approached the dwelling. One was immediately on guard—it was too silent. They did not hear the grunts of the wounded or the laughter of the healers' child.

The warriors exchanged looks and ran toward the hut. The faster of the two pulled back the curtain and cried out at the sight that met them.

There, on the floor, the two healers lay dead—eviscerated. Their organs spilled from their bodies, and lacerations covered their faces, arms, and legs. In the corner, naked, covered in finger-shaped bruises, with blood coating their thighs, was the child. They simply sat there, staring silently at their parents' corpses.

The first warrior calmly approached the small child. "Kwey. You're all right now," they whispered, trying desperately not to scare them. They put their hand on the child's shoulder. The child sucked in a breath and flinched, so the warrior withdrew their hand.

"I'm here to help. Do you remember me?" the warrior asked calmly.

The child continued to stare at their parents.

The second warrior grabbed a blanket and placed it over the healers' corpses.

"Go, get a firekeeper and the chief. They'll need to know about this," said the first warrior. "And a nurturer!" they added as the second warrior headed out. They found another blanket to try to cover the child, but the latter paid no heed to what was happening.

"Do you need anything?" the first warrior asked, maintaining their distance while trying to engage the child. But the child stared through them, at the blanket covering the bodies of their parents.

Hours later, the firekeepers had cremated both bodies and burned any evidence of the bloodshed that had occurred. All warriors were roused, and hunting parties were sent out to try and find the murderers responsible for this offence. It took three nurturers to calm and bathe the child and dress their wounds.

Many attempts were made to house the child with another family, but every time, the child ran away and returned to their own dwelling. They were always found staring at the same spot. After months, it became clear the child was not going to speak. The elders took it upon themselves to teach them the language of hands, which the ancestors had passed on.

No one ever discovered who was responsible for the atrocity that had taken the lives of the two healers. The transgressor's identity died on the lips of a child no longer able to use them to form words.

The villagers and the child forgot their name. From then on, they were known as Nitàwesì.

CHAPTER XVI

MIJINGE

Bèl and A'tugwewinu decided to remain in Riordan's compound. Bèl resumed warrior training with the kids. Riordan and Yun-seo sometimes joined, though they often paired off, sparring for hours at a time, speaking not with words but with their bodies. When Yun-seo didn't use their gift, Riordan always won, but as soon as Yun-seo called on their ability, Riordan couldn't measure up. Riordan never lost patience, though, and instead demanded that Yun-seo keep attacking. Again and again, as if by some miracle, xe mustered the strength and speed to evade Yun-seo's gift. Thirds were supernaturally gifted to be stronger and faster than anyone else, but Riordan could retaliate with xir tech; xe could build faster and stronger wheels. Sparring was xir testing ground.

"I admire your dedication," Bèl called out, "but the result will always be the same. No other gender can hope to surpass a third." She stated it very matter-of-factly.

Riordan puffed out xir chest. "Doesn't mean I can't try."

Bèl looked on with pride.

In the evening, A'tugwewinu sat with the younger children and shared stories. Her work sharing the teachings of her people was by no means done. Bèl sat in on these story sessions from time to time, using them as opportunity to sharpen her tools or fix her pointed nails, shaping them into even deadlier claws. She was always within reach of her lover. After a few weeks, some of the children had memorized several of the creation stories that A'tugwewinu carried, and she had gifted them with marks of their own. Riordan protested this.

"If you mark them, the Madjideye will put targets on all of them," xe seethed.

"This is a calling, Riordan. The marks are an honour," A'tugwewinu said.

"Not all my kids are eighths like you! They can't hide."

A'tugwewinu flinched. Her face went slack. Anything else she might have wanted to say died in her throat.

■

Bèl darted between rubble and discarded metal overhangs, weaving her way easily through the throng of people gathered at the market. On her left, A'tugwewinu crawled under the merchants' carts, hands moving quickly, taking small tins of food and stuffing them into her coat before scuttling off to the alley where Riordan watched. Bèl was never more than the space of two people apart from A'tugwewinu.

The trio set off with their bounty, hurtling through the maze of concrete until finally they were safe again in the dwelling that Bèl's family had owned for generations—a room large enough to fit a dozen or so people, with beds stacked on top of one another. The place was a haphazard mismatching of random objects, from tech to weapons to trinkets. No one actually knew what they were, but Bèl insisted on keeping them, as her ancestors had held on to them for generations. Bèl's entire family had yet to return from their mercenary job in another city, so for the time being the three of them hunkered down, Riordan and A'tugwewinu poor substitutes for the blood relations whom Bèl missed dearly.

A'tugwewinu cried out softly—Bèl looked and saw that she had cut her finger on the tin can she'd been attempting to open with a knife. Bèl shot over, took A'tugwewinu's finger, and put it in her mouth to seal the wound. Once it stopped bleeding, Bèl took the tin from Winu and finished opening it herself. She fed Winu first before passing the tin to Riordan.

"Why do ya always do that, eh?" Riordan asked.

"Ita'? What?" Bèl questioned.

"Come to her rescue for every little thing. Even today, in the market— she can do this herself, but ya still stuck to her like a shadow."

Bèl sighed. "Listen, Riordan, I know you've been with us a while—"

"Months, actually."

"—but there's still a lot we haven't told you yet."

"Really?" Riordan exclaimed. "Like the fact she's actually an eighth?"

Bèl rounded and put her arm to Riordan's throat. From the corner of xir eye, Riordan spotted a small concealed blade between Bèl's fingertips. Should xe inhale too deeply, it would slice xir skin.

"How much longer do ya got to know me before I don't gotta be held at knifepoint anytime I ask a question?" xe said through gritted teeth.

"That's enough, Bèl," A'tugwewinu whispered from across the room.

Immediately, Bèl dropped her arm and backed away. She sat next to A'tugwewinu, so close their thighs and shoulders were touching. Riordan rolled xir eyes.

"You're right. It's time I told you how I ended up in Zhōng yang," A'tugwewinu started. Riordan sat down, ready to listen and understand.

Near the end of her story, A'tugwewinu broke down sobbing. Bèl pulled her into her arms.

Riordan tossed xir head back. Honestly, these two, *xe thought.*

"Anyway," A'tugwewinu continued, sniffling and rubbing her face with the back of her hand, "after Bèl found me, we started living here together. I was emaciated and on the verge of death. She had to feed and bathe me, and it's because of her that I'm even alive to tell you this. One day, Bèl started to tell me the story of her warrior ancestors and the history of the Taino Nation. Before I knew it, marks appeared on me. Since my secret was out, I told Bèl all about the Andwànikàdjigan and who we were."

"I pledged my services to her," Bèl interjected.

"What does that mean?" Riordan asked.

"Complete protection, until my death."

"So yer gonna be her shadow until ya die," Riordan said mockingly. Xe turned to A'tugwewinu. "And yer gonna let her do everything for ya like a spoiled baby."

A'tugwewinu was crestfallen.

"I don't expect someone who's been alone xir whole life without anyone to lean on to understand," Bèl said.

"Exactly! Me, a lowly, good-for-nothing second. Don't ya see yer ruining any chance Winu ever has of surviving? What happens when ya die, huh?" Riordan shouted.

"The honour of the Taino Nation and this dwelling are all my family has left," Bèl seethed. "She is the last of her people. The Madjideye annihilated them, knowing that those who can keep stories on their skin are a threat to their dominion. We live like this because we know nothing about how to fix this broken world. But in the stories are the answers. Her fate is greater than any of ours."

"No one life is better than another," Riordan fumed.

"I have nothing to live for unless I am protecting someone. My family trained me for this from childhood. I don't know how to do anything else," Bèl stated sadly. "I waited an entire year for my family to return before I took in Winu. Her spirits brought me to her. It's been two years since that day. My family is never returning—I know that now. The least I can do is follow in my ancestors' footsteps and continue the honourable guazabara way."

"Then teach her!"

"The warrior way is passed down through blood memory and years of dedication to the practice. Not everyone is capable."

"Then simplify it, make it so she can learn something, because bein' an eighth won't be enough to survive. Soon, the Madjideye will catch on."

"How do you know that?" A'tugwewinu asked.

"I've seen yer features shift when you panic. At first, I thought it was yer power, until ya shifted so much that I noticed the marks. That's when I realized yer an eighth." Xe paused. "I've never met one before."

A'tugwewinu sighed. "Yes, we are rare. My Nokomis and I were the only people in our village who weren't firsts or seconds. But our village was very small—barely eight hundred people. They called us ayahkwewak."

Riordan tilted xir head, confused. Xe tried to repeat the word but completely destroyed its pronunciation.

"It's our word for someone whose gender is neither first nor second, someone whose gender also grants them special abilities," A'tugwewinu explained. "It's for any of the six other genders that people are born with. Those who were chosen by Kichi Manido to be the bridge between this world and the spirit world."

"So then why not be an eighth? Why do you shift yer features and spirit to that of a first?" Riordan asked. "If I could change my gender, I'd do it in a heartbeat."

A'tugwewinu smiled. "I find I look more like my mother like this—I stay this way to honour her memory. If you want to change your gender, then change it. Just because eighths have the ability to shift our physical features and bend our spirits, that doesn't mean we're the only ones who can. You can choose whichever gender you feel closest to, regardless of what you were born with."

Riordan looked shocked. "I ... I think I'm a sixth," xe stated.

A'tugwewinu beamed. "That's wonderful! Nokomis's dearest friend was a sixth, but I never got to meet her. Sixths carried a sacred role for my people, when we young ones went through our adulthood ritual."

"What was it?" Riordan asked, throat dry in anticipation. The world was filled with firsts and seconds, and even thirds were quite numerous, but fourths to eighths—some of those genders, Riordan had only heard about. Knowledge about the gifts each gender carried ranged from fact to myth, depending who you spoke to.

"Why do you say you're a sixth?" A'tugwewinu asked.

"Because I see the way the two of yas can't breathe unless one of ya exhales while the other inhales, and I feel annoyed," Riordan teased.

A'tugwewinu blushed. Bèl raised an eyebrow in defiance.

"If the two of yas being together was also a secret, it's the worst you've kept."

"It's a recent development," Bèl stated. A'tugwewinu turned scarlet. Bèl reached out and gripped her hand.

Riordan rolled xir eyes and continued. "Ever since I started sellin' myself to merchants fer tech or food, I've felt nothin'. I honestly think more about what I'm going to get to invent than anythin' else. At first, I thought maybe that was just it, sex wasn't fer me. But now, seeing the two of yas so into each other, I don't want any of it. Sex or love."

Bèl sighed and shook her head. "If you don't at least receive some kind of pleasure from sex, Riordan, you don't have to do it. We'll steal or find some other way to get the food and tech you need."

Riordan nodded. "Fer me, it feels like a chore—sex, love, all those things that other people get desperate fer. I just don't see the need fer it."

"Sixths are born complete," A'tugwewinu explained. "The only gender that doesn't need to search for a partner or several. They are born capable of spending their entire lives with only themselves, and of feeling completely at peace with that. When we had our adulthood rituals, sixths would sit with us, and teach us to be with ourselves for a few years before we began looking for partners. They also counselled people in relationships, to help them not become too overwhelmed with the person or people they were with and maintain some semblance of self."

"Wait! So, I'm doin' that!" Riordan replied gleefully.

"Yes." A'tugwewinu returned the smile. "By sharing with us your concern for how attached we are, you are in fact doing your gender's role."

Bèl sighed.

"What about seconds?" Riordan asked.

"Also very sacred. While the other genders carried gifts inside of themselves, seconds' gifts came from outside, by working for their families and communities in whatever ways were needed. They were vital in ensuring our communities thrived." A'tugwewinu's tone grew wistful. "But in Andwànikàdjigan, people had abilities regardless of their gender. The elders said it was because Kichi Manido had blessed us as Anishinabeg. All genders were viewed as equal there. It was only when I came to Zhōng yang that I understood the way outsiders view gender is very different. It is clear to me that the Madjideye have had a role in creating disparities between the genders."

"I think I want the world to still see me as a second, with only family knowing that inside I'm a sixth," Riordan stated.

A'tugwewinu got up and knelt in front of Riordan. She grasped xir face with both hands and looked xir in the eye. "The people who matter will sense who you truly are on the inside, regardless of what's on the outside," *she said softly. Tears welled in Riordan's eyes. A'tugwewinu brought xir into her arms and held xir close.*

"Xe's right, Bèl," A'tugwewinu said softly. "Tomorrow, you start training me."

Bèl huffed. "Figures," she said.

Riordan looked up to see her smiling softly at the pair of them.

CHAPTER XVII

FOUND

Nitàwesì woke and shook their head, trying to extinguish the lingering dream of Shkitagen. They groaned, frustrated, and looked at Ojiwan.

"We're almost at the city," they signed. "We need to start looking for them."

Ojiwan raised his arms, signalling that he wished to be carried. Nitàwesì picked him up and placed him in their coat, and together they began the last day of their arduous trek to Zhōng yang. There were many other cities on the continent, with great distances separating them and not much between except a smattering of struggling villages. It took weeks to reach another city on foot. The machines the Enforcers rode in were the only other mode of transportation.

Nitàwesì was terrified of Zhōng yang. They would never have ventured outside their village had Shkitagen not supported their decision to leave. Whatever small amount of courage they'd felt back when they began the long hike up the mountain range that surrounded their village had been ripped away by Shkitagen's capture.

By the light in the sky, they estimated it had been about ten days since Pasakamate was destroyed by the flood. If they could maintain a steady pace and not falter too much from lack of food and the additional weight they now carried, they could perhaps reach the city before kizis disappeared. They trudged along, feeling the child's tiny tender arms around their neck. Their eyes scanned constantly, their mind alert, as they listened and watched for any sudden sound or unnatural movement in the rocky wilderness.

"Ready, Ojiwan?" they signed, close to their face so the little one could see.

The young one nodded and signed back, "Yes, Nmama."

Nitàwesì flinched but tried to keep their expression neutral. They kissed the top of Ojiwan's head and saw a small smile tug at the little one's lips. Unsure how to respond, they simply walked, hands still, for the remainder of the day. Budding in their chest was a stirring sensation of wanting to protect this child at any cost. It terrified them more than any of the dangers a city like Zhōng yang might possess.

CHAPTER XVIII

ENFORCER ATTACK

It had been months now since their capture. Yun-seo had been freed from the pipe in the dingy corner of the dwelling and now spent all their time with the children, eating with them, working with them, explaining their armour, and sharing anything and everything they could about the Madjideye.

Yun-seo had been only eleven when the Enforcers kidnapped them. After a decade of training, they had begun their duties, and after only a few years of being Elite Enforcer H-09761, they had murdered 137 people. Nightmares still plagued them. There were nights when Yun-seo screamed and sobbed for the lives they'd ended, forced to watch a never-ending loop of their victims' faces. They sensed their victims' hopelessness, smelled their fear—a stench only a warrior could breathe. Riordan told them time and time again that this was necessary retribution; it would be worse if Yun-seo ever had a peaceful night's rest. Bitterly, Yun-seo agreed. Their torment was but a small price to pay in the balancing of their wrongdoings.

A'tugwewinu was the most soothing balm during moments like this. Riordan was emotional whiplash personified, and Bèl seemed promising, but remained wary of the former Enforcer, which Yun-seo didn't blame her for in the slightest.

It was during a conversation with A'tugwewinu that Yun-seo stopped speaking midsentence and sniffed the air. It was thick with the scent of ochre and ozone, carrion and burnt flesh. They grabbed A'tugwewinu by the shoulders.

"Enforcers. Hide your marks!" they ordered.

As if in reflex, A'tugwewinu's skin glowed and started to tremble. Her features shifted as the marks disappeared. "If I start to panic," she said fearfully, "I can't control my form. I'll revert to an eighth, and the markings will show." She helped Yun-seo to their feet. "Who's looking for me?" she asked.

"An Elite Enforcer. I can smell their gift—it's death, cleaved bone, and melted skin. Warn the others, but we need to be quick and quiet."

A'tugwewinu nodded, her shoulders tense. She headed off in search of Bèl and Riordan. Yun-seo followed.

They found Riordan seated in a corner with a few of xir inventor kids, pieces of Yun-seo's old armour strewn about, with perfectly fabricated replicas sitting next to the originals. Bèl stood a few feet away with a dozen younglings around her, practising elaborate defence manoeuvres.

A'tugwewinu put a finger to her lips and signed to Bèl via a complex series of hand gestures. Bèl went rigid. She silently relayed the information to the younglings, the flurry of her hands betraying their steadiness.

What absolute genius, Yun-seo marvelled.

Riordan calmly wheeled behind A'tugwewinu and Yun-seo. Xe hunched down to speak directly into Yun-seo's ear. Warmth bloomed inside them at the close contact.

Riordan whispered, "How many?"

Yun-seo shivered as Riordan's lips brushed their ear. They swallowed and responded just as quietly: "One. Elite class. Stronger than me. Evacuate those who can't defend themselves. The rest, get them ready to kill."

Riordan purred xir approval. Yun-seo's heartbeat quickened in response. Xe pulled away and silently relayed the information to those standing by.

In the corner, a young one shouted, "Soup's on! Come get it before I eat it all!"

No sooner were the words spoken than the older children grabbed the littler ones and sprinted away with them, disappearing through the cracks in the walls. The inventor kids grabbed their tools and important tech, ran, and hid. The compound cleared of all but several dozen older children, who took formation alongside Bèl, various weapons in their hands. Yun-seo recognized many of the children as those who had played a part in immobilizing and capturing them. They weren't sure, however, if it was going to be enough to take down this particular Enforcer. They inhaled again and located the smell—it was coming from the dwelling's southeast corner. They approached, Bèl close behind. Yun-seo held up a hand at a safe distance. Bèl nodded, understanding.

A sudden explosion hurtled concrete toward them as a portion of the wall disappeared. The Enforcer, a second almost as tall and twice as wide as Riordan, burst through. Yun-seo charged without hesitation, their hands outstretched and glowing, fists enveloped by orange and yellow flames. They screamed; their power intensified, and spheres of fire erupted from their palms, striking the attacking Enforcer. The Enforcer retaliated with power of his own—from his palms he sent beams of searing hot light at Yun-seo, piercing the ex-Enforcer's arm and right side, below the ribs.

Yun-seo grunted in pain. They looked down and saw blood pooling from their wounds. They felt suddenly dizzy. Shots rang out behind them, and they felt a strong arm wrap around their lower back.

"Come on! Don't give up now!" Riordan's voice echoed in their ears.

Yun-seo stretched out their hands again like they'd experienced a jolt of newfound strength. With a slap, they snuffed out the flames on their fingertips, black smoke erupting from their palms.

Bèl inhaled the chaos of the moment, felt the vibrations shift with each swipe of her arm. Felt her vascularity, her fingers denting the handle of her machete as she poured her strength into each swing. The Enforcer deflected her strikes with maddening accuracy. Bèl spun, rounded back around, and crouched low to the ground as one of her warriors ran up her back like a ramp, leaped over her and, with a knife in each hand, brought the blades down into the Enforcer's left bicep and shoulder. Their enemy howled in pain. He took hold of the warrior by her head and threw her against the nearest wall. Her head and back hit with a sickening crunch somehow audible over the cacophony of battle. The warrior slid down the wall, a streak of blood in her wake.

Bèl cursed and jumped to her feet. Shots thundered from all angles, bullets striking the Enforcer but never seeming to slow him down. Bèl and the other warriors hacked at him with machetes and knives, yet he continued forward—he dodged their blows with incredible speed and launched several of them away with just a sweep of his arm. He was bleeding, knives protruding from his arms and legs like quills, yet nothing stilled his attack.

The black smoke lifted from Yun-seo's body and wafted over to the Enforcer. It surrounded him, entering his body through every visible orifice.

The Enforcer sputtered and choked. He paused his assault for a brief moment, giving Bèl the opportunity she needed. With a vicious gleam in her eyes and her ancestors' blood coursing through her veins, she leaped toward the Enforcer and bore down on his exposed neck. Cleaved skin from bone with three powerful swings that separated his head from his massive body. His head rolled free while the rest of him collapsed to the earth.

Yun-seo whispered to the smoke. Immediately, it started to consume the Enforcer's body. Soon, his figure had melted into ash and dust. Yun-seo felt their eyes roll back into their skull and their body go weightless. Their legs shook and crumpled beneath them. Riordan's arm around their waist was all that kept them from kissing the ground.

Riordan dropped the gun in xir hand and clutched the unconscious third. Xe put xir ear to their chest—their heartbeat was strong and clear, but their breathing was shallow.

Riordan wheeled over to xir quarters. "We gotta move!" xe barked. "Bèl! Find out who's hurt and who didn't make it. Winu! Round up the kids and get ever'body packin.'" Xe gently deposited Yun-seo on a pile of pillows and began looking for the first-aid supplies xe had stashed. Xe found some bandages and cleansing lotion the medic had made a few weeks ago and crouched next to the unconscious third, lifted up their shirt to assess the damage.

Bèl came up the steps to xir quarters. "Four dead, seven wounded— two of them are critical."

Riordan exhaled. "Give 'em their last rites and have Cass give them shots," xe said, referring to a solution they used to speed along the inevitable. "Then bury 'em with the dead. We leave once that's done. We'll handle grieving rites when we get to our new place."

"Got it," Bèl replied, her voice steel edged.

Riordan wiped the blood pooling in the fingertip-sized holes left by whatever the Enforcer had attacked Yun-seo with, then proceeded to bandage them. The wounds were small, but there were dozens of them up and down Yun-seo's body. Only time would tell if they would be able to recover.

"Don't die on me, ya hear?" xe threatened, staring into the peaceful, unconscious face of xir informant.

An old feeling stirred in xir chest. *Dammit! When did my feeling toward Yun-seo become like what I feel for Bèl and Winu?* Xe cursed and tamped it down. Xe wheeled over to see how xir kids were faring.

A'tugwewinu was crouched in a corner. She closed the eyes of the first in front of her. As she did, a tear slid down her cheek.

"I'm sorry we couldn't keep you safe, Sumiha," she whispered.

An onslaught of images suddenly assaulted her: her mother walking back toward the village; the prisoners she'd left behind at the compound facing torture and starvation; Bèl getting shot and dying before her eyes.

Her chest felt tight. She inhaled, but her breath lodged in her throat. She made soft choking sounds. Her heart was beating too fast, her hands trembling. She fell back, nails scratching at her throat. It was too much, everything was too much. She couldn't breathe, she couldn't—

"Shhhh."

Warm arms enveloped her from behind. She felt Bèl's chest against her back, Bèl's hands grasping hers, crossing her arms over her chest.

"With me now," Bèl said, exhaling into her ear. A'tugwewinu felt Bèl's chest expand against her. Gently, something loosened in her own chest, and she was finally able to release the breath her body had been holding in. She continued to follow the slow, measured breaths that Bèl demonstrated for her. After a few minutes, the panic wore off, and sorrow took its place.

"Six of our children are dead because of us," A'tugwewinu sobbed.

Bèl hummed her agreement, tears pooling on her lover's shoulders. She vibrated with rage.

The three of us will be the death of these kids, she thought bitterly.

■

Walking in front of A'tugwewinu and Riordan, at the end of the street, Bèl stalked quietly between the food stands in the market. She waded through much taller adults, coming close to several stalls but never lingering, never so much as touching anything. But A'tugwewinu and Riordan knew better. After hitting a few more stalls, Bèl weaved through the crowd and hurried toward them. Together they entered the alley and began fishing through the many layers of Bèl's clothes, removing cans of food, strange-looking vials of precious medicines, pretty metals, and other pilfered goods.

Riordan beamed. "What a haul!"

Bèl returned xir smile. The trio marched to a small dwelling hidden behind a hill of rubble and crawled under an opening in the floor to an underground room. A'tugwewinu lit a small gas stove to warm up some of the canned food, so they could feast on their spoils.

"Ya know, I've been thinkin' of getting some other kids involved," Riordan said.

"What do you mean?" A'tugwewinu asked.

"Well, it's been the three of us fer a few years, and we've been doing good fer ourselves, but this city is filled with orphans, and all of 'em are starving. We could give 'em a place to stay, teach 'em how to steal, and take care of 'em, ya know?"

Bèl sighed. "We could, but the more of us there are, the more dangerous this becomes—the more endangered they become."

"Nah," Riordan retorted. "Zhōng yang's already eating 'em alive. I think if you train 'em to fight, I teach 'em to build things, and Winu teaches 'em to survive, we'll have ourselves an army, one this city'll never see coming. And the best part is, they'll get a family out of it."

A'tugwewinu's eyes shone. "What do you think, Bèl?"

Bèl sighed. "I still think it's dangerous, but I sure ain't going to let some kids get used up, not if I can teach them to defend themselves."

"We'll look for a bigger place tomorrow," A'tugwewinu promised.

CHAPTER XIX

FOUNDLINGS

As soon as they arrived in Zhōng yang, Nitàwesì immediately started scouring the city for any sign of hunters or Shkitagen. He'd said he would leave a sign so that Nitàwesì could find him. They searched high and low for any telltale scorch marks or scratches, but before long, all the rubble and destroyed buildings started to blend together. Nitàwesì had never been taught to orient themselves in such a place. Barely three days went by before they understood: they were truly lost in a maze. Hopelessness filled their chest. To make matters worse, no one there understood sign language, and Ojiwan refused to use anything but his hands to communicate.

"Ojiwan, please," Nitàwesì signed, "can you talk to someone, ask them if they've seen your mother?"

But it was useless. At the mere mention of his mother, Ojiwan looked away and ignored any further signing.

Nitàwesì gently raised the child's chin with one hand and with their other, signed, "I. CAN'T. SPEAK." They furiously punctuated each word. "So you need to do it for me," they continued, hoping he would comprehend their dire situation.

Ojiwan pondered for a moment. "No," he signed. He turned away and continued eating the last bit of rations they had.

Nitàwesì screamed internally. They had tried eavesdropping on some Enforcers, getting as close as they dared, only to discover their oppressors did not make much small talk. They'd caught a glimpse of one of the machines the Enforcers carried, but the faces projected on it didn't show anyone familiar.

The denizens of Zhōng yang were a quiet folk. The markets scuttled with whispers and only the occasional bout of raucous laughter. People stood bundled in layers of mismatched, patched, and threadbare clothes. Enforcers marched about in pairs, guns drawn, their helmets betraying no emotion whatsoever. The people looked down and away, some going so far as to collapse to their knees and bow whenever an Enforcer stormed past. Nitàwesì steered clear of the Enforcers and their worshippers, looking out for more sociable merchants, seeking someone, anyone, who could sign. But Nitàwesì was routinely ignored. Some even ridiculed them for the funny way they moved their hands. It was infuriating.

Shkitagen could already be dead and—no! No. They couldn't think like that, they simply couldn't.

Nitàwesì sighed and looked to the sky, watching the ebb and flow of eerie oranges and greys and blacks as they swirled around each other. There had to be someone else like them in this city. The elders at Pasakamate had spoken of other villages, other Anishinabeg and other nations of first peoples that Kichi Manido had placed on this land. But Nitàwesì couldn't seem to find anyone else capable of communicating with their hands—perhaps this was something only those from Pasakamate knew how to do.

The healer felt an intense pang in their chest that stole their breath from them. They missed the way Shkitagen's eyes, filled with specks of fire and gold, focused intently on whatever task was at hand; the way his large, strong hands, which were dark sepia, gently tended to his flames; the way his full lips moved when he muttered the four-direction prayers and softly lulled his fire songs. Being away from him was like having a limb severed. Nitàwesì felt a constant ache at the back of their skull, an ache that grew more insistent by the day.

They returned their gaze to the streets. Their eyes landed upon a child slightly older than Ojiwan, peering at them from the corner of an alleyway. Nitàwesì waved to the child, who immediately vanished into the dark. Nitàwesì was startled. They grabbed their pack and Ojiwan and darted after the child.

Deep in their gut, they knew this child had been watching them out of more than simple curiosity. All this time in the city, Nitàwesì had asked adults for help, and all of them had proven useless. They should have looked down—children always saw and heard more than adults did. They were always more aware of their surroundings than those who noticed only what mattered to them and them alone.

Nitàwesì reached the alleyway. They saw the child standing a few feet away, waiting for them.

"I think you should follow me," she said.

Nitàwesì was wary, but didn't feel like they had a choice in the matter. The child approached them and took their hand. Nitàwesì hoisted their pack and held Ojiwan tight with their other hand. The latter seemed confused but said nothing.

The mysterious child led them through the city, past other alleys and piles of rubble, underground, then back into the open again. After an unknown length of time—an hour, maybe, give or take—the three of them reached the outskirts of the city, where they were confronted by a ruin of a large building, all dirt and sand and brush and not much else. Nitàwesì was confused—shouldn't there be people where they were headed?

The little one who was guiding them stopped in place and stomped the earth three times. In front of them, a hatch in the ground opened up, and three people—older than children but younger than Nitàwesì—climbed out. They wore pieces of armour and clutched long metal weapons—knives and swords and spears.

"What's this?" one of the guards asked the child.

"They're like us. They smell like Winu. She'll want to see them," she responded.

The guards nodded and led the way underground, shutting the hatch behind them.

After a series of dark, narrow tunnels, the path ahead expanded into a large cavern, the top of which was open in places so they could see the sky.

Nitàwesì found themselves unexpectedly surrounded by children. The child who'd led them there ran off toward a very tall second in the corner of the room. Nitàwesì noted the weapons and the warriors among them and felt a sudden swell of fear and trepidation.

They signed to Ojiwan, "Stay close to me."

The tall second, who had red hair and pale skin the likes of which Nitàwesì had never seen, approached them with unnatural speed. Beside this second stood a third with a staggering array of weapons strapped to their body and a person whose gender shifted—Nitàwesì assumed they must be an eighth. What struck Nitàwesì more than the person's fluctuating gender was how similar their facial features, angular cheekbones, and jutting nose were to Nitàwesì's. The two of them looked very much alike. They were even similar in stature. Their only differences were eye colour and hair.

Nitàwesì froze.

A'tugwewinu regarded the newcomers with interest, a small questioning smile and a curious look in her eye. She surveyed Nitàwesì, their small stature and the tangle of curls swept into a tight bun atop their head. Noted their open cloak, revealing a tight cropped undershirt and soft belly, thick arms and thighs, and the pouch slung over their shoulder, which was filled to the brim with medical supplies of all sorts. Their left ring finger was adorned in tattoos and a thin band of metal, the only decoration on their entire body.

"Where are you from?" A'tugwewinu signed.

Nitàwesì could have cried with relief. "Pasakamate. Where are you from?"

A'tugwewinu smiled genuinely. "Andwànikàdjigan." She spelled the village's name with her hands.

Nitàwesì let out a gasp. "My parent from the wolf clan is from your village. I'm Nitàwesì." Their hands were a flurry.

The storyteller tilted her head, confused. "Is that your name or your condition?" she asked verbally.

"Name."

A'tugwewinu read from Nitàwesì's closed-off expression that they did not wish to elaborate on the meaning of their name—"mute." She stepped forward. "My name is A'tugwewinu." She paused her fingers between symbols.

"Nice to meet a fellow Anishinabeg. How is your village?"

A'tugwewinu's features hardened. She shook her head.

A wave of emotion took hold of Nitàwesì. Somehow, they had figured there would be others like them in Zhōng yang, and that they would have come from villages filled with Anishinabeg who could heal and make fire dance on their fingertips and who had tattoos from stories and walked beside the resurrected spirits of their ancestors.

They had thought perhaps some remnant of their family was still alive, that they might hear stories about their parents—stories no one in Pasakamate could have told them.

"Well, I didn't think I had any family left, but my father was wolf, so anish na', cousin?" A'tugwewinu offered a smile and extended her hand. Nitàwesì grasped her arm and brought their face to hers, gently touching their foreheads together in greeting.

Something small built inside Nitàwesì then, and they rushed into the arms of this stranger. Held her tight, as if this person was all that remained of their lost villages. They felt it then: they could never let go of her, no matter what happened. Then the wailing began. Both clutched the other until Ojiwan managed to sneak between the two of them, and then they held him too.

Eventually, Nitàwesì pulled away. They noticed everyone else had scattered to give them some space. They divulged their story, detailing their journey and how they and Ojiwan had ended up here, in A'tugwewinu's home.

"I've never encountered hunters," A'tugwewinu signed.

"They cover their skin in ash. They abuse the spirits to shape-shift. They come in packs in the darkest times and take away any gifted villagers they find. We've been at war with them since before I was born," Nitàwesì replied.

They signed to one another until late. A'tugwewinu was not fluent and had to speak occasionally, when her hands couldn't form the right words. Ojiwan fell asleep at some point, nestled on Nitàwesì's shoulder while they gently rocked him.

"Is he your child?" A'tugwewinu asked.

"He is now." Nitàwesì smiled tenderly as they stared at the sleeping child, whose soft puffs of breath tickled their skin. A bond was forming—they felt tethered to the little one.

The tall second approached then, with the third close behind. Both carried containers filled with hot food. Nitàwesì's stomach growled—they had not eaten anything substantial in some time.

"I'm Riordan, this is Bèl," said the tall second as xe handed the container of food to Nitàwesì. The healer nodded their gratitude. They noticed that several children around the cave were crying softly. In the centre of the room lay several objects surrounded by funeral stones.

"Sorry to bother yas, but we started the grievin' rites. See, we just got here late last night, and we lost some of our family 'cuz of an Enforcer attack. So, if ya don't mind waitin' to eat 'til we've feasted 'em." Riordan spoke with an accent that Nitàwesì had heard only in the streets of Zhōng yang.

A'tugwewinu smiled sadly and left her newly discovered cousin alone. She whispered something to Bèl, who nodded before lifting the back of A'tugwewinu's shirt and pressing on a tattoo on her upper back, close to her spine.

Nitàwesì couldn't help but notice the scarred flesh there. *Torture by Enforcers, perhaps?* They shuddered. Life here clearly wasn't any easier than in Pasakamate.

They watched in astonishment as A'tugwewinu's irises vanished beneath a white haze. She opened her mouth, and a story emerged about a people called the Taino, led by a fierce first guazabara. Nitàwesì noticed that as A'tugwewinu spoke, Bèl's shoulders straightened with pride. The young warriors listened intently, their eyes filled with wonder.

Once the story was finished, Bèl stood up and recited a prayer in a language Nitàwesì had never heard before. They understood that maybe Bèl was from the south, like their birth parent and Shkitagen's father. A place the village elders had once called beautiful and warm, islands filled with some of the most resilient people—a lineage of stolen people and first peoples. Shkitagen was of that bloodline mixed with the first peoples of the north. Nitàwesì knew that those islands were gone now; the waters had risen so high there was nothing left.

Next, Riordan stood and spoke kind words about each child who had given their life to protect their family. Xe broke down sobbing after only a few sentences.

"I jus' wanted to make a family with all of yas," xe said. "I knew the risks. I knew it would be dangerous. I knew this was a possibility. I hope ya can all forgive me. I'm going ta do better. Work harder ta make sure this doesn't happen again." Xir accent seemed even thicker with xir heartfelt declaration. Riordan's shoulders crumpled; xir repeated apologies grew unintelligible.

A'tugwewinu came up behind xir and placed a hand on xir back. Bèl stood on xir other side and placed one arm around her beloved and a hand on Riordan's shoulder. Slowly, the children got to their feet and encircled their leaders. The group of them reached out and held one another's hands.

Nitàwesì looked away. They felt like an intruder, a voyeur during this family's most vulnerable moment. They raised their eyes skyward and muttered a silent prayer for Shkitagen, wherever he was, asking the Kichi Manido to whom the elders prayed to be kind enough to keep him safe and to reunite the two of them one day soon.

The next day, Nitàwesì, Bèl, and A'tugwewinu spent some time signing together. A'tugwewinu wasted no time informing the children about the kidnapped nurturer and firekeeper from Pasakamate. A few days earlier, one of the children had spotted hunters bringing in people who matched the descriptions Nitàwesì provided. Riordan tasked a dozen kids with searching the city for them.

For the first time since their beloved was taken, Nitàwesì felt hope swell in their chest.

They found Ojiwan playing with a few children his age, signing with some of the ones A'tugwewinu had taught to communicate in this way that was birthed from the first peoples.

The elders in Pasakamate had taught that long ago, when the land was filled with only first peoples, their common language was to communicate with their hands, because the first peoples were divided into different nations, each with different oral languages and dialects. Some people in Pasakamate, like Shkitagen, still spoke the original language. And even though the firekeeper had been teaching Nitàwesì, the healer was by no means fluent. Nitàwesì learned that Bèl spoke some Taino as well as Anishinabeg. A'tugwewinu was fluent and would often tell entire stories in Anishinabemowin, teaching some of the children.

"My name is from another nation, from the east, the Mi'kmaq people that Nokomis's husband was from," A'tugwewinu signed. "He passed away before I was born, and those villages were all lost when the waters rose."

"The waters destroyed Pasakamate as well," Nitàwesì said. "Only the mountains protect Zhōng yang. What will you all do when the waters rise above them?"

A'tugwewinu and Bèl both shrugged.

"We've lived every day trying to escape the Madjideye," Bèl signed. "We've never thought about the waters."

"You're a healer, eh?" A'tugwewinu asked suddenly, changing the subject.

Nitàwesì nodded.

"I wonder if you wouldn't mind helping out a new friend of ours. They got hurt in the Enforcer's attack, and they haven't woken up yet. We're getting worried."

Nitàwesì shrugged. "I'll do what I can."

They were led to a place far in the back, where Riordan sat cross-legged and hunched over an unconscious third, gently, almost lovingly, rubbing their forehead and hair. It looked to Nitàwesì that this person was part of the small, close-knit family they'd stumbled into.

"What happened?" they signed.

Riordan sighed. "An Enforcer shot Yun-seo with some fire gift we've never seen before. And they're not healin'. They don't look infected—they're just not gettin' better. And they ain't wakin' up, neither."

Nitàwesì nodded and extended their hands. They placed one palm on the third's bandaged stomach and the other on their forehead. Next, they called in their spirits and those of the person lying before them. Every time Nitàwesì used their gifts, they did so with the guidance of their patients' helpers and spirits. Every human was connected to a portal; most were unaware of this, but no one in this life walked alone. From deep within Yun-seo's core, figures emerged: tall, broad warriors covered in ornate armour, with thick, black hair tightly clasped in neat topknots. Long swords were strapped to their waists, bows tied to their backs, with quivers containing lightweight arrows. These fierce protectors, the likes of which the healer had never seen, glared at Nitàwesì but let them do their work, as their intention was clear. Not letting fear taint their work, Nitàwesì took a few deep breaths and allowed their spirit to leave their body, to fully submerge into the portal within Yun-seo, where they were able to survey the weakened third.

Deep levels of exhaustion rose to the surface. Dug deep into the spirit realm, Nitàwesì spotted a beautiful carved well that should have been filled with the shining particles of fire dust that fed their patient's gift—only the top was visible. This well pulsed with stagnant energy. Nitàwesì peered over its edge and saw only an echoing emptiness. This third's gift was completely depleted, they realized, which was why they weren't waking up. Nitàwesì's spirit looked to the protectors and pleaded with them to give the wounded person some of their gift. A few came close and placed their fingertips on the edge of the well. Their corporeal forms disappeared. Suddenly, the well started to glow, and the third inhaled deeply, their eyes fluttering open.

Nitàwesì smiled at the third and then thanked the spirits for their work as their own spirit returned to their body. They removed their hands from the warrior.

Yun-seo sat up shakily. Before they could speak, they caught Riordan's lifted eyebrows, xir lips tilting into xir usual smirk.

"Hey, thanks for not dyin' on me," xe whispered.

Yun-seo grinned. "Not unless it's by your hand, right?"

Riordan laughed. A'tugwewinu slapped xir chest.

"Unless it wasn't clear *before* you saved all our lives," A'tugwewinu said, "you've more than proven yourself these last few months. Welcome to the family, Yun-seo." She smiled and approached Yun-seo, bringing their foreheads together. Then she stepped back, and Bèl did the same, touching her forehead with Yun-seo's.

Nitàwesì looked on, once more feeling out of place. It was as if being separated from their life's love had left them incomplete, constantly feeling like an outsider.

Yun-seo pulled back and peered at the stranger standing next to A'tugwewinu. They sniffed the air. "You're a fourth!" they exclaimed.

Nitàwesì cocked their head to one side. They signed a series of complicated gestures like the children had done before the Enforcer attack.

Yun-seo shook their head.

"This is Nitàwesì," A'tugwewinu said. "They are wondering why you're so surprised."

"I've never met a fourth before," Yun-seo replied.

Nitàwesì shook their head and continued signing.

"There were several fourths in Pasakamate, the village they're from," A'tugwewinu continued. "They're wondering why you've never met one before."

Yun-seo nodded. "I guess fourths don't get recruited as Enforcers." They shrugged, a long-lost memory tingling at the back of their mind. "Anyway, thanks for whatever it is you did. It felt like I slept a long time."

"It's been days," Riordan said. "Ya even slept through our move. This is one of our other homes. It's on the outskirts. We'll spot Enforcers comin' a long ways b'fore they get here. It's safest fer now."

"Riordan carried you on xir back. You were strapped to xir like a toddler!" A'tugwewinu teased.

Yun-seo blushed.

"Don't worry, you probably didn't weigh more than a toddler. Anyway, look at this giant," Bèl said, gesturing to Riordan's arms.

"Hey!" Riordan exclaimed. "Why does that feel like an insult?"

"Because the bigger you are, the slower you are," Bèl retorted, casually picking at her nails.

"Yer a giant too!" Riordan exclaimed.

"I am lithe and tall."

A'tugwewinu looked at Nitàwesì. "They're always like this. Siblings," she signed, rolling her eyes but smiling.

Nitàwesì smiled, too—they couldn't help it.

A'tugwewinu laughed. "Come on, let's get you something to eat."

CHAPTER XX

MÀGÒDIZ

One evening, after their training, Yun-seo came and sat down next to A'tugwewinu, Nitàwesì, and Riordan. "I—I think I'm to ready to share how the Enforcers kidnapped me," they stated.

Riordan gestured for them to continue.

Yun-seo shuddered, their eyes cast in shadow. "They came to my home and murdered my mother in front of me. My father sacrificed his life, killing both himself and the Enforcers sent to retrieve me so that I could run away. I ran for months, but eventually they found me hiding in the desert and stole me away in the middle of the night. After that, life was just torture and pills until I became this . . . this *soldier*!" They spat the word. "I bent to their every whim. The Enforcers that trained us didn't care if we lived or died, if we bled or cried. They used our minds and bodies for their sick pleasure." Yun-seo sped up, as if unable to stop the flow of horrid memories.

"This!" They touched the scar that spanned half their cheek, the skin gnarled and melted from the base of their left nostril to their ear. "I got this on my first mission. I was sent to recruit a child and kill her family, and … I guess I froze. I couldn't lift my hands, use my gift—nothing. My Commander killed everyone out of spite while I just stared. I couldn't move." Yun-seo took a deep breath. "Then he turned to me and told me … told me that I was the biggest disappointment in my unit, and then … I passed out. And when I woke up, I had this. I've no memory of what happened, and I only remembered the rest about a week ago." Their words ran into one another, and their breath came in quick gasps.

A'tugwewinu reached out and pulled the taller human into her arms, enveloping them in a tight embrace. She gently shushed them.

"Thank you for sharing your story with us, as painful as it was."

Yun-seo let loose a few tears and wiped them away against A'tugwewinu's breast.

Watching this, Nitàwesì noted how similar it was to the way they would scent Shkitagen with an action familiar to most wolf clan members—homage to the animal, now long gone, to which they belonged. They shuddered.

"I'm sorry, that was a lot," Yun-seo said, noticing Nitàwesì's reaction. They laughed shallowly while trying to still their tears.

Nitàwesì shook their head. "You didn't bother me. I just miss my beloved. You two remind me of us," they signed, offering a bittersweet smile.

Riordan laughed. "It's not like that. We're family."

Nitàwesì looked away, not remembering enough about their parents to understand how typical families acted. Shkitagen and his father were very close, though. They presumed this was how families were supposed to be, but they weren't sure. Shkitagen was often their reference point for socially acceptable norms. Having been forced to raise themselves, Nitàwesì was a recluse—although loved by

Pasakamate for the healing they provided, the villagers had been confused as to why someone as beautiful and well spoken and charming as Shkitagen had married Nitàwesì.

A'tugwewinu startled—a sudden realization. "Yun-seo! When you were an Enforcer, where did the hunters deliver their captives to the Madjideye?"

Yun-seo looked despondent. "I can't remember. Every time I try, it's like there's this void. After completing a mission, I simply disappeared; then I'd reappear somewhere completely different. The Enforcer camp I belonged to was one of hundreds. Your firekeeper could have been taken to any camp anywhere in the world. If he is gifted, they'll probably start his torture soon, to make him into one of them."

Nitàwesì looked absolutely terrified.

"He'll last longer than I did, though," Yun-seo added to try and reassure the fourth. "The Enforcers want us as children because it's easier to mould us—the older we are, the longer it takes to bend our minds to their will. So there's still hope."

"What if they can't bend his mind?" Nitàwesì signed, thinking of how furiously stubborn their lover could be.

Yun-seo shook their head.

"Would your device tell us how to get to a camp? Or where Shkitagen might have been taken?" A'tugwewinu asked.

"No. We don't report on new arrivals, just bounties and information pertinent to their capture. Nothing else."

"Would one of the children know how to get to an Enforcer camp?" Nitàwesì signed to Riordan.

"No," xe said. "Anytime one of our kids trails after an Enforcer, they don't come back. I don't let 'em do that anymore."

Dejected, Nitàwesì slumped and turned away.

"We'll figure something out," A'tugwewinu promised.

CHAPTER XXI

ANSWER

Bèl woke to the soft snores of her lover. A'tugwewinu slept with her back pressed tight against Bèl, Bèl's long arm wrapped around A'tugwewinu's torso. Bèl smiled and leaned over. She breathed in the scent of the eighth, her sweat and musk, cupped her breast and kissed the outside of her ear.

"Let me make your dreams even sweeter, nanichi," she whispered.

The snoring ceased, but A'tugwewinu's eyes remained closed. A small smile appeared. Bèl kissed around her ear, lips travelling south as she sucked down her neck. They were quiet so as not to wake anyone else in the early morning hours. It was dark enough still, the fires mere embers, that no one would be able to see exactly what they were doing. And besides, they were in the very back of the dwelling, away from everyone else. Just to be safe, though, Bèl pulled their blanket up to cover both their bodies. She slipped her hand underneath the waistband of A'tugwewinu's loose trousers. Felt her warmth there, rubbing slow circles and gently teasing the skin of her lover's neck between her teeth. A'tugwewinu brought her hand up behind her and rubbed the apex of Bèl's thighs. Bèl gasped as A'tugwewinu moaned.

"Please," the eighth whispered, begged. Bèl acquiesced and pulled A'tugwewinu's trousers down, leaving her bottom half naked. The third removed her own clothes and then pinned her lover down roughly. A dark, guttural laugh bubbled up from A'tugwewinu's core—how easily Bèl could manoeuvre her body. Bèl relished the trust the storyteller placed in her. The air between them was thick, every sensation heightened. Bèl cherished the feel of the raised symbols that covered A'tugwewinu's body—the small grooves, dark skin overlapping darker skin. Bèl hoisted the storyteller's legs around her waist and pushed forward, joining their bodies, fingers between them as blood rushed to their groins. Small gasps, quick breaths, and A'tugwewinu's *oh*s with every hard thrust filled the silence around them.

A'tugwewinu reached out and clawed Bèl's back. Her moans turned to squeals, and she bit into Bèl's shoulder to muffle her climax. Bèl followed suit, inhaling her lover's neck in an attempt to silence her grunts of satisfaction. She tightened her hold, relishing in A'tugwewinu's soft parts, in the wetness down there. The storyteller giggled. Bèl rolled off her then and used her shirt to wipe the sweat and fluids from them both.

Bèl peeked her head out of the blankets to search for her discarded pants. A pillow smacked her in the face. She scowled and looked to the left, catching a glimpse of Riordan's clear, amused eyes.

"Quieter next time—don't want to scar the children." Xe tutted. Bèl snorted and threw the pillow back. Riordan caught it easily, much to her frustration. Bèl quickly found her pants and slipped them on, then hid back under the blanket.

"Ignore xir, Bèl," A'tugwewinu whispered, their mutual glow easing the shadows caused by recent events. Getting too warm, Bèl pulled the blanket down. A'tugwewinu brought her head to rest on Bèl's naked chest. Bèl sighed. They both dozed a little longer, content to share each other's air, their hearts beating as one.

Yun-seo woke to Riordan chuckling as xe wheeled toward them.

"What's so funny?" they whispered.

Riordan shook xir head. "Why're ya awake so early?" xe asked.

Yun-seo shrugged. "I was barely asleep to begin with."

Riordan hummed. "Well, how's 'bout we scrounge up some break-fast for sixty kids?"

Yun-seo nodded, grateful for the distraction.

■

"Before your final adulthood ritual, you will need to fast. This ceremony is meant to bring us closer to the spirits; it is to ask questions, seek answers, and learn more about why Kichi Manido put us here. This ceremony also helps you grow and heal," Nokomis explained.

A'tugwewinu nodded.

"I'll help you prepare your bundle and anything else you might need," A'tugwewinu's mother stated.

In the days that followed, A'tugwewinu gathered the essentials for her ceremony. Together, she and her grandmother went away from the village, to the side of a hill, where there was a cave.

"For generations Andwànikàdjigan has used this sacred place to fast. But you can do this fasting ceremony anywhere," he explained.

A'tugwewinu marvelled at the drawings carved into the rock that surrounded her, beginning at the base of the cave and extending far above them.

"You will set up your bedding there." Nokomis pointed to the farthest wall.

Nearby was a pit filled with kindling for a fire. A'tugwewinu set up her small mat and pillow and blanket where Nokomis had indicated. Anticipation swirled inside her as Nokomis sat next to the fire and began the four-direction prayer. A'tugwewinu held her small bundle in her hands. It was filled with sacred items that had been passed down through her parents' families, and from Nokomis's ayahkwew bundle as well.

Nokomis beckoned her over. He took out a pack of cigarettes from his back pocket. A'tugwewinu stared in disbelief. She had seen asema only a few times in her life. Nokomis took one out and broke it in half, crinkling the asema loose with his thumb and forefinger. He deposited half of it in A'tugwewinu's palm and the rest in his own.

"We only need a little bit," he said. They both prayed with their asema before sprinkling it on the charcoal bricks. Nokomis struck pieces of flint together until they sparked and the kindling caught fire.

"Let's sing the fire a song," Nokomis said. A'tugwewinu nodded. Together their voices mingled and echoed inside the cave.

That night, A'tugwewinu ignored the pangs of hunger that gnawed at her insides. She turned instead to the fire, watching as the flames licked and swept into figures. They illuminated the shadows of the spirits in the cave. The flames crackled, and the spirits spat stories in her ears, answering some of her deepest questions.

■

A'tugwewinu slowly blinked awake. Bèl softly snored with her head on A'tugwewinu's breasts.

"I know how we can find Shkitagen!" A'tugwewinu exclaimed, startling Bèl. She jumped up and ran to the other side of their dwelling, where the children slept huddled together for warmth. Most of them were awake already. A'tugwewinu smelled food cooking and hurried over to it. She spied Nitàwesì with Ojiwan, the two of them eating a brown mush with green sauce spread overtop.

"Nitàwesì!" A'tugwewinu called. Her cousin looked up. "I know how we can find Shkitagen!" she signed gleefully.

Tears welled in Nitàwesì's eyes. A'tugwewinu continued to sign, explaining the dream she'd had and how the spirits could help them.

"I've never done that ceremony before," Nitàwesì signed, worried.

"That's fine, I'll help you. Let's leave after you finish eating. There's a tall hill nearby. We can climb to the top and fast there. It's secluded— we'll be safe," A'tugwewinu added, to assure them.

Nitàwesì stared at their food.

"Are you going to finish that?" A'tugwewinu asked.

"Go ahead, I've felt nauseated for days now." Nitàwesì grimaced as they handed the plate to their cousin.

"Suit yourself. I got like that before my first time too. Listen to your body—if you don't feel like eating, don't force yourself."

Later that day, A'tugwewinu packed a duffel bag with some bedding and the few sacred items she had been able to gather since leaving her village.

Riordan came up to her. "I have something for you," xe said, and handed her a pack of cigarettes. The label was faded, and the plastic around it was crinkled and old.

A'tugwewinu stared at the gift with disbelief. "Where did you find this?"

"There're still a few secrets left for me to discover in this city," xe replied with a twinkle in xir eye. "Was waitin' to give it to ya on our birthday, but I figured this was more special, ya know?"

A'tugwewinu clutched the precious gift to her heart. She lunged forward and hugged Riordan. "Miigwech," she whispered.

"Yer welcome." Riordan held xir sibling close. "I'm gonna stay here and watch the kids. But take Yun-seo with you. This ceremony's from their people, too."

A'tugwewinu smirked. "Are you sure they can be apart from you for that long?"

"What?"

"You should tell them soon."

Riordan shook xir head, still not understanding.

"That you're a sixth," she elaborated.

"Oh, okay. It ain't a secret. I'm sure they know."

"Really, Riordan? You haven't been paying any attention to the way they look at you?" She shook her head. "I don't think they know."

Riordan sputtered, realization finally dawning. "I held them captive—I terrorized them!" *No one in their right mind would develop feelings for someone who hurt them so much ... would they?*

"Your methods were brutal, yes, but they did try to capture and kill you first. What you did was warranted. Honestly, I don't think Yun-seo holds anything against you—if anything, they look to you like you liberated them."

"Then why go outta my way to tell 'em I'm a sixth?"

A'tugwewinu finished collecting her things. "Because Yun-seo looks at you the same way I look at Bèl."

"Shit." Riordan ran xir hands through xir matted hair, unsure of what to do. A'tugwewinu simply laughed and walked away.

CHAPTER XXII

SPIRIT SONG

The group reached the top of the hill right as kizis was setting. They had just enough time to make a fire and plop themselves down on their bedding. Bèl and Yun-seo were accompanying them to tend the fire as they fasted, since A'tugwewinu and Nitàwesì would be sacrificing their bodies to gain access to the spirit world.

Nitàwesì shrugged nervously. They were worried about leaving Ojiwan with Riordan, but they knew the toddler would be safer back there with xir. Nitàwesì needed to focus on their prayers if they were to find Shkitagen, and that meant seclusion from other humans and as few distractions as possible.

"I've never really prayed or asked Kichi Manido for much before," Nitàwesì signed. "Shkitagen did that for the both of us." Their hands trembled at the mention of their lover.

"Praying is good," A'tugwewinu said. "But our people have always understood that simply asking for something isn't going to make it happen. We've always worked for our healing. When we pray, we offer something of ourselves or provide an offering, because taking something without offering something in return is theft. The mother whose soil and rock we stand on taught us that. It's why I have asema, the first gift she ever gave us. We return that to her in gratitude. It's also why we fast. We offer our hunger, our thirst, and our sleep. This makes our bodies weak, so our spirits can be strong."

Nitàwesì nodded.

"Nokomis told me that long ago, we also honoured one another by giving each other asema as a sign of gratitude, or if we needed something from someone, so we wouldn't be greedily taking from them. It was doing a trade, acknowledging that we saw their spirit by gifting them this earth's first gift to us."

"Asema became too rare to continue doing that, right?" Nitàwesì signed. Pain flowered in their chest. They remembered how sparingly the elders in Pasakamate had used this medicine.

"Yes, exactly," A'tugwewinu signed, dejected.

"Why can't we get more? I asked the elders once, but they just stormed off."

A'tugwewinu nodded. "Nokomis told me that asema used to grow from the earth, but when the Madjideye took away kizis, everything stopped growing."

"Kizis?" Yun-seo piped up from a few feet away. They were busily unpacking the gear while Bèl made a shelter.

"The shaky thing in the sky that goes away," A'tugwewinu clarified.

"You mean the sun?" Yun-seo asked.

"The sun," A'tugwewinu repeated, eyes sparkling as she memorized this new word.

Inside a circle of smooth stones, far enough away from the fire that they couldn't see its light, A'tugwewinu and Nitàwesì sat down back to back, eyes closed. The wind offered a constant cold bite that would keep the cousins awake through the night. Nothing happened at first; it was quiet except for the occasional sound of A'tugwewinu shuffling to get comfortable or Nitàwesì yawning. Then, very suddenly, the storyteller looked up and smiled as dozens of grandmothers flitted around the two of them, small pearls of blue light inching closer and growing into hazy humanlike figures. The grandmothers gazed down upon their descendants sitting in ceremony. They wore long silver braids down their wide, elaborate ribbon skirts. Their wrinkled, heavy cheeks quivered gleefully.

"Pjashig, Ànike-nokòmisibaneg!" A'tugwewinu greeted the spirits. She marvelled as more spirits materialized from the portal they had opened. Upside-down and backward faces emerged; wisps of clawed and fanged creatures that had once had names and stories of their own flickered in through the mist that surrounded them.

Nitàwesì was fearful and hesitant; they could make out only hazy shapes and whispers, while A'tugwewinu was having what sounded like entire conversations in Anishinabemowin.

After what felt like minutes to Nitàwesì but must have been hours, A'tugwewinu turned and grasped Nitàwesì's arm.

"The spirits say your fast is done now," she signed.

"What? I thought I was supposed to be here with you for three more days?" Nitàwesì signed.

"You didn't hear what the grandmothers said?"

Nitàwesì shook their head. "All I heard were whispers."

"That's all right. They come to you as they want you to see and hear them. But you need to leave the circle now. Put some more asema in the fire and thank them for the time you had. And ask Bèl to come see me."

Confused, Nitàwesì got up and left the circle. They tore the precious cigarette open, placing the loose asema in their hand. Then they walked over to the fire on the other side of the hill, just beyond sight of where they were fasting, and looked to Bèl for permission.

Bèl nodded, and Nitàwesì offered the asema to the fire.

They felt a pang in their chest. *Why was my ceremony cut short? Was I not worthy of completing it? Is something wrong with me? Is Shkitagen already dead—was this fast pointless?*

Bèl stood in front of Nitàwesì and gently held their chin. Their thoughts floated away as they gazed into Bèl's captivating eyes. Her large calloused hands wiped the tears from their cheeks—Nitàwesì hadn't even realized they were crying.

"A'tugwewinu said I'm done and asked for you to go see her," they signed.

Bèl nodded. "Thank you for your prayers. Did you receive what you were looking for?"

Nitàwesì shook their head. They turned and stared off toward the horizon.

"Yun-seo!" Bèl called.

Yun-seo rolled out of the makeshift shelter and rubbed their eyes. They were groggy and sore from sitting with the fire all night. They got up and jogged over to the pair.

"Can you stay with Nitàwesì? I need to go check in with Winu."

Yun-seo nodded.

"Their fast is done, so make them something to eat, okay?" Bèl turned and headed toward A'tugwewinu.

Yun-seo approached Nitàwesì, shrugging out of their coat. "Can I wrap this around you? It's going to be cold soon."

Nitàwesì watched as kizis set. *It's been only one day and one night.* They nodded.

"I know it's too big for you," Yun-seo said, wrapping Nitàwesì in the oversized jacket. "Or me, for that matter, but it was Riordan's."

They recalled the encounter they'd had just before the four of them set off for the hilltop.

"It's gonna be cold out there," Riordan barked. Yun-seo stared at the jacket xe was holding. "Take it," Riordan muttered, thrusting the jacket at the third.

"Why?" Yun-seo caught the jacket, which was easily twice their width.

"Consider it the first of many reparations."

"Wait—what?"

"For how I treated ya when ya first came here."

"But ... I was sent here to kill you. None of you should trust me, let alone make me part of your family."

"Would ya hurt us now?" Riordan asked.

"No! Never!" Yun-seo shouted.

"Right. So, we trust ya. Had I known that Enforcers were just scared kids in armour, drugged out of their minds, I probably wouldn't have killed so many of ya. I wouldn't have tortured ya like I did." Riordan looked away, regret in xir voice.

"You know, I've never met an Enforcer like me. Most of them are like the bastard who attacked us—mindless, violent. I don't think they can all be saved, no matter how hard you try."

"What makes ya different?"

Yun-seo shrugged the coat on. "Maybe it's because I'm small for a third, and all the other Enforcers treated me like shit. Or maybe it's because deep down, I really wanted to be saved."

Riordan hummed.

"You can't save anyone who doesn't want to be saved in the first place." Yun-seo sighed.

"When did ya get so wise?"

"Well, it certainly didn't happen while I was around you."

Riordan let out a deep, bellowing laugh that made Yun-seo's toes curl. Xe wiped xir eyes, noticing the deep blush in Yun-seo's cheeks. Xir eyes narrowed, becoming laser focused. Xe gripped Yun-seo's shoulder. Yun-seo flinched slightly, and Riordan quickly withdrew xir hand.

"You know I'm a sixth, right?" xe stated.

Yun-seo's eyes widened slightly. "Um, no, I, uh, didn't know—sorry," they stammered.

"Yeah. I just thought ya should know." Riordan turned and began to wheel away.

"Riordan!" Yun-seo called. Riordan turned. "You don't need to give me any more gifts. Reparations are useless. I tried to kill you, you tried to kill me. You broke me down, I broke your nose. You yelled, I yelled—we're even."

Riordan inhaled as if to retort, but was cut off.

"Besides, if you keep doing nice things like this, it's going to send mixed messages. I might get the wrong idea."

"Yun-seo . . ." Riordan breathed.

But Yun-seo walked away. The connection, the friendship that had been steadily growing between them these past several weeks, now had a gap in it, one that got wider with each step Yun-seo took in the opposite direction.

Yun-seo shook off the memory and sat down close to the fire with Nitàwesì. They took out some old cans and opened them, mixed together some food on a plate.

"Here. It's a little bit of everything. It must have been hard not to eat for so long." Yun-seo handed Nitàwesì the plate.

I didn't even have time to think about food or water—I was so focused on praying for Shkitagen, Nitàwesì thought bitterly. They took a sip of the muddy water offered to them, then a small bite of the mush on their plate.

"So, uh, this is awkward, me just rambling at you and you not being able to talk back," Yun-seo muttered.

Nitàwesì shrugged.

"Do you want me to stop talking?" Yun-seo asked.

Nitàwesì thought about it for a moment, then shook their head. Listening to someone else was a much-needed distraction at the moment, and the sound of Yun-seo's voice was soothing to them.

"I was thinking ... maybe you could teach me how to talk with my hands?"

Nitàwesì looked at Yun-seo.

"Unless you don't want to! Which is totally fine. I can ask Winu," Yun-seo added quickly, heat rising to their cheeks.

Nitàwesì giggled. "I'll teach you," they signed, nodding to make clear their intention.

"Miigwech. Did I say that right?" Yun-seo asked.

Nitàwesì nodded again.

Bèl stepped gracefully out of the shadows right then.

"Hey! How's Winu?" Yun-seo asked.

"Fine," Bèl uttered. "I'm going to finish this fast for you," she signed to Nitàwesì.

"Why? Why couldn't I do it?" Nitàwesì asked, exasperated.

"I don't know, but Winu said the spirits need someone to step in for you, so I volunteered. Keep the fire going until we come back. Keep eating and drinking while thinking of us, and pray for our protection," Bèl signed.

Nitàwesì nodded.

"Don't come over to us unless Enforcers are approaching," Bèl said to Yun-seo. "Help Nitàwesì with the guatu. You gonna be okay?"

Yun-seo stared, dumbfounded. "Have you ever done this before?"

Bèl raised an eyebrow. "You think the Anishinabeg are the only first people to have fasting ceremonies? The Taino had them, too."

Yun-seo nodded, soaking in the new information.

Bèl packed up her small altar filled with sacred items—trinkets that represented various spirits and helpers, tokens of the spirituality Bèl and A'tugwewinu practised that had been passed down from their elders. "You good?" she asked the other two.

Both Nitàwesì and Yun-seo nodded. Bèl took one last look at the pair. Strangers who had just met and couldn't really communicate with each other—but they would have to make it work. She shrugged and returned to the fasting site.

Nitàwesì felt sleep tugging at them. They looked at Yun-seo and pointed first to themselves and then to the bedding.

The third nodded. "Have a good rest," the ex-Enforcer, now warrior, said softly.

■

Long ago, there was a village in Anishinabeg aki. This village was filled with warriors and nurturers, elders and children. One day, a warrior insulted a nurturer, and the two fought viciously. More villagers became involved. Dozens of warriors sided with the warrior, and dozens of nurturers sided with the nurturer. Soon the village was segregated, warriors on one side and nurturers on the other. The fighting continued. So much so that the elders were pushed to the side, and the children were left neglected.

During this time of civil war, a child was born. This child took their first steps, but none of the adults around them noticed. The child walked away from the village and into the wilderness, where the four-leggeds, the flyers, the swimmers, and the backward and upside-down spirits took pity on the child and cared for them. This child wailed and cried day and night for the village they had left behind, decimated by the two genders there at war with one another. The animals were so concerned that some went to Kichi Manido to beg for the child's village to know peace, so the child could return home. Kichi Manido was also concerned with the village, and gave instructions to the animals and the spirits to pass on to the child. They returned, and by this time the child was grown, having passed puberty. The animals told them that Kichi Manido said Child Now Grown would need to fast and pray and then climb the tallest tree and wait for Kichi Manido to instruct them on how to bring peace to their village.

So Child Now Grown fasted and prayed and found the tallest tree, and they climbed and climbed and climbed, until their head peeked out from the top. A storm pulled in suddenly. Dark clouds and thunder boomed, and Child Now Grown was very afraid, but then the swimmers and crawlers, the four-leggeds and the flyers all appeared to support them. Child Now Grown stayed at the top of the tree and looked up in wonder as a single lightning bolt extended down from the heavens and into both Child Now Grown and the tree. The storm dissipated. Then Kichi Manido spoke, telling Child Now Grown that the lightning strike had blessed them as a new gender altogether, not warrior or nurturer, but two-spirit. With the in-between ways, the nij-manidowag ways, they could counsel couples, name children, be a nurturer or a warrior if needed, or fill any role within the community that was lacking. Now they could understand the perspectives of both genders and also sit in an altogether different perspective. This was what the village needed; bringing in a third gender would help usher in peace.

Child Now Grown accepted this gift, returned to their village, and sat with each nurturer and warrior until both sides understood the other's perspective. Many were admonished and realized the error of their ways. As the years went by, more and more babies were born with third genders, fourth genders, and so on, until finally we were gifted the eight genders we have today. And with each new gender came a new perspective and more *balance, more gifts, and more understanding. And with all of this, our villages thrived.*

■

Nitàwesì awoke suddenly, jarred by the bite of the wind and their unfamiliar surroundings. Though it was hazy, they recalled their dream of the story their parents had told them. The fourth could barely remember anything about their childhood, yet here was a gift they'd never thought to ask for—no doubt it was from the grandmothers. Nitàwesì sighed, feeling some internal peace, a small flutter in their lower abdomen. Confused, they peered down at their hand, which was protectively covering their stomach below their belly button. A single thought emerged: *Have Kichi Manido and the spirits gifted me with both this memory and a child?*

They barked out a laugh. Was it a gift or a bad omen that they now carried Shkitagen's child? *Shkitagen, you'd better stay alive, and you'd better let me find you soon—I can't raise this child on my own.* The healer cried, despondent at the thought of what should have been a miraculous revelation.

Overwhelmed, they turned and faced the fire and a softly snoring Yun-seo. They let the flames gently melt away their anxieties.

CHAPTER XXIII

HOME IS BEHIND

It had been eight days since Riordan's siblings left to find answers, and xe was wary. When Bèl and Winu had fled the city over a year ago because the Enforcers were closing in on them, it had left a giant hole in Riordan's chest. Having them back made xir feel whole again, but now that they were away for ceremony . . .

"Hey, Streetking!"

Riordan looked over to see one of xir medics, Ajax, staring at xir. "Whadya want, Jax?" xe barked.

"Enforcers'r startin' ta sniff 'round. We need t'move 'gain," pe said.

Riordan exhaled and rubbed xir face, moving the matted hair out of xir eyes. "'Kay, get ever'body packin'. We move out as soon as the rest'a the family gets back."

"Riordan, y'already lost almost forty kids with this move. More'r gonna leave—if yer home ain't safer than the streets, what's the point?"

Riordan let out a grunt. "I know. I'll figure it out." Xe went to pack xir scant belongings, organizing items into what was essential and what could be left behind. As long as the Enforcers didn't find this place, they could one day return to it.

"Bèl and Winu are back!" one of the kids shouted a few hours later.

Not a moment too soon, Riordan thought as xe wheeled xir way over.

Bèl and Winu appeared gaunt and thin, but they had a glow to them.

"We need to talk," A'tugwewinu stated.

"Clearly." Riordan gestured to the children packing all around them.

"Enforcers close by?" Bèl asked as she observed the frenzied packing. Cans of foods and dehydrated packs stolen from Enforcers lay in hand-pulled wagons with mismatched wheels. Tech and gadgets made from scraps were stuffed into dilapidated duffel bags. An old bicycle had been piled high with plastic bags full of warm clothes that were more patched than whole, but still capable of providing warmth for the fast-approaching cold season.

"Yeah, we gotta go. Moving to our home on the other side of Zhōng yang."

"The kids can go there, but we're leaving," A'tugwewinu stated.

"What? Where ya goin' now?" Riordan asked, incredulous. *They can't leave me again. I won't survive it this time—I can't take care of this family alone.*

"We know where Shkitagen is. Nitàwesì, Bèl, and I are going there right now. We just need to grab some weapons and food and Ojiwan."

"Wait—what? The kid's safer here, no?" Riordan was befuddled.

"We need to bring him with us in case we never come back here," Nitàwesì signed.

"Why wouldn't yas come back here?" Riordan shouted.

"Riordan." A'tugwewinu placed her hand on xir arm. "The spirits showed us a compound far west of here. It will take us months to get there by foot. We're going to make a plan on the way, but the Enforcers are after us—you, me, and Bèl. If the three of us leave, the kids will be safe."

"You want me to leave my family?" Riordan roared. *This can't be happening, it just can't be.* Xe turned to wheel away but was stopped. Xir children were lined up and staring up at xir. Two of the medics, Ajax and Cassiopeia, and Mohammed, one of the warriors, stepped forward. Though only seventeen, they were some of xir oldest kids.

"Streetking, you've trained us well. We'll be all right on our own," Cassiopeia said softly.

Riordan felt a pang deep within xir chest. Xe let out a breath. "Fine. Yer the parents now." Xe turned to A'tugwewinu and Bèl. "We leave within the hour." Xir eyes watered as xe spoke.

Ajax, Cassiopeia, Mohammed, and a dozen other children, those who had been there the longest, ran forward and surrounded xir. Some cried, while others looked at xir with hope in their eyes. Riordan swallowed back tears, fighting to control xir emotions.

"All right. Keep packin', kiddos. We don't want Enforcers beating down our doors." Riordan's voice broke as xe spoke. The children wiped their faces and went to finish their tasks. Only Ajax remained.

"We're gonna be fine," pe stated. "Besides, aren't ya getting a little old to be hangin' out with a buncha kids?" Pe let out a laugh.

"Shaddup," Riordan said, smiling. Xe turned then to see that Bèl, A'tugwewinu, and Nitàwesì had gone. Yun-seo remained and was staring at xir.

"Shouldn't you be packin'?" Riordan asked.

"Everything I own is already on my back." Yun-seo stepped closer. The tall sixth was swaying, fists and jaw clenched. "Hey." Yun-seo took Riordan's hand. "You okay?"

Riordan reached out suddenly and pulled Yun-seo into xir, crushing them into xir chest. Xe sobbed into their shoulder.

Yun-seo was momentarily surprised. Then they wrapped their arms around Riordan and ran their fingers up and down xir back. They felt the wetness from xir tears soaking through their shirt, but they didn't mind.

"I need to apologize for what I said before I left," Yun-seo said as Riordan's sobs began to subside.

Riordan pulled back and wiped xir face with the back of xir hand. "What?"

"My feelings are my responsibility, not yours. Just keep doing whatever you want. You're a kind person. It's my fault for reading into things."

Riordan looked confused. Xe mulled over the word "kind," letting the bitter taste of it sit in xir mouth. Xe nodded.

"Friends?" Yun-seo extended their hand.

"No."

Yun-seo looked confused.

"We're family," Riordan said, and pulled the small third in for another hug. Yun-seo smiled. "This okay?" Riordan asked as xe inhaled Yun-seo's scent.

Once more, Yun-seo rubbed the taller sixth's back. "Yeah, this is okay," they whispered.

Ojiwan was once more strapped to Nitàwesì's back. The toddler was overjoyed at being reunited with his new mother.

"Let me carry him," Bèl signed.

"It's fine. I carried him for days before arriving here. He's only three—he's not heavy," Nitàwesì signed.

Bèl frowned. "I insist. We should all take turns carrying him. It will be a long journey."

Nitàwesì untied the wrap holding the toddler in place, shifted him from their back to their front, and then lifted him toward Bèl, who took him and held him to her chest. Ojiwan shuffled slightly and wiped his snot on Bèl's shirt. Bèl smiled at the young one.

Nitàwesì looked on, bemused. "I've not seen you look that way at anyone except A'tugwewinu," they signed.

"I can be kind when I need to be," Bèl huffed.

Nitàwesì smirked. "Would you ever have one of your own?"

Bèl rolled her tongue in her mouth, pondering. "Well, technically I've already had over a hundred children in this lifetime. But one from my own lineage? I've never had the peace to even think about it." There was bitterness in her words. "Are you ready?" she signed, changing the subject. Nitàwesì nodded.

"'Skoden!" Riordan bellowed from the cave entrance.

They walked on, A'tugwewinu and Riordan glancing back every few minutes to see the children carefully departing the area in small groups, scattering to their various new homes throughout the city. They would regroup later on, when it was safe to do so.

"I've never left Zhōng yang before," Riordan whispered. "It's like my blood is screaming at me with every step I take." Xe clutched xir shirt, a white-knuckled grip.

The group offered looks of sympathy, but no one knew what to say; all of them had felt the loss of being forced to leave the familiar, of having to venture out into the unknown—the sharp sting of not knowing whether you would ever be able to return. For some, the pain was greater, knowing it was impossible to cross oceans or return to a land or village that no longer existed.

"Let's rest over that hill and come up with a plan." Bèl pointed with her chin to a large hill up ahead. It would take a few hours to get over it, but with kizis setting soon, it would be a good place to rest.

Bèl carried Ojiwan the entire way, never getting out of breath. It made Nitàwesì slightly jealous that third-gender beings were so much stronger and faster than any of the other genders. Bèl and Yun-seo could both lift things that were three times their body weight, and they could easily move twice as fast as Nitàwesì. And then there was Yun-seo's gift. Nitàwesì often felt like they were at such a disadvantage. In Pasakamate, they'd never felt inadequate; there were warriors and nurturers and firekeepers and they themselves, the healer. Everyone looked out for one another. But here in the wilderness with this ragtag group, they felt like being a healer wasn't nearly enough.

"I can hear you thinking from over here," A'tugwewinu signed. She was walking next to Nitàwesì and had noticed her cousin's deeply furrowed brow and set jaw.

"I've been told my face is very expressive."

A'tugwewinu laughed. "That it is! What's on your mind?"

Nitàwesì stared at the dried brambles that jutted out from cracks in the arid earth, the sand and garbage that swirled in the dark-grey and orange fog. And behind it all, the metal skeletons and detritus of the concrete city getting smaller with every new step they took.

"Shkitagen and I left Pasakamate because the waters were getting too high. We foolishly thought we would find someplace better and that everyone from the village would join us there. I never thought I would be in this situation, where I'm just not ... enough, I guess." Their shoulders dropped.

A'tugwewinu nodded. "Nokomis told me that we would always live in villages together, everyone with their role, and that together we would thrive. We weren't meant to survive on our own. But don't you think we're almost a village?"

"The six of us?" Nitàwesì's eyebrows shot up. They scanned the landscape in front of them.

"Two warriors, a storyteller, an inventor, a child, and a healer—two thirds, an eighth, a sixth, a second, and a fourth. Doesn't that sound like a village to you?"

The healer thought for a moment, then shook their head. "A village without nurturers? Or elders? Also, Yun-seo and Bèl can't protect us all! And you and Riordan can fight, too, but I can't."

"You can always learn. I had to. Riordan too. Bèl has also memorized some of the stories I carry, you know. It's one of the gifts that comes with being forced to learn to survive on our own—we all need to take on multiple roles."

"I've only ever healed. I wouldn't even know where to begin."

"You already have. Look at how you care for Ojiwan. Is that not what a nurturer does? Will you and Shkitagen not automatically transfer into that role as soon as your child is born?"

Nitàwesì was taken aback. They'd thought no one else was aware of the fetus growing within them. Then they rolled their eyes internally—there was very little one could hide from spirits. The grandmothers had most likely told their cousin far more than Nitàwesì could fathom. They understood now why the spirits hadn't let them continue their fast.

They considered A'tugwewinu's question. It was true that when people in the village had children, they would take care of them *and* fulfill their traditional role. Some people were solely nurturers, but many carried different roles, and regardless of their gender, parents would still take care of their own children.

"It is also within our abilities as ayahkwewak to be in a position of service wherever we are needed," A'tugwewinu said. "Ojiwan needed to be looked after. Not only did you do that, you also adopted him. I needed to protect myself, so I trained to be a warrior."

"But you can shift between genders," Nitàwesì protested, stabbing the air.

"True, eighth genders can shift our features. However, as ayahk-wewak, we don't need to transform our bodies. Our spirits can tackle that role if our community needs us to. It's one of our responsibilities as in-betweens," A'tugwewinu explained.

Nitàwesì nodded, understanding. "So, when do I learn to fight?" they signed, smiling.

A'tugwewinu laughed. "Guess what, Bèl?" she called out.

Bèl whipped her head around. "What?"

"My cousin wants to train." A'tugwewinu put her hand on Nitàwesì's shoulder.

Bèl beamed.

CHAPTER XXIV

THE EARTH THAT WAS

They reached the top of the hill and spotted, in the distance, the Enforcer base some distance from Zhōng yang. Like most Enforcer bases, it resembled a large fortress made from salvaged materials. Unlike most buildings that existed within the city, however, there were no holes in its massive concrete walls. The sight of it, its enormity, the dozens of Enforcers within, made them all fearful. It would take another half-day of walking to reach.

Nitàwesì fed Ojiwan and then excused themselves to empty their bladder behind an outcropping of tall, jutting rocks. To steady themselves, they put their hand on the rocks, whose surfaces had been smoothed by years of soilstorms. They paused when their fingers brushed an unfamiliar texture and looked down to see a pattern of ash and flaked blood on the stone. They screamed, the familiarity of the symbols dawning on them.

Bèl and Riordan were by their side within a minute.

Bèl touched the symbol. She brought the soot and blood to her nose, rubbing the mixture between her fingers. "This is about two weeks old. Maybe a bit more."

"It's Shkitagen! He always drew that symbol on my palm. It means love," Nitàwesì signed, sobs overtaking them.

"The arrow below it points away from Zhōng yang, to the west. Winu was right!" Bèl said.

"I had nothing to do with it," A'tugwewinu stated, approaching from behind. Riordan held the bleary-eyed Ojiwan, who was rubbing his face with chubby fists. "I just translated what the ancestors told me.

"Go, do your business, Nitàwesì, then it's time I tell everyone what the other side revealed to me."

"Nokomis is my tether between the realms. If I'm a few steps away from a cliff but cannot get close enough to peer into it, it is he who hangs over the edge. He is inside the abyss but can still come to me. As long as my body remains in this realm, I cannot step closer to the abyss. But Nokomis's body is no more—his spirit can roam freely. That is our power as ayahkwewak, those who possess the gift of the in-between. We are bridges between the spirit and physical worlds."

A'tugwewinu turned to Yun-seo. "Nokomis told me to trust you, Yun-seo, so I did, and I instructed the others to do the same." She turned her gaze to her lover. "Nokomis told Bèl to find me and gave her the life force necessary to cling to this world and save me from prison."

Yun-seo had many questions, but they recognized this as a moment that should not be interrupted. If they kept listening, the answers would come.

"Nokomis came to me on the hill while we fasted, and for seven days and seven nights, he showed me the Enforcers' camps—dozens and dozens of them, each filled with hundreds of Enforcers, scattered all throughout the continent. He showed me how ravaged this land truly is, the cliffs and cracks within the earth, canyons so deep it would take us days to climb down and weeks to go around. How the waters continue to rise and surround us from every direction." A'tugwewinu paused to inhale. "But there is hope. There are villages everywhere. Neighbouring nations—the Nêhiyawak to the north and the Haudenosaunee to the southeast. I even saw villages containing all kinds of people, descendants of those from across the ocean."

Riordan and Yun-seo perked up, not knowing much about that side of the world, despite its being where some of their bloodlines were from.

"There's life there too," A'tugwewinu shared, giving the pair hope. "Though I wasn't able to see it all, I know it's there—your ancestors told Nitàwesì so when they healed you."

Yun-seo put their hand to their chin and extended it outward, palm up—a sign they'd been taught meant "thanks." Nitàwesì smiled at them and nodded.

"Nokomis even showed me your child." A'tugwewinu beamed at Nitàwesì. "A seventh. She looks like Shkitagen but has your eyes."

Nitàwesì started to cry, so grateful for the vision their cousin had received. Their hands went to their stomach.

"But what Nokomis wanted most of all to show me was the Madjideye," A'tugwewinu said fiercely.

"You saw 'em!" Riordan said. Bèl slapped xir shoulder, shushing xir.

"We fear their name despite having never seen them," A'tugwewinu continued. "This is because the Madjideye have no form. They have no souls and do not belong in this world.

"Long ago, the first peoples were the only inhabitants of this continent. We were far from perfect, but we understood one universal truth: balance. That should we ever consume from this earth more than what was needed for our survival, there would be retribution. Then a new people arrived from across the ocean. A colonizing people who believed they held dominion over the earth. These people did nothing but consume. For hundreds of years, the first peoples pleaded with them, tried to maintain the balance, but were killed and beaten and jailed by them. Our ancestors' cries were ignored."

"This is my understanding of what I saw," A'tugwewinu continued. "Nokomis showed me a spirit made up of everything that was green and good. And from her eyes fell black blood. Her mouth wrenched open in a scream. Her hair spilled out behind her, stretching as far as the eye could see, and in front of her were the spirits of all who aided human beings. Spirits or helpers whose names I have not earned the right to speak stood with her in council, and one by one they decided whether they would stay and continue to protect the humans or, after having witnessed us pitiful humans refuse, for thousands of years, to learn reciprocity with all the living and nonliving beings around us, they would leave us to our own devices." A'tugwewinu paused to wipe away her tears with the back of her hand, leaving streaks of dirt in their stead.

"The mother of this earth, Ahkigowin aki or Ah-ki', with more pain in her heart than she could bear, started by telling the spirits that she was leaving. With her leaving, everything living, every plant and medicine, all the four-legged animals, the flyers, the crawlers, and the swimmers in the lakes and oceans, would die off. And so, too, would humans. Several of the spirits agreed this was the best way. Too long had they warned humans, too long had they been abused. It was time for this pitiful species to die off.

"But a few spirits stepped forward to defend us. There were humans who were still trying to heal this land, they said. Led by first peoples, people from all over the earth, they were doing their hardest to protect what was sacred, to give back, to keep the balance. These spirits said they would stay behind to offer gifts to those humans, and perhaps with their help, we would survive without the mother of this earth. So, the storytelling spirit said they would stay and dissolved their spirit into thousands of pieces, each entering different first peoples so that stories would survive. Then the fire spirit said they would stay, and they, too, split themselves into thousands of pieces, tiny embers that floated through the air until they were inhaled by those fighting to maintain balance. Then the spirit of medicine, the spirit of grandmothers who watch over babies, the shape-shifting spirit, the backward spirit, the warrior spirit, and the in-between spirit all did the same, until finally nations and villages of first peoples bearing these gifts rose up." A'tugwewinu paused, observing her family's reactions.

Bèl's eyes were visibly damp. She held Ojiwan close. Riordan was stunned. Nitàwesì clutched their hair and sobbed quietly, while Yunseo placed an arm around their shoulders.

"The rest of the story we've guessed, or know quite well. Once the spirit of this earth left, everything died, and the people fought. Fire filled this world, and it wasn't the animals or the plants leaving that killed us off—we did it to each other. Entire continents went to war. And for a while, it seemed like the spirits were right—humans were indeed the plague of this earth. But while weapons were employed and massacres were committed in greater and greater numbers around the world, many of us escaped the chaos by staying in our villages, continuing our traditions, and doing our best to maintain whatever balance remained. We sacrificed what little food, water, and medicine we had, and when we had nothing left, we offered ourselves, our very bodies, as trade and reciprocity between us and the spirits." A'tugwewinu exhaled shakily. She rubbed her arms to warm them. Kizis was gone now, and it was eerily quiet save for a cold, biting wind.

"That was when the Madjideye came, when we were at our weakest and most pitiful, the minds of humans so warped and full of hatred, distrust, and hunger. They came through then, feeding off our pain, growing by killing or brainwashing every human who still carried with them some particle of a gift bestowed by the spirits. They fed off our hopelessness, our weakness, our fear. Nokomis showed me where they came from, where we need to send them back to. I don't believe it's coincidence that they took Shkitagen west. We were all destined to meet, to retrieve the last firekeeper of this generation. And once we do, Nokomis is going to show me what we need to do to set the balance right once and for all. That is what I saw, and all that I know." A'tugwewinu released an exhausted sigh.

Bèl cleared her throat. She looked to A'tugwewinu, as if asking permission to speak. The storyteller nodded.

"I've been thinking," Bèl said. "This journey will exhaust us if we continue on foot. We're going to have to steal an Enforcer vehicle if we're going to make it."

A demonic grin split Riordan's face. "Now yer talkin'," xe said. The metal piercings in xir face gleamed in the firelight.

"They don't work at night," Yun-seo whispered. Everyone turned to them. "They're powered by the sun, what little of it manages to shine through the pollution. Even then, sometimes they don't work for days on end."

"It's still better than walking," Bèl argued. "Can you get into the base and take one?"

"No, they scan our tattoos when we enter a camp." Yun-seo scratched the ink on the back of their neck. "At this point, I'm either marked dead, or I have a bounty on me like the rest of you."

"Then we'll have ta sneak our way in." Riordan cackled and cracked xir knuckles. "Do ya know where they keep the vehicles at this base?"

Yun-seo nodded. "Enough of my memories have come back. They're kept outside the camp itself. They've never even considered that someone might try to steal one, since non-Enforcers wouldn't know how to operate it."

"That's true, though. No one knows how their vehicles work," A'tugwewinu said.

"But I do." Yun-seo shrugged. "There isn't much to it. They start remotely. We just have to get inside one, and we're off. The problem is how to get me close enough."

Riordan laughed, brimming with mischief. "Seems ta me like yas'll need a distraction."

CHAPTER XXV

MADJIDEYE

"Creep along the side of the base opposite the vehicles," Yun-seo instructed. "You'll need to draw attention to yourself. There are hundreds of Enforcers here, so you need to do something big, or only a few will be sent to arrest you."

Riordan laughed. "Oh, I'll give 'em somethin' big, all right," xe muttered gleefully.

"How are you going to make sure they don't capture you?" Bèl asked.

Yun-seo shrugged. "As long as the vehicles have enough of a charge, I should be able to get one started."

"And if none of them are charged?" A'tugwewinu asked.

"Then this fails and they execute us all."

"We won't let that happen," Bèl said. "A'tugwewinu, Nitàwesì, and Ojiwan will meet us at the base of the hill to the west of the camp. They'll leave now, which gives them the day to make it there on foot. Meanwhile, you, Riordan, and I will wait until nightfall. You will get as close to the vehicles as you can, while Riordan and I circle around the back and make our move."

"And trust me, ya'll know when we make'r move." Riordan fiddled with a long hand-held tool adorned with various buttons and gears. Xir fingers moved chaotically, pressing junctures that split the tool in half, revealing other parts that protruded from the device. When pressed, some of these parts ignited, while others were for cutting.

"What exactly is that?" Yun-seo asked, pointing at the device taking shape in Riordan's lap.

A'tugwewinu giggled. "Xe doesn't know, but trust me, it'll work."

"What do you mean?"

"Ya see, the little machines and forgotten gadgets that're all broken up and shoved in dumps and left on street corners, they've been speaking t'me ever since I could remember," Riordan explained. "And this little guy says that if I twist in a few screws here and melt a few wires there, it'll make a nice big bang for me."

"What's a guy?" A'tugwewinu asked.

"This," Riordan said, holding the strange contraption out to xir sibling, "is a guy."

A'tugwewinu looked at the device with wonder. She was always excited to learn new words or names—a constant form of resistance against the Madjideye.

"Now all yas, gimme some space and some silence. My guy is kinda shy."

Yun-seo crouched down and crept silently toward the base. The vehicles were on the north side. There was very little in the environment they could use to hide themselves, which made them nervous.

They took a deep breath and oriented themselves. They were aware of the muscles, tendons, and ligaments that intertwined in their body;

the sharp gravel poking under the thin soles of their shoes; the itch they felt from the cold sinking into their bones. It would be the cold time soon. Yun-seo wondered if A'tugwewinu had a word for that season, or if she even knew what seasons were, since the pollution made for an almost unchanging climate with only minute differences in temperature throughout the year.

This time would be colder than usual, though. Yun-seo knew this as clearly as they knew the scars on their body. A feeling in their gut told them the Madjideye were up to something that would ensure suffering—theirs and everyone's. Maybe they were going to round up the freed humans who still scurried around the concrete skeletons of cities or lived in travelling villages, and force them to live in Enforcer camps, if they wanted to survive.

I'm sure many would rather choose death, Yun-seo thought bitterly. Living among Riordan and the others since being captured all those months ago had caused some forgotten ideology to resurface within them. This *need* they felt, to have the open sky above; to search through remains and rubble for food; to wait for hours for drop after drop of water to drip into a cup, until there was enough for a single swig. Entire communities came together to support each other and to ensure each other's survival, instead of putting their individual needs or desires first.

Everything they'd experienced since their capture flew in the face of the training that had been drilled into them for over a decade.

The warrior was assaulted suddenly with a cavalcade of images—a memory long forgotten, pulled from the deep recesses of their mind and violently pushed to the forefront.

"H-09761!" *barked the metallic voice of the Elite Commander in charge of their unit.* H-09761 *flinched. The sound of the Elite Commander's voice* caused their skin to sweat and their heart rate to increase. In an instant, he was in front of them, sneering.

"What's this I hear, that you walked away from torturing the latest arrival?"

The Elite Commander's spittle splashed H-09761's cheek. Why was he so close? H-09761 tried to shuffle backward, but was stopped by the Commander's massive barrel of an arm wrapping around their back and pulling them forward. Closer.

"Got nothing to say? Seems like you need a reminder!" The Commander dragged H-09761 inside the base and marched them right into his quarters, where he threw them to the concrete floor.

H-09761 was dressed in their training attire, sweatpants with a tight shirt that framed their almost-nonexistent muscles. The Elite Commander threw his entire body weight onto H-09761 and straddled their waist as they struggled.

"Get off!" they pleaded.

"Think you're in any position to make demands?" the Elite Commander teased. "Why the Almighty wanted to recruit a tiny, weak thing like you astounds me. I will purify your weakness. I will pluck out every thread of compassion from this body until you rise to the ranks of perfection that all Enforcers in my unit achieve. Only then will you be fit to serve the Almighty." The Elite Commander brought his hands to H-09761's chest and gripped the flesh there. Squeezed hard.

"I think you'd be much prettier without these, don't you?" he hissed.

H-09761's body went numb. The only thing keeping them from spiralling into madness was the hard, cold concrete they were pinned to. They couldn't breathe. Their tears held the only warmth left in them.

"Uh-uh! None of that." The Commander tutted. He retrieved a pill from a compartment in his belt and shoved it down H-09761's throat.

"That's right," he said as H-09761 *gagged on his large fingers, choked, and swallowed the pill against their will.*

Their body went limp. Fear, sadness, powerlessness—it all slipped away, and their eyes glazed over.

"That's better, isn't it?" the Commander said. H-09761's *mouth went slack, and their eyes slowly drooped closed.*

Bile rose in Yun-seo's throat at the memory of the assault. They turned quickly and violently heaved onto the ground next to them.

"Fuck, fuck, fuck," they muttered as their stomach clenched painfully. They broke out in a cold sweat. It was one thing to know instinctively what had happened, but another thing entirely to remember it to the last detail—the smells, the sensations, the taste of blood and bodily fluids. They slapped themselves across the face.

They were so busy trying to bring themselves back to reality that they didn't hear the approaching Enforcer. Suddenly, they felt a gun pressed to the side of their temple. The cold weight against their scalp, cushioned only by their growing hair, sobered them in an instant.

"What are you doing outside Enforcer compound 3491?" asked the Enforcer in a robotic monotone.

Yun-seo's mind raced. They had to think fast. One wrong move and the Enforcer would pull that trigger—or worse, they'd be captured and tortured. That couldn't happen. They would do *anything* rather than be sent back into the clutches of their former Commander.

Which left only one course of action.

"Elite Enforcer H-09761 reporting for duty. I was captured by an enemy to the Almighty, Riordan Streetking. I have pertinent information. Take me to the Commander."

■

Bèl hoisted Riordan up on top of her shoulders, clutching xir ankles above xir wheels—a feat that would have been impossible for anyone but a third. Riordan's great bulk and weight barely phased Bèl at all. The warrior extended her arms and raised her sibling to a hole in the wall.

"Oh shit," Riordan whispered. Xe gripped the rough, dry stone and peered through the small opening. The air smelled stale. Mechanical whirring and ticking echoed both in the walls and below, where dozens of Enforcers roamed, some in full armour, while others wore only training uniforms. They marched about, dronelike and methodical.

Riordan gasped.

"What is it?" Bèl whispered.

"It's Yun-seo," Riordan said. "I think they've betrayed us."

■

"H-09761! We thought you were dead," the Commander stated warmly. But Yun-seo heard the suspicion in his voice. It underlined every word.

The Commander stepped forward and placed a palm on Yun-seo's cheek, caressing the scarred flesh there with his thumb.

In that moment, feeling cornered, Yun-seo called to every spirit that A'tugwewinu had taught them about.

Nothing happened.

The Commander stared into their eyes. "You should have died from withdrawal ages ago, yet here you stand before me." He moved his hand to the back of Yun-seo's neck. He gripped it firmly and forced the third to their knees.

Pain radiated from where Yun-seo's knees hit the concrete. "I have information!" they shouted.

The Commander laughed.

Yun-seo calculated their options. They had very few. "I know the location of the street kids' hideout. It's underground—it's where they keep their stolen goods!"

The Commander contemplated the information. "Good. And?"

Yun-seo searched their racing thoughts. "I—I ran away. They're weak but numerous. They got lazy guarding me, and I was able to get out and make it back here. I am loyal to the Almighty, I swear it!"

"Pray tell the exact details of your capture and subsequent escape?"

He doesn't believe me, Yun-seo realized. *He knows something's up.*

"I thought so," the Commander said, when Yun-seo failed to respond. "Take this one to my chambers—it seems we have a deserter. And what do we do to those who leave the grace of the Almighty?" he asked, a sadistic twinkle in his eye.

Yun-seo screamed as loud as they could. It was their last resort, which would either free or damn Yun-seo and the people they called their family.

■

"Can you hear what they're saying?" Bèl whispered. Riordan continued to grip the hole in the wall with both hands. Bèl used xir as a ladder of sorts and climbed up to the hole, almost tearing xir shirt in the process. She gripped the wall next to Riordan and peered through to the open courtyard below, where Yun-seo and a small group of Enforcers surrounded them.

Riordan was beyond grateful for all the labour-intensive training Bèl had forced xir to do. Xir hands and fingers were trembling, going white from exertion, while the muscles in xir forearms bulged from the effort. "I don't think I can stay up here much longer," Riordan said through clenched teeth.

Bèl glared at xir. "You should think less and train more," she said, watching the scene before them as it played out. They tuned their ears to what was happening below, hearing only Yun-seo's shouts.

Riordan radiated anger. "The Enforcers'r gonna find our kids," xe seethed.

Bèl shushed xir. "Watch objectively," she said.

"They have a guy!" they heard Yun-seo shout. "They're going to use a guy!" Their voice was panicked. Bèl and Riordan noticed then that the third's gaze was directed at the two of them.

Riordan let go of the wall and jumped down. Xir wheels didn't catch properly, and xe slipped and fell backward, twisting onto xir side. Xir forearm and hip took the brunt of the impact. Bèl landed next to xir in a perfect crouch and extended a hand.

"They're telling us to use your machine," Bèl said, hoisting Riordan upright.

Riordan reeled back. "What? No, they're rattin' us out. We need to run before they send Enforcers after us. Try to regroup with Winu, leave the traitor."

"That's not what this looks like to me. Just do it, Riordan. I'll get Yun-seo out of there, you wheel over to the vehicles and meet up with us later." Bèl ran off then, heading for the compound's entrance.

Riordan let out a groan. "Ya better be right," xe muttered.

■

Yun-seo waited, listening for anything but hearing nothing—no cavalry coming in response to their scream. *That was it,* they thought, *my only chance of surviving this.* The seconds ticked by painfully as the Enforcers ignored their pleas and dragged them to the Commander's chamber.

They were deposited on the floor. The door was slammed shut behind them.

With only a few moments to act, they got to their feet and immediately catalogued the interior: no objects large or sharp enough to do any damage, and the furniture was bolted down. No windows or other openings through which to mount an escape.

The door burst open, and the Commander stormed in. He wasted no time barrelling toward his prey. Yun-seo took a deep breath and called upon their gift. They screamed with all their might and lunged at the Commander, hands out in front, fists a fiery red.

The Commander swept out his right leg. Yun-seo managed to grab his thigh and held it tight before bringing a fist down into the meat of it. And into that punch, they poured every last ounce of their heat, their pain, their fear.

The Commander laughed and grabbed Yun-seo by the back of the neck, peeled them off his thigh, and sent them careening backward.

"What useless tricks," he said dismissively.

Yun-seo lay flat on their back, sweating. They still did not have full control over their gift or how it manifested. But this should have worked, they were sure of it. They stuck their hand out and called upon the energy they had successfully sent into the Commander. They felt it, reconnected with it, and started guiding it from his thigh to his heart.

The Commander halted in place. He stared down at himself, at the red glow slowly emerging from beneath his skin. "What ... I—I didn't teach you this!" he stuttered as the veins of energy travelled toward his heart.

No sooner did Yun-seo clench their fist than an iron grip squeezed the Commander's heart. He let out a yelp and went down on both knees, clutching his chest.

"There is more power in *one* of my ancestors than in everyone on this base *combined*," Yun-seo seethed. They stood up, their fist in front of them, tight and shaking and deadly. Slowly, they approached the Commander.

"Entire legions guide my bloodline," Yun-seo spat. "Your pitifully sparked match is nothing compared to the blazing hellfire that's within me now." They were standing in front of the Commander now. "I want you to know that this was supposed to be slow, this was supposed to hurt. But I've come to realize you're just a tool, a worthless pawn in a game you don't even know you're playing." They enunciated every word as the Commander wheezed, batting his hands and feebly attempting to call upon his own gift. His heart was fading.

With one last painful grunt, Yun-seo felt their gift crush the Commander's heart. They released their grip and watched his eyes roll back into his skull, his body fall limp.

"I curse your spirit for all eternity. May it never know rest or peace!" Yun-seo screamed to every spirit listening.

They felt a sudden wave of nausea bowl into them. From the exertion, they realized. *Come on, ancestors, get me out of here.* With what strength they had left, they limped out of the room that was to have been their place of execution, had they not been able to call upon their ability.

Suddenly, a loud boom echoed across the compound, shaking the walls and the ground. They heard the aftershocks of crumbling rock and the panicked cries of startled Enforcers. *They're coming for me.*

Yun-seo breathed a sigh of relief and leaned against the wall. They felt warmth trickling down their face and wiped it away. Looking down at their hand in horror, they realized blood was streaming from their eyes. They had barely a moment to panic before Bèl appeared in front of them, haggard and out of breath, but otherwise fine.

"Come on," she said. She ran over and placed an arm around Yun-seo's waist, taking on as much of their weight as she could.

They rounded a corner and saw two Enforcers running down the hallway toward them. Bèl pushed Yun-seo aside, took out her machete, and quickly cut one down with a single strike. Yun-seo found a gun a few feet from where they'd fallen and crawled over to it. Picked it up and steadied it with both hands. Their vision was partially obscured with red, but they squeezed the trigger twice in quick succession, and the second Enforcer crumpled to the ground.

Bèl wordlessly scooped them up again, grunting as she did.

"You're hurt?" Yun-seo asked over the roar of fire and the cracking and crumbling of concrete.

"This way!" Bèl yelled, ignoring Yun-seo's question. The two of them lumbered toward the compound's entrance.

An Enforcer followed them out. Yun-seo spun back around and fired two more shots, hitting their pursuer in the gut and neck.

Bèl guided them over to the fourth vehicle in a row just outside the compound. Yun-seo collapsed to the ground next to it.

Riordan wheeled over and hoisted them up by their shirt. "Oh no ya don't!" xe fumed. Xe slapped Yun-seo across the face to wake them up. "Does this one have enough of a charge?"

Yun-seo could barely think, much less stay awake. They shook their head, trying to rip through the fog to check the battery monitor on the vehicle's dashboard.

"It's fully charged," they replied weakly, staring at the vehicle's readout.

Riordan opened the door and tossed Yun-seo into the driver's seat. Bèl climbed into the back and lay down on the floor, groaning and clutching her ribs. Riordan jumped over to the passenger side, moving frantically as Enforcers spilled out of the burning compound and started running toward them with their guns raised.

"Skoden! Get us outta here!" Riordan screamed.

Yun-seo groaned. They'd already pushed their body far beyond its limits. All it wanted to do now was sleep, but they couldn't stop yet. They pulled the lever at the base of the vehicle, put their foot on the pedal, which they knew would force the gears to move, and yanked the cord to start the engine. It slowly sputtered to life. Feeling a sudden burst of adrenalin, they slammed their foot on the accelerator pedal and spun the wheel in their hand, turning the vehicle away from the base.

"Gimme the gun!" Riordan ordered. Yun-seo tossed it at the sixth. Riordan whispered something and kissed the metal of the vehicle before opening the window to xir right. Xe twisted a few levers on the exterior bars that wrapped around the vehicle as shielding, dismantling the ones that covered the window, and shimmied their head and shoulder out the window—arm extended, weapon in hand.

Xe fired several shots at the remaining vehicles as Enforcers sprinted toward them.

Another loud eruption. Yun-seo looked in the rear-view mirror and saw destruction in their wake: the burning shells of the vehicles. The explosion had even launched some of them dozens of feet from where they had been parked. There was no way the Enforcers could pursue them now.

"How?" Yun-seo asked as Riordan pulled xirself back inside the vehicle.

"Always have more'n one guy!" xe answered.

Yun-seo nodded and returned their gaze to the road ahead. Some of it was paved, but most of it was just hard soil.

It took thirty minutes of driving at full speed to reach the spot where they'd arranged to meet A'tugwewinu, Nitàwesì, and Ojiwan. Yun-seo stopped the vehicle, and Riordan jumped out.

"It's us!" xe shouted.

The hidden trio emerged from a nearby cave.

"Where's Bèl?" A'tugwewinu demanded.

"In here," Bèl called from the back seat. "I think I broke some ribs." She grunted in pain.

"I can heal that," Nitàwesì signed.

"It'll have to happen on the way. We need to get as far away from here as possible," Riordan said.

"I don't think we're going anywhere." A'tugwewinu pointed at Yun-seo, crumpled against the window. Their eyes were closed, and blood dripped down their face.

CHAPTER XXVI

BACKWARD IS FORWARD

Yun-seo's head was pounding. Their body ached in a way it hadn't in a long time—they weren't even sure where they were. Groggily, they opened their eyes as the vehicle door opened and Nitàwesì appeared. The healer held their palms out. Waves of heat and soothing light extended from them and entered Yun-seo.

"Stay still, you've been hurt pretty badly," A'tugwewinu said from behind Yun-seo. She was on the floor of the vehicle with Ojiwan, asleep on a pile of blankets, running a hand over his back.

In the distance, Yun-seo heard shouting.

"Ignore them," A'tugwewinu said.

But Yun-seo couldn't help but overhear.

"So what—you think the next time we find Enforcers, Yun-seo's just going to turn us in?" Bèl screamed.

"Yes!" Riordan roared. "If my guys hadn't half blown up their compound, the Enforcers would be on their way ta our hideouts in Zhōng yang to kill our kids."

"You will never understand the desperation of being captured," Bèl retorted. "Yun-seo stays with us."

Riordan growled. "I'd rather be killed than tell the Madjideye anythin' about this family! The traitor goes!"

"Have you ever been in so much pain and misery that you would do anything, anything to make it all stop?" Venom coated Bèl's words.

"I'm very familiar with pain, Bèl."

"But you've never been at the mercy of Enforcers. You can't even imagine the things they do to you. A'tugwewinu knows, they had her for two months. And trust me, what you saw when we made it to your home was just the surface of it. But more than anyone, Yun-seo knows. They experienced more years of pain from the Madjideye than any of us. So don't you dare sit up on your high and mighty throne and speak of loyalty! The Madjideye are the akani, not Yun-seo," Bèl finished with a hiss.

Yun-seo swallowed back tears. "I didn't tell the Enforcers anything they didn't already know. I would never—"

"I know," A'tugwewinu whispered. She moved forward, sitting on the console between the two front seats.

Nitàwesì pulled away, flustered. "I don't know how you use your gift this way ... it's wrong somehow ... it's eating away at your life force," they signed, then clenched their fists.

A'tugwewinu translated.

"I don't know how to use fire any other way," Yun-seo said. "I thought the plan had failed, I thought Riordan and Bèl were captured or worse, and I thought death was better than ..." Yun-seo's voice cracked, and their breathing was ragged. The fear, the desperation of recent events rushed back into them.

"For all Riordan's genius with machines, xe's an idiot when it comes to people. Just ignore xir. Xe'll come to xir senses," A'tugwewinu explained. Yun-seo nodded.

"I'm afraid," Riordan whispered, absent any bravado. Xir shoulders slumped.

Bèl turned and glared at xir. She noted her sibling's crestfallen expression and trembling hands. She knew then it was not scolding Riordan needed. Bèl went over and wrapped her arms around Riordan, holding the sixth close as xe bent down and burrowed xir head into Bèl's coat.

"I don't know what I'm doin'," Riordan admitted, xir voice higher and shakier than Bèl had heard it in a long time. Xe recoiled suddenly, not used to being so overwhelmed.

"I think you need to let go," Bèl said. "Trust that Kichi Manido is watching over your kids, and focus on the path in front of us."

Riordan nodded shakily. "Yer right. But … don't ya dare tell anyone I said that."

Bèl laughed.

The duo returned to the rest of their family. Yun-seo looked away as they approached.

Riordan inhaled as if to speak, but xe was at a complete loss for what to say.

"Let's get a move on," Bèl ordered. Everyone scrambled into the vehicle and tossed their belongings in the back.

Riordan swung xirself into the passenger seat next to Yun-seo. "Show me how to drive this thing," xe asked kindly. Yun-seo looked at xir, terrified. Riordan shrugged, offering only a slight twitch of xir lips and an imploring stare.

It seemed this was the closest Yun-seo would get to an apology, at least for the time being. They nodded and quietly began to explain the various pedals and buttons. They started the vehicle again and began driving west.

CHAPTER XXVII

SMOKE

"Can we stop somewhere?" A'tugwewinu asked. They'd been driving for a few days now.

"Whadya wanna stop around here fer?" Riordan asked.

"The prison they took me to—it's close. Last time, we had to run away, but maybe this time, we can do something for those we left behind."

Bèl and Riordan roared their outrage at the same time.

"Forget it," Riordan stated firmly.

"Why would you want to go back, Winu?" Yun-seo asked, silencing the others.

A'tugwewinu sighed. "There are storytellers there, ones who asked to stay behind. I have this feeling, this awful feeling in my gut that something's happened."

"Winu ..." Bèl started.

"I know!" A'tugwewinu exclaimed. "I know it's dangerous and we could get caught, and this might be the stupidest thing I ever ask any of you to do. But you weren't there. You didn't see the looks on their faces as they learned stories and inhaled words like they were the sweetest water they would ever drink. Like the words would fill their stomachs and ease the pain the Madjideye inflicted upon them. Last time we were on foot. This time, with the vehicle, let me at least try and give some of them a real chance to escape."

Riordan groaned, knowing full well from the tone in xir sibling's voice that A'tugwewinu was going to do something stupid, no matter what. "What's the plan?" xe asked.

"We make a hole in the fence, then head around back and have the Enforcers chase us? What then?" Bèl asked.

"Do you have any more guys?" A'tugwewinu asked.

Riordan shook xir head.

"That's fine," Yun-seo piped up. "We can puncture the wheels of their vehicles, let the air out slowly. They won't notice right away. Then we drive them out far enough that it will take them hours to return. That should give the prisoners time to escape."

Bèl thought about it. "That might work."

Riordan nodded. "What's my headin'?"

Bèl pinched the bridge of her nose. "Northwest thirty by seventy-four, then south by fifteen."

Riordan turned the wheel and began driving in the new direction.

A'tugwewinu touched Bèl's shoulder. "Want me to do your hair?" she asked softly, trying to quell the roiling anxiety she sensed inside Bèl. The third nodded and sat in front of her. A'tugwewinu knelt and began to deftly undo the messy braids that lined Bèl's scalp, starting from the bottom, at her lower back, and working her way up.

"How do you do that?" Yun-seo asked, twisting around in the passenger seat to watch A'tugwewinu work.

"Did your parents not braid your hair?" she asked.

Yun-seo shook their head. "My mother frequently washed my hair in ceremony when I was little. She told me it was to get rid of bad spirits, but she never braided it."

A'tugwewinu spoke wistfully. "Our braids are the physical manifestation of our spirits. It's why no one should ever touch your hair except for family and loved ones."

"Wh-why did you shave your hair?" Yun-seo asked quietly.

"Enforcers."

Riordan gripped the wheel tighter. There was a noticeable creak from the piece of metal xe'd placed on the accelerator so that xir wheels could push it comfortably.

Yun-seo lowered their head. "Oh."

"When we braid," A'tugwewinu continued, taking a deep breath, "we take three strands, representing the mind, the body, and the spirit, and we weave them together as one—a reminder to walk this path in a good way. Braiding hair is a ceremony."

All passengers fell silent then, the only sounds coming from outside as Riordan drove over rocks and sand and garbage and swerved to avoid pits and potholes in the road ahead.

A'tugwewinu began to sing in ancient tongues, vocables rising and falling, and Bèl joined in every so often, tapping out a rhythm on her thigh with the palm of her hand. When the songs ended, Ojiwan pushed himself out of Nitàwesì's grasp.

"Me too," the little one signed to A'tugwewinu.

"Nitàwesì, do you know how to take care of tight curls?"

Nitàwesì shook their head, embarrassment heating their cheeks. "Shkitagen had looser curls, like me, and I never got close enough to anyone else to learn," they signed.

A'tugwewinu nodded. "Come closer. You'll need to learn for Ojiwan." She grabbed a vial of precious oil they had traded for and gently finger-combed it through Bèl's thick locks. Once moisturized, A'tugwewinu took strands of hair from one side of Bèl's scalp and wove them until she'd made a neat braid the thickness of her thumb. "And then you keep going until all the hair is in braids. Sometimes you have to measure first, but Bèl always wants this style. I've done it hundreds of times now."

Ojiwan made grabbing motions with his little hands.

"Come here, guaili." Bèl sat the child down on her lap. "Nitàwesì, can you pass me the oil?" Nitàwesì did as asked, and Bèl started gently smoothing through the many tufts of hair on the child's head. "How do you want your hair, guaili?" she asked.

Ojiwan pointed to Bèl's scalp. A'tugwewinu was starting on the third braid.

"Like me? All right, then." Bèl smiled.

Nitàwesì turned their attention to Bèl as she gently braided Ojiwan's hair. His hair was much shorter, so the braids ended at the nape of his neck, in little curls.

It took some time, but eventually both sets of braids were complete.

"Happy?" A'tugwewinu signed to Ojiwan. The second patted his braids, smiling.

Bèl dug through her pack until she found a broken piece of mirror. She handed it to Ojiwan, who peered at his reflection and cackled gleefully, showing his teeth. The adults melted at the sight.

Bèl nodded and gently kissed A'tugwewinu's forehead.

"Want me to braid yours, too?" the storyteller signed to her cousin.

Nitàwesì looked surprised. "You can try, but I've never been able to do anything with these tangles."

"You should take better care of your curls!" Bèl said.

A'tugwewinu made a braid on either side of Nitàwesì's head. They lined the healer's scalp and fell down their upper back.

"I'm giving you two braids because you have your life's love," their cousin whispered.

"Is there a braid for those who are married but have hearts large enough to love more than one other?" Nitàwesì asked.

A'tugwewinu chuckled. "That's beautiful. Let's add a third braid." The storyteller wove her fingers through her cousin's curls. "You have a different hair type from Bèl and Ojiwan. It's closer to mine, but I don't have curls, so the type of braids they have wouldn't work. Also, their style of braiding is sacred, specifically from their ancestors, those who were stolen from across the ocean." She gently combed through Nitàwesì's locks, undoing tangles as she wove their hair.

"My other parent, the one not related to you, was from the south, from a first people called Mexica," Nitàwesì signed. "They had hair like mine. It's the only thing I have from them. My parent always wore it loose or tied up. It was beautiful, curly hair." A sad smile.

"Thank you for sharing that with me," A'tugwewinu whispered. "May I sing for your parents?"

Nitàwesì nodded. Then A'tugwewinu softly sang them a song full of hope and pain and gratitude. The meaning somehow came across, even though only Bèl and Riordan could translate the words.

"When my hair gets long enough, could you ... could you braid mine too?" Yun-seo asked after the song had ended.

A'tugwewinu nodded.

"At the next stop, me and Winu are gettin' sheared!" Riordan exclaimed.

Everyone laughed.

"Are you sure you won't let it grow?" Bèl whispered in A'tugwewinu's ear while the others excitedly discussed stopping soon for a rest.

A'tugwewinu shook her head vehemently. "Never again, Bèl. No one will ever touch it again." She shuddered.

Bèl nodded sadly. "I understand. Are you sure you're okay to go back there?"

"I'll force myself to be." A'tugwewinu took a deep, bracing breath.

Riordan felt the clipped hair at the nape of xir neck. The choppy length was "ruggedly beautiful," A'tugwewinu had said. Xe peered back at Winu. Her hair had grown some over the past few weeks, but now it was shorn once more, the stubby black hairs that remained a poor substitution for the long mane that had once reached her lower back.

"We're almost there," Yun-seo declared from the driver's seat, waking Nitàwesì and Bèl.

Riordan caught A'tugwewinu peering directly at xir. Her gaze was hard, frightening.

If I get captured, it said, *kill me. Promise me.*

Riordan nodded once.

Over the horizon, the vehicle's occupants spotted small plumes of grey smoke billowing up from the prison's location.

"That's strange," Yun-seo said.

"What's strange?" A'tugwewinu asked, growing anxious.

"The smoke. There's a lot of it, don't you think?" The storyteller hummed in agreement. "I say we circle around first—an Enforcer vehicle patrolling the perimeter shouldn't raise any alarms."

The closer they got, the tighter the pain in A'tugwewinu's chest became. Her breath grew shallow; her vision started blurring at the edges.

Not now! she thought desperately.

From behind A'tugwewinu, Bèl's large arms pulled her back and embraced her. A'tugwewinu listened to her lover's slow, deliberate breathing. She matched the rhythm of Bèl's inhales and exhales, her racing thoughts slowing to a more measured pace. Eventually, the panic subsided, and her vision cleared.

A'tugwewinu gripped Bèl's arms firmly—for comfort, for grounding, for some indication that this was all real. That this time, she wouldn't be going in alone.

They drove in near silence except for Ojiwan's quiet whimpering—he had picked up on the tension in the adults around him. Nitàwesì held the child tight.

Nearing the prison, the family saw that A'tugwewinu's gut feeling had been justified. The building was on fire—or it had been some time ago. Where once had stood a roof and four walls, there was now little more than rubble and charred remains.

"Did the prisoners escape?" A'tugwewinu asked hopefully.

Yun-seo swallowed audibly. "I don't think so."

In the distance, they spotted the tall chain-link fences. They appeared to be coated in what looked like blood. At the centre of the fenced-in area was a blackened mound. As they got closer, the mound's horrible nature became clear: it was a pile of burnt, still-smouldering corpses.

And on the outermost gate, strung up for anyone passing by to bear witness, were the bodies of the storytellers—those whom A'tugwewinu had marked. Their clothes were torn, revealing the marks adorning their chests.

"Pull over! Stop!" A'tugwewinu screamed. Yun-seo stomped their foot on the brake.

The storyteller burst out of the vehicle and sprinted toward the bodies on the gate. She stopped beneath them, too short to reach their feet even if she jumped. She let out a piercing wail and collapsed to her knees, sobbing hysterically.

Bèl gripped Yun-seo's shoulder. "Is there any immediate threat?"

Yun-seo shook their head, eyes wet at the sight of their sibling in mourning. "No, the Enforcers wouldn't have left the compound in ashes if they planned on staying here. We should be safe."

With those words, Bèl jumped out of the vehicle and went straight to A'tugwewinu, wrapped her in her arms, and held her.

Riordan exhaled. "All right, let's get ta work," xe muttered.

"What?" Yun-seo asked.

"Somebody's gotta start diggin' graves," xe responded bitterly. Xe went to the back of the vehicle where xe'd stored xir tools.

Yun-seo swallowed their tears. They looked at Nitàwesì, who was busy holding one hand over Ojiwan's eyes while they tied a piece of fabric over them with the other, to try and shield the little one from the atrocity he had most likely already glimpsed.

Nitàwesì held the child's hand and made the sign for sleep on his palm. Ojiwan nodded and curled into the fetal position on the pile of blankets that was now his bed.

"Go help Riordan," Nitàwesì signed to Yun-seo. "I'll make something for us to eat, even if no one has any appetite at the moment."

Yun-seo nodded. "I understood 'go' and 'eat'?"

"Close enough."

Yun-seo exited the vehicle and followed Riordan. The two of them dug for hours.

A'tugwewinu never stopped crying.

Nokomis had explained to A'tugwewinu that massacres caused wrinkles in the fabric between the spirit world and the physical world. Everything in the physical world, including all living things, rested in a delicate web—murders and suicides tore at these strings, leaving gaping, garish holes.

A'tugwewinu glanced up at Bèl as the warrior unsheathed her machete and pulled the blade across her forearm, lightning quick. Blood trickled down, a rivulet of red soaking the earth. Bèl handed the blade to A'tugwewinu, who used it in the same fashion, slicing even deeper. It was up to the two of them to offer their flesh to patch up the torn web, to appease the spirits of those who were massacred and to mollify the spirits of the land currently festering in anger.

Some distance behind them, Yun-seo cried out in alarm.

"What are they doing?" they exclaimed, getting ready to run toward the two of them. They were stopped by an arm encircling their midsection. They turned to see Nitàwesì holding them, gently shaking their head. Riordan approached from the other side with Ojiwan in xir arms, the blindfold still in place.

"This is the payment," Riordan whispered.

"Payment for what?" Yun-seo asked.

From a distance, they heard A'tugwewinu shouting in Anishinabemowin and watched as an incandescent portal opened beneath them and swallowed her blood. They observed as Bèl's entire body shuddered, and translucent hands appeared in front of her, rising up from the murky depths of the portal and pulling at her veins.

"What is ... can you ... Can you see that?" The terror in Yun-seo's voice was evident.

Nitàwesì nodded. They removed their arm from Yun-seo's and started to sign. Riordan translated for them: "To walk with the spirits is a calling that many of us carry. But to be able to summon them is something that only trained ayahkwewak can do."

Yun-seo shook their head. "I don't understand."

Riordan added, "Winu's giving them the same funeral rites she would give one of her own people. If she had hair left to cut, she would have offered that too. They're both asking the spirits to right the wrongs of these deaths."

"How? How can a spirit fix this?"

"Giibi have access to infinite realms, while we can only glance through one. Divine retribution awaits those who tamper with the thread of life—unrest for eons," Nitàwesì signed.

Yun-seo trembled at the enormity of the statement, which the healer punctuated sharply. "Why blood?"

"Look around you." Riordan waved xir free arm over the barren earth, the remains of the prison—shattered bits of rock, plastic, and rusted metal. "The only thing we got to offer the spirits that's precious is our blood."

"Have you ever made this offering?" Yun-seo asked.

Riordan glared at them. Xe nodded.

"And you?" Yun-seo signed at Nitàwesì.

The healer exhaled audibly before responding in a flurry. "I offer them a sacrifice daily in trade for exacting revenge on those who massacred my parents."

"You do this daily?" Yun-seo searched the healer's arms and noticed scattered scratches, but nothing like the deep scars that A'tugwewinu and Bèl would carry after this ceremony.

"I offer them something far more precious to me than blood," Nitàwesì signed.

"What?"

They smiled sadly. "My voice."

Yun-seo's breath hitched. Questions remained heavy on their tongue.

"All right, enough," Riordan said before Yun-seo could ask anything more. "Let's leave 'em to it and get ourselves some sleep."

Just then, dozens of hazy figures appeared and started dancing around Bèl and A'tugwewinu. The couple swayed to a visible blue wind as a far-off warble sounded. Ancient tongues speaking backward echoed against Yun-seo's skin.

"But I've never seen anything like this!" they pleaded.

Nitàwesì gently gripped their wrist. "This is not our ceremony. If they had wanted us to watch or participate, they would have asked us to."

Yun-seo nodded. They hung their head and followed the healer back to the vehicle. They held the fourth's hand the entire way.

CHAPTER XXVIII

THE VILLAGE WITH THE RED FLAGS

The silence in the vehicle was palpable as the group drove away from the prison. Ojiwan was uncomfortable and trying to entertain the others by babbling and waving his hands in hopes of getting some sort of rise out of them. Only Nitàwesì would sign with the little one.

A'tugwewinu sat in the vehicle's rear with her back to everyone. She had refused to eat and hadn't even moved for the past few days, though Bèl had at intervals successfully poured small amounts of water into the storyteller's mouth. Other than that, A'tugwewinu was listless. This in turn made Bèl irritable. She snapped at everyone, save Ojiwan. Whatever peace still existed between Bèl and Riordan was burned away entirely. Yun-seo was sure that if it weren't for the vehicle confining them, the two would have resorted to using their fists by now.

Whenever they pulled over and rested, Nitàwesì and Yun-seo gravitated toward each other, finding comfort in the fact that they were both new arrivals to this family. In the scant few months the group had been together, the newcomers had barely scratched the surface of the original trio's dynamics. Both Nitàwesì and Yun-seo resolved to stay completely out of this situation. Nitàwesì tried to get Ojiwan and Yun-seo to engage with one another, but Yun-seo had never picked up a child before and could barely remember what it was like to be a child or to play, and to Ojiwan, Yun-seo was more of a nuisance than a nurturer.

It was Yun-seo's turn driving when Riordan, in the passenger seat, exclaimed, "Village! Up ahead!" It was enough to make most of the vehicle's occupants jump.

"Do you see any flags?" Bèl asked Yun-seo.

Yun-seo squinted. "I think I see red, but that's it. I can't make out anything else."

"That's good, red means a merchant village. We should be fine so long as Enforcers haven't already found them," Bèl stated.

"Just in time, too—the solar reserves are dwindling. We need to park for a while to let the batteries recharge," Yun-seo informed her.

"How long?"

"The haze isn't too thick today. Half a day should do it, hopefully."

Bèl nodded. "All right, me and Winu will stay here. The rest of you go and see if you can find some supplies."

Yun-seo veered to the left, toward a grouping of tall boulders that would provide the vehicle with a small amount of camouflage, enough to perhaps give them time to make a getaway, should the need arise.

Merchant villages were rare. Nitàwesì had encountered only one in their whole life. They were entire villages made up of scrap metal and plastic, with small domes or huts on wheels—some even had motors. That way they could open up shop anywhere they pleased and roll out again at a moment's notice. Constructed from dilapidated tarps, random objects, and whatever pieces of metal could be found, most of the merchants' vessels were poorly constructed things, often too slow to outrun Enforcers, should they be discovered. The safety of the villages rested on their constant, unpredictable movement.

Nitàwesì held Ojiwan's hand as the toddler waddled next to them, his wide eyes drinking in the colours and smells and sounds of over a hundred people bustling around them.

"I can fix things fer trade," Riordan signed. "Other than that, we don't have valuables to trade—except the vehicle, and that obviously ain't happenin.'"

"I can also heal minor injuries if needed," Nitàwesì added.

Sweet fragrances filled the air—smoke from shoe leather cooking on grills, strange compositions of canned mush boiling in buckets and handmade pots. The bustle was joyous, as people greeted and bartered with one another. It was a very different atmosphere from the shifty mistrustfulness Riordan and the others were accustomed to in Zhōng yang.

"What is that?" Yun-seo asked, staring at a merchant grilling creatures skewered on sticks over a fire.

"Dessert!" Riordan squealed as xe and Nitàwesì dashed toward the stand.

Riordan quickly assessed the merchant's cart, noting that it needed a few tweaks here and there—the wheels were stuck, and the engine was uncalibrated. It needed strong arms to crank it back to life.

Meanwhile, Nitàwesì noticed a severe burn on the merchant's hand, which they offered to heal.

Within moments, the two had successfully bartered with the merchant. Nitàwesì's hands glowed as they healed the burn on the merchant's hand, and Riordan slipped underneath the cart, whipped some tools out of xir belt, and tinkered away. Xe moved a few gears into place and greased the wheels.

Yun-seo approached just in time to hear the merchant thanking Nitàwesì. The healer turned around and handed Yun-seo a dessert.

"What exactly is this?" Yun-seo asked, wishing they had their telecom to look up whatever it was they were holding.

The merchant looked at them with surprise. "You've never had dessert before?" she asked.

Yun-seo shook their head.

"Well then, you're in for a treat! I just caught these buggers a few miles back, biggest ones I've seen in years. Thought they could hide in this cave. It wasn't easy, let me tell you, but I got 'em!"

Yun-seo observed the critter on the stick. They could have sworn they'd caught one of its legs twitching. "Is it still ... alive?"

The merchant shrugged. "Eh, probably ... damn near impossible to kill dessert. Just start eating the head and make your way down."

Yun-seo stared at it, horrified.

"I'll eat it if you won't," Nitàwesì signed as they took a huge bite out of the dessert in their own hand. The audible crunch offended Yun-seo's nerves.

"What taste?" Yun-seo signed.

"Salty and smoky and crunchy." Nitàwesì grinned.

Yun-seo didn't know the last sign, but decided life was too short. They took a deep breath, opened wide, and bit off the creature's head, a piece half as big as their palm.

It's salty, and the crunch isn't so bad, they thought as they chewed.

"Oof! That oughta do it," Riordan muttered as xe slid out from under the cart and got back on xir wheels again. Xe dusted off xir hands. The merchant gave them several more desserts, as well as a number of cans containing different foods and a jug of water. Riordan placed their spoils in xir thick canvas pack before hoisting it onto xir back.

The trio thanked the merchant and walked off together.

"Does the little one need anythin'?" Riordan signed to Nitàwesì.

"Do you think we could see if there is a doll or something for him to play with?" the healer responded.

"Oh!"

The trio paused at the sudden exclamation. A first stood before them, alert.

"I apologize for stopping you," he said to Nitàwesì. "I just . . . I used to know someone who could speak with her hands. You remind me of her, how similar you look . . . For a moment, I thought you were her."

Riordan carefully observed the stranger shift in place, as if to turn. In that moment, the fabric that crossed over his chest moved just enough for Riordan to make out a series of telltale scars. Xe inched forward and gently touched the stranger's shoulder, then bent down and whispered, "Storyteller?"

The stranger recoiled. Nodded hesitantly. Worry appeared on his face as she quickly absorbed every detail of this quartet—the three adults and the child at their feet. Yet she didn't feel the presence of a threat or a trap.

"I have a feelin' we might know the same person. We can take you to her," Riordan offered.

The stranger hesitated, then nodded again.

The five of them slowly made their way back to the vehicle, along the way finding a doll for Ojiwan, a few other useful trinkets, some more food, and blankets—all of which they stuffed into Riordan's pack.

As they approached, Bèl jumped out, machete raised. "Who's this?" she demanded, tilting her chin to the first walking behind the others.

"My name is Sachit. We briefly met when you freed me. I believe I am here to speak with A'tugwewinu." The first's deep voice exuded confidence.

Bèl's eyes narrowed. She maintained a defensive posture—she did not remember this person.

"It's all right, Bèl," A'tugwewinu whispered from behind. Her voice was hoarse from disuse. She stepped forward.

Sachit went to her, stopping when the two of them were within arm's reach.

"You look like you've been pounding on Death's door, begging for entrance," Sachit stated. He reached out and cupped the storyteller's cheek. A'tugwewinu looked away. "I take it you've seen the prison?"

A'tugwewinu nodded. Fresh tears rolled down her cheeks.

The first opened her arms wide and held the storyteller close.

Sachit shared stories both beautiful and horrible: of the strength that A'tugwewinu had displayed at the hands of the Enforcers; of Sachit's own journey after being freed and finding the Village with the Red Flags; of how he found Mama Hato and per bar and worked there for some time, tending to wounds and listening to the stories of travellers and merchants. Of Mama Hato's moonshine, which "might make your heart stop, but damn, what a way to go."

A'tugwewinu laughed at that—it was the first time in days she'd so much as smiled. At first, she clutched her knees to her chest as she listened, but eventually she relaxed and leaned on Bèl's shoulder.

They talked well into the night.

Riordan got up and moved away from the vehicle, which xe'd been huddled against. Xe extended xir arms in the air, rolling xir shoulders until they popped.

Xe spotted Yun-seo sleeping in a similar position on the other side of the vehicle, their arm over Nitàwesì's middle, while the healer rested their hand on Ojiwan, whose chubby fist nestled under his chin.

Riordan rolled xir eyes skyward. *Kichi Manido, give me patience for whatever this is becoming.*

The sixth opened the vehicle door as dull light broke through the haze above—somewhere behind it all, kizis had risen and was trying valiantly to bring light to the darkened world. To xir left, A'tugwewinu and Bèl slept, completely intertwined. Riordan had never understood how that could be comfortable, since xe knew for a fact that Bèl had an entire arsenal of weapons strapped to every possible location on her body.

A'tugwewinu snored lightly and shuffled closer to Bèl, trying to stay warm.

Next to the vehicle, stoking some embers and cooking something that smelled divine in a pot, Riordan spotted the new storyteller they'd found.

"I assume yer responsible for this?" Riordan said just loud enough for Sachit to hear. Xe nodded toward the peacefully sleeping couple.

Sachit chuckled. "Seeing old friends again and speaking of pain can sometimes bring healing that no medicine can, yes. But your sibling there is stronger than she thinks. Her grief is palpable, and by no means should it be minimized."

Riordan shook xir head. "I thought we were gonna lose her. She was ... she was lettin' herself die."

"Perhaps," Sachit mused. Riordan approached the coals. "Or perhaps that was simply her grieving process."

Riordan looked at her, confused. "We cry when we grieve, we hold ceremony—we don't shut down."

Sachit shook the spoon in his hand. "Not always. Sometimes our bodies need time to catch up to overwhelming feelings. Be grateful she had a process at all, no matter how worrying it was for the rest of you. Be grateful she didn't bury it, letting it eat at her day after day. Be grateful it didn't prolong the torture from which she is so desperately trying to heal."

Riordan contemplated the storyteller's words. "They're all I have." Xe motioned to the couple snoring on the ground and the three asleep inside the vehicle. "I had over a hundred children, but now this is all I got left."

"You still have all those children," Sachit said with a twinkle in her eye. "Just because you are not physically with them does not mean you are no longer a parent. I have a feeling you will see them again someday."

Nearby, Ojiwan began to wail, waking the four sleeping adults.

"Guess that means it's time to eat." Sachit spooned warm food from the pot and passed around cups for each of them as they approached the fire.

"Eat," she said to the group. "Then come with me to visit Mama Hato. We'll see about getting you the information you need."

Riordan swallowed the fear xe felt at the thought of venturing to another Enforcer camp, knowing full well their survival to this point had been predicated on luck. Perhaps this next leg of the journey would mean the death of them.

CHAPTER XXIX

OJIWAN'S ADVENTURE

Ojiwan fussed and whined all morning. The toddler refused to eat; he threw the doll and the four blocks that Nitàwesì and Riordan had given him and spent his time whimpering softly.

Bèl and A'tugwewinu had left earlier with the elder, Sachit. Yun-seo and Riordan were working under the vehicle, having removed several screws and mechanical parts. They still weren't speaking about what had happened at the Enforcer camp or Riordan's accusations. The two of them silently agreed that it was best to just move on. And it did actually seem to be working—Riordan's rough edges were difficult to deal with, and Yun-seo simply preferred peace. At some point, though, it was bound to blow up in their faces. Or so Nitàwesì mused.

Nitàwesì felt a lurch in their gut—a sudden bout of nausea. They raised a hand to their mouth to try to stifle it.

"I'm going to be sick," they signed to Ojiwan, but the toddler paid them no attention—he was otherwise occupied, staring up at the rolling grey and dark-orange clouds. Nitàwesì hurried over to the rocks just past the vehicle and threw up.

They waited a few minutes to see if the nausea would pass. It didn't—they threw up a second time. So far, this pregnancy was not as bad as some others they had witnessed back in Pasakamate, but it still rendered them useless every once in a while. It was worse when things were tense, as if the baby could tell that A'tugwewinu wasn't eating; that Bèl wasn't sleeping, instead staying up to watch over her lover; that Riordan was obsessively fixing everything in sight.

Nitàwesì wondered if their pursuit of Shkitagen was simply a distraction from the larger problems facing this world. They were curious what would happen after they rescued the firekeeper. Would Riordan run back to Zhōng yang to try and find xir lost children? Would Bèl and A'tugwewinu return to roaming Ahkigowin aki, sharing stories with the people they found and birthing new storytellers along the way? Where would Yun-seo go to make reparations for the crimes they'd committed as an Enforcer? And what about Ojiwan's mother, Nodin? Would they find her alongside Shkitagen, or was she already lost? Would Nitàwesì and Shkitagen find another village to welcome them? It didn't seem like there were any Anishinabeg villages left.

The thought of an "after" was incomprehensible and not worth mulling over. This entire time, Nitàwesì had prided themselves on the hope they maintained that they would find their life's love and that somehow, some semblance of the peace, no matter how tainted, would be returned to this band of misfits.

But the stories that A'tugwewinu shared scared them. She alluded to change so profound that it would completely shake up their world. Living in constant fear of hunters, rising waters, Enforcers, starvation, sickness—their world was pain, but it was familiar. And sometimes, when A'tugwewinu whispered of a world free of the Madjideye,

Nitàwesì realized that getting rid of them wouldn't remove the rest of their problems too.

The fourth sighed and stood up. The nausea had ebbed and was bearable now. There wasn't anything left to regurgitate.

They made their way back to the fire pit, now nothing but cold ash, and remarked to themselves how well the boots Riordan had given them were holding up. They paused—they didn't hear Ojiwan crying anymore. Nitàwesì smiled. At least the toddler had self-soothed, which was better than some of the rest of them managed to do.

But as Nitàwesì got closer, they realized Ojiwan wasn't where they had left him. They turned to the vehicle—Riordan was shimmying out from under it now, followed by Yun-seo.

"Where's Ojiwan?" Nitàwesì signed to Riordan. The inventor raised an eyebrow in question and then immediately segued into panic.

"Ojiwan?" xe called. The trio collectively held their breath, waiting to hear a whimper, or even just some pebbles moving. But there was only the silence of the chill afternoon.

Riordan shot up on xir wheels, grabbing Yun-seo by the elbow and hoisting them up. "We need ta find Ojiwan!" xe yelled. Yun-seo nodded.

Nitàwesì went to the vehicle and started tearing apart the inside, undoing all of Riordan's meticulous organizing. They darted around the nearby rocks, searching, while Riordan and Yun-seo screamed Ojiwan's name over and over again.

Riordan wheeled over. "When was the last time ya saw him?"

"Fifteen or twenty minutes ago. I was sick, I just left for a little bit." Nitàwesì was despondent. *How could I be so stupid? Of course a toddler wouldn't stay put. I should have just thrown up right next to him.*

Riordan looked them in the eye. "It's not yer fault. We all shoulda been payin' better attention. I'm gonna go on ahead—I have a feelin' he went toward the merchants. Yun-seo, both of you keep searchin' around here—move in circles around the vehicle and keep doublin' back, in case the kid comes back here."

Yun-seo nodded, came over to Nitàwesì, and put a hand on their arm. Nitàwesì started sobbing into the third's shirt. Yun-seo held the healer close as they cried. After a moment, Nitàwesì inhaled sharply and pulled away. They dried their tears with their sleeve.

"I'll search this way," they signed, motioning to the left.

Yun-seo nodded, then went in the opposite direction, calling the toddler's name.

Riordan took off at full speed. Xe headed toward the Village with the Red Flags, weaving around debris, metal deposits, and pits in the earth from wars long ago, only stopping when xe arrived at the outskirts of the village.

Still no sign of Ojiwan. Riordan wheeled toward Mama Hato's bar, where Sachit had said she was taking xir siblings.

The bar was at the heart of the village. It was one of the larger movable businesses, with walls made from canvas and plastic tarps. The inside was filled with people, some whispering closely like lovers, others raucously cheering and celebrating. What they were celebrating, Riordan did not know. In the corner, steeped in shadows, xe saw xir family huddled close together by Sachit, who stood behind a long counter. With them was an elderly seventh with a hard, punishing gaze—Mama Hato, Riordan presumed.

Riordan hurried over. At the sight of xir, Bèl and A'tugwewinu got up off their stools, visibly concerned. Bèl moved her hand to her machete.

"Ojiwan's missin'," Riordan blurted. "Yun-seo and Nitàwesì are searchin' around the camp. We need to look here."

"The child?" Sachit asked softly. Riordan nodded. Sachit looked at Mama Hato.

"If it's a child that's missing, we can find them very quickly," the bar owner said.

"How?" A'tugwewinu asked.

"What does the child look like?"

"Second gender, three years old, about this tall." A'tugwewinu raised her hand to just above her knee. "Dark hair in braids like these"—she motioned to Bèl's neatly lined scalp—"and russet skin."

Mama Hato nodded, then reached behind the counter and grabbed a massive bell whose handle was the length of per forearm. Pe stormed to the entrance of the bar, waving per arm back and forth to swing the bell, which clanged loudly, attracting half the village.

"These people's child went wandering," Mama Hato yelled to the assembled crowd. Pe motioned to the three adults standing close by before rattling off Ojiwan's description. "First one to find him and bring him to my bar gets drinks on the house until the next encampment."

No sooner had pe uttered the words than the crowd erupted, people scattering in all directions to search for Ojiwan.

Mama Hato approached the dumbfounded trio.

"Why would you do that for us?" Bèl asked.

"You saved the person who would wind up becoming the love of my life. Consider this my thanks." Pe looked at Sachit with shining eyes. The first blushed and took Mama Hato's wrinkled hand. "Come get something to eat. This shouldn't take long." Pe waved them over to the bar.

They had barely taken their first bites of food—some mixture of grey sludge and bits of dark green niblets—when they heard a distant wailing, already getting closer. The group looked to the entrance as a frazzled fourth carried in a screaming Ojiwan. The toddler was distraught, crying loud enough for the whole world to hear. A'tugwewinu rushed over, gently tutting as she took the child and held him in her arms.

"Oh, gigi, were you scared, Ojiwan? Auntiuncle's got you now." She soothed the child. Ojiwan reached around her neck and held on tight. His cries quieted to gentle hiccups.

"Here, take this food with you," Sachit said. "You'll need it for your journey." She swept the rest of their meal into a dirty plastic bag.

"Yas know how to get where we're goin', then?" Riordan asked Bèl. The third nodded.

"Chi miigwech, thank you for everything," A'tugwewinu called to both Mama Hato and Sachit. The two elders beamed.

Bèl and Riordan clasped the elders' hands in gratitude before they exited the bar, waving goodbye to the villagers and thanking the fourth who had found Ojiwan. The fourth waved them off cheerfully, a second drink already in hand.

A'tugwewinu marched toward the vehicle with Ojiwan still clutching her neck. Riordan and Bèl hurried to catch up with them.

"If what Mama Hato told us is true, we need to leave right away," Bèl stated.

"Why? What's the hurry?" Riordan asked.

A'tugwewinu paused. "The camp Shkitagen was taken to is the site of the very first Enforcer camp on this land."

"So?"

"That means it's the location of the first portal."

Riordan shrugged. "How does that make it special?"

A'tugwewinu stopped and stared ahead. Nokomis stared back at her gravely. "I'm starting to piece together the messages from our fast," the storyteller said. "I think if we find Shkitagen, we can open the portal between this world and the next and drag the Madjideye back to wherever it is they came from."

Riordan gripped A'tugwewinu by the arm, stopping her in her tracks. "What, what does that mean? How?"

Bèl gently held xir hand. "Mama Hato has lived a long time and has travelled to many places—pe's even travelled on a boat! Something that floats on water! Pe explained so much to us. We will need a firekeeper to open the portal, but beyond that we're not sure. Shkitagen should know more."

Riordan regarded both of their faces, saw the resolution in their eyes. It suddenly dawned on xir. "Portals don't just open. It took the end of the world fer the Madjideye to come through the last one. Just what is one firekeeper gonna do to open it again?"

A'tugwewinu shook her head. "We don't know what it will take."

"How many'r gonna die this time?" Riordan asked bitterly.

"Hopefully no one. But we won't know without Shkitagen."

"Fuck! Why him? How do ya know some second ya never even met is gonna help, eh?" Riordan shouted.

Bèl sighed. "It has to be a first person closely connected to the spirits—so close that they can call upon them. From what Nitàwesì has shared, Shkitagen's trained with the elders his entire life. He knows prayers and songs and ceremonies. We're hoping he can do it."

"And to answer your other question," A'tugwewinu said, "he'll help us because it's the only way our world can ever be free.

"Opening portals—at what cost? Ya'll die, and fer what? To free a world that doesn't even know our helpers left us alone to die out? Ya think the Madjideye will ever let us live long enough ta pull this off?" Riordan spat. Before the others could respond, xe unleashed a roar and wheeled away.

"Is it naive of us?" A'tugwewinu asked, watching Riordan depart.

Bèl shook her head. "It's the only option we have. Xe can't see that because xir biggest fear is losing us. Being left to survive alone in this world."

A'tugwewinu inhaled sharply. "Oh."

The two marched back to the vehicle. Nitàwesì ran out to greet them and reached for the toddler.

Riordan was already in the passenger seat. A'tugwewinu explained to Yun-seo and Nitàwesì that it was vital they leave soon.

"Why the haste?" "Nitàwesì asked.

"The sooner the better, no?" A'tugwewinu signed back.

What she didn't say was that the longer they waited, the greater the chance that the firekeeper would end up fully brainwashed—or worse, dead.

If he wasn't already.

CHAPTER XXX

SOILSTORM

The silence in the vehicle was intense once more. It was becoming clear to Yun-seo and Nitàwesì that this was simply how Riordan was; the silent treatment was childish but expected.

Riordan sat in the passenger seat, refusing to drive, leaving Yun-seo behind the wheel for ridiculously long stretches that left them exhausted.

"I can't take it anymore. I need rest," Yun-seo exclaimed after a long while.

"Pull over there." A'tugwewinu pointed to the right, to a relatively sheltered spot next to a hill of debris. The ground there was littered with wires of all lengths, colours, and widths; random assortments of plastic and metal containers strewn around; and various items and pieces of technology piled high, their many uses lost to time.

Riordan perked up at the sight of the pile of trash. Xe opened the door and got out of the vehicle. The others watched as xe wheeled xirself over to the pile and started digging into the junk.

Yun-seo sighed and got out. They went around to the back of the
vehicle and opened the rear doors to let in some cold air, then hopped
in next to Nitàwesì. Yun-seo smiled at them; they felt warm inside
their chest, and slightly queasy, too. Nitàwesì looked up timidly and
kissed them. The action caught Yun-seo by surprise. Blushing, they
returned the kiss.

"This is good?" Yun-seo signed hesitantly.

Nitàwesì signed back, "This is very good," their eyebrows rising at
the word "very."

The two gazed shyly at one another until the sound of Bèl clearing
her throat yanked them back to reality.

Bèl and A'tugwewinu sat huddled together, watching them.

A'tugwewinu offered a sly smile. "I'm going to catch some sleep."

Yun-seo turned even redder. Nitàwesì nodded.

A'tugwewinu curled into the fetal position with her head on Bèl's
thigh. She was asleep within minutes.

Bèl looked down at her tenderly. Careful not wake her, she pulled
out one of her favourite knives and used the tip of it to pick at the dirt
under her long, pointed fingernails.

"Could you tell me more about the other genders?" Yun-seo asked
Bèl shyly, quickly adding, "If you don't mind."

Bèl smiled. "You've heard Winu use the word 'ayahkwewak,'
right?" Yun-seo nodded. "She told me ayahkwewak is the plural form
of 'ayahkwew,' a word that translates to something like a gender-fluid
person, someone who can fulfill any role their community needs
them to. A'tugwewinu's aracoel knew many words in his language.
'Nij-manidowag' is another word the Anishinabeg used. I guess the
literal translation is 'two spirit,' but what it really means is those closer
to Kichi Manido due to their gift of being bringers of balance, living
in a sacred in-between space—someone who is at the service of their

community, regardless of their gender. All of us thirds to eighths are these in-betweens, these keepers of the balance. Many creation stories from various first peoples mention how in the beginning there were only firsts and seconds and how limiting such perspectives turned out to be. Some nations talk of great strife, wars, famine ... And then suddenly, as if to answer their prayers, Kichi Manido gifted the people the other six genders that we have today. Some nations have even more than eight genders, and there could be others out there, people with gifts we can't even dream of. First peoples across this continent have different words for people like us. Us Taino have 'naguakio,' which is someone like me, a third."

Yun-seo processed the information for a moment. "Miigwech for sharing that with me. I made a small gift for you and one for Winu to thank you both for everything you've shared with me. Every time you share, it feels like a piece of sunshine inside me."

They smiled shyly as they handed Bèl a small, rectangular piece of metal. There were several grooves in it, thin enough to fit a blade within. Bèl stared at it for a few moments, confused about the object's purpose. Noticing Bèl's furrowed brow, Yun-seo explained.

"It's a knife sharpener. I saw some merchants using something similar and decided to make one for you. I noticed you sharpen all your weapons by hand, and it takes you a long time. Hopefully this helps."

Bèl smiled broadly, showing her teeth. She clutched the knife sharpener to her chest and nodded in thanks. Then she proceeded to pull a knife out of the holster at her side and to slide the weapon into her new tool.

After a few minutes of silence, Yun-seo couldn't help but stare at Nitàwesì.

"What is it?" Nitàwesì asked, blushing slightly.

Yun-seo opened their mouth to speak but quickly shut it again. Finally, they said, "I want to ask you about something you told me before, but it's ... sensitive." They glanced at Bèl, who was busy sharpening her various knives.

Nitàwesì nodded. "It's fine, I can guess. You want to ask about my voice?"

Yun-seo was confused, trying to read the various gestures. They couldn't piece it all together.

Nitàwesì snapped their fingers at Bèl—she looked up from what she was doing. "Can you translate for Yun-seo?" Nitàwesì signed. Bèl nodded, and the healer began to tell their story.

Bèl took a deep breath. "When Nitàwesì was a child, two Elite Enforcers attacked their home."

Yun-seo flinched, knowing where this was going. Nitàwesì rolled their shoulders. They glanced at Ojiwan to check that the child was still asleep.

"Their parents were both healers. They had all been sitting down to eat when the Enforcers came. It was very sudden. They didn't have any warning. Then there was just ... blood everywhere. Nitàwesì remembers looking at their parents' faces, the shock of it all. They both looked like they'd been slashed over and over with some invisible knife. They hadn't even had a chance to scream."

Bèl shuddered. Tears formed in Yun-seo's eyes.

"It got much, much worse."

Nitàwesì bit the inside of their cheek. Fingers trembling, they continued.

"The Enforcers said something about Nitàwesì not being a threat, not yet being a storyteller. And then they took turns with ... with their body." Bèl gripped the handle of her machete so hard it creaked. She signed to Nitàwesì, "Are you sure you want to share this?"

Nitàwesì nodded. "I need to tell this story. I've never shared it with anyone, and I have a feeling I may never share it again."

Bèl nodded. "I will honour your truth."

Nitàwesì resumed, and Bèl continued to translate. "All Nitàwesì remembers is the pain, the anger, the despair they felt wanting these Enforcers dead but knowing they were too weak to do anything. They were transported somewhere, then ... they thought that they were dying, that wherever they were, it was the next place, the place where we go after we die. They saw so many things that they still don't understand and can't explain. They remember a voice, though, asking if they wanted justice. And though Nitàwesì was still so young, they knew what that word meant. 'Yes,' they said, with absolute, righteous confidence. The voice said it needed something from them, an exchange, to come into this—our world. If it was their eyes, a mere look would strike the Enforcers down, though Nitàwesì would no longer be able to see. If it was their hands, a simple touch would cause the Enforcers to combust from within, but they would never be able to use their hands to heal. So, they thought, what could they give that they wouldn't regret losing? The answer came: their voice. Nitàwesì told the spirit, 'Take my voice.' Suddenly, their throat felt tight, like they couldn't breathe, but the sensation lasted only a second.

"And then, with a snap, they were returned to their body. Everything still hurt so much, like they were on fire. It took every ounce of their strength not to pass out, to just sit up. And then Nitàwesì remembered what the spirit had told them. They looked at the two Enforcers, who smiled lecherously. And with every ounce of force Nitàwesì possessed, they said, 'I want you both to disappear from this world.' Every word they spoke rang in their ears, and then it was like the air pressure suddenly dropped, and everything went deathly quiet. They stared in astonishment as the Enforcers simply dematerialized—their skin, their armour, every part turned into dust."

Yun-seo's eyes widened, an unspoken *how* trapped on their lips.

"Nitàwesì doesn't know which spirit gave them this gift, but after that moment, they vowed to never again utter a word lest they destroy more lives. They know they will never speak again, but honestly, they're happy this way. Offering their voice as trade didn't take away their ability to communicate, and it gave them the gift of strength at the time they needed it most."

Nitàwesì sighed.

Bèl's shoulders drooped. "Thank you," she said, "for allowing me the honour of sharing your story. Do you need anything right now?"

Nitàwesì's eyes watered. "Maybe someone could hold me?" they signed. Their heart was beating rapidly. They'd shared something of themselves that very few knew, a story they had buried so deep within that it ached to have it out in the open. They looked around and saw not pity in Yun-seo and Bèl's eyes, but love and the fire to protect that both warriors carried within.

Yun-seo reached out and wrapped their arms around Nitàwesì. Bèl followed suit.

It felt like a weight had been lifted from Nitàwesì's shoulders. They glanced from Bèl to Yun-seo, and they knew: these people, their new family, understood the sacrifice they had made. Yun-seo had felt the pain of being kidnapped and brainwashed by Enforcers, their body used and experimented on. And Bèl had died once already at the hands of Enforcers.

Nitàwesì wondered if they would get the same response from Shkitagen. The firekeeper had been raised by a wonderful father, and their other father had visited occasionally with the travelling merchant village they lived in. Shkitagen had been brought up in an environment of warmth and love, with teachings from the elders. He was so good that sometimes it hurt to look at him. Nitàwesì wondered if he might pity them, or fear someone who had so mercilessly killed their parents' murderers and was glad to have done it.

Nitàwesì breathed in the scents of the two thirds holding them: Bèl's musk, and the metal and leather she wore around her body; and the sharp, electric scent of Yun-seo, like there was magick on their tongue. Both exuded strength and safety. It eased Nitàwesì. They felt their eyes begin to droop as steady hands lowered them onto the pile of soft blankets next to the sleeping Ojiwan.

Yun-seo's eyes shot open. They'd been startled awake by voices yelling outside. Nitàwesì was still asleep next to them, Yun-seo's shirt clutched tightly in their hand. Just the sight of that brought a smile to Yun-seo's face, though it faded once they made out what was being shouted.

"This is the stupidest you've ever been, Riordan. Get back in the vehicle and we'll figure this out along the way!" Bèl shouted.

"No! The sooner ya reach Shkitagen, the sooner I lose yas both. I'm stayin' here. If you wanna die so bad, do it without me!"

Yun-seo sat up and gently tapped Nitàwesì's shoulder, rousing them.

"You know we can't storm an Enforcer camp without you!"

"Then maybe we shouldn't rescue him at all!"

"You would do that?" A'tugwewinu said, her voice high.

"Oh please! Countless people get slaughtered by the Madjideye ev'ry day. The only reason ya wanna save this one is so he can open yer stupid portal!"

Nitàwesì inhaled sharply.

"He's still—" A'tugwewinu started.

"Still what?" Riordan screamed. "He's a fuckin' stranger! Some firekeeper yas never met, and just 'cuz he's shacked up with yer cousin, that somehow makes him important?"

"It's more than that!" A'tugwewinu yelled.

"Pu-lease! I bet when ya fasted the spirits told ya exactly who Shkitagen was and what he could do—that's why ya were on that hill fer so long. Stop with this saviour act of yers, yer just as selfish as the rest of us."

"Selfish?" Bèl retorted. "We're doing this to save this world! To free it from the Madjideye for good!"

"At the cost of both yer lives and the very firekeeper yer trying so hard to save!"

"We don't know that!" A'tugwewinu shouted.

Nitàwesì had heard enough. They jumped up and barged out through the back of the vehicle with Yun-seo at their heels.

Nitàwesì glared at the trio. Riordan's chest was heaving. Bèl stared back, resolve etched into her features. A'tugwewinu looked at the ground.

"So, this is what you were doing all along?" Nitàwesì signed. "When were you going to tell me this? After I got to hold my life's love again after months of imprisonment? Were you going to wait until his baby was born? Let him hold them just once? When. Were. You. Going. To. Tell. Me?"

A'tugwewinu sighed. She finally made eye contact. "We don't know what the toll will be for opening a portal—only Shkitagen does. But even if the cost is our lives ... What's the difference between potentially dying now or in a few months, when the Enforcers finally catch us?" She was defeated, tired, and it came through in her words. A tense silence followed.

Nitàwesì was furious. Some part of them still dreamt of sharing a beautiful home with Shkitagen—and now, perhaps, with Yun-seo too. A place where they could all raise Ojiwan and the child who was coming. They refused to give up any of the hope they held for this future.

They took a deep breath, looking for someone to blame for this rift in their hope, this breaking of their trust. They glared at Bèl, who glared right back, then they shifted their sights to Riordan.

"Hey, don't look at me like that—I only found out back in the Village with the Red Flags," Riordan signed.

Nitàwesì turned their full anger onto their cousin and her lover. Getting nothing further from Bèl or A'tugwewinu, not even an acknowledgment, Nitàwesì spun on their heels, fully intent on fleeing, taking Ojiwan and maybe Yun-seo and getting as far away from the rest of them as they could.

They glanced at the sky as fierce rolling clouds descended, drifting toward the ground. They let out a cry of surprise.

Yun-seo spun to see what was wrong. "Soilstorm!" they yelled. Yun-seo grabbed Nitàwesì's hand and dragged them back inside the vehicle, followed by the other three adults.

"Stuff the blankets into the cracks!" Yun-seo ordered, and the others frantically obeyed. Nitàwesì peered out the windows as the clouds plunged down upon them.

"Here!" Yun-seo ripped a blanket into thick strips twice the length of their forearm and just as wide. "Wrap this around your face, lie down, and breathe through it. Don't take it off! The air is toxic."

Within moments, they were all down on the floor inside the vehicle, strips of cloth covering their faces as they huddled together under the largest blanket they possessed.

Then it came. Violent, roaring winds shook the vehicle. The metal exterior groaned as untold numbers of pebbles pelted it, ricocheting in every direction. Ojiwan let out a long scream, but the piercing wail was almost drowned out by the storm raging outside.

They waited for what felt like hours, until the last of the wind finally died down and they could see outside once more. Riordan threw off the protective blanket and opened xir door, whistling as xe surveyed the damage.

Hundreds of tiny dents marred the outside of the vehicle, and every window was a web of cracks. Luckily, one could just about see through them still, so they wouldn't accidentally drive off a cliff.

"The windows are supposed to be bulletproof," Yun-seo stated with some measure of awe.

"Some of those rocks were a lot bigger'n bullets," Riordan said.

"Can we keep going?" Nitàwesì signed.

"The batteries!" Yun-seo screamed. They quickly climbed up on top of the vehicle's roof, followed by Riordan. Several of the panels were cracked beyond repair, but miraculously, some had survived the storm. Still, Yun-seo was crestfallen. "More than half are destroyed. That means the vehicle will only run for half a day at best, and that's only if we have a thin haze overhead."

"We don't get soilstorms in Zhōng yang," Riordan said, "but I've heard travellers say that after one, the sky thins out a bit. At least we have that goin' fer us."

They both jumped down to find Nitàwesì still fuming, glaring distrustfully at Bèl and A'tugwewinu.

Riordan sighed. "I think it's only fair ya tell us what ya want us to do now, Nitàwesì."

Nitàwesì shook out their hands, almost like they were at a loss for what to say.

A'tugwewinu appeared downtrodden, borderline pitiful. She held her knees to her breasts, making herself as small as possible in the far corner of the vehicle. Bèl crouched next to her in similar fashion, accepting of whatever fate Nitàwesì doled out, though she did not appear contrite, not in the slightest.

"I've understood for a long time that we each have a role to play," Bèl started. "I was raised in a warrior tribe by wise, fierce, honourable people. They taught me that the greatest thing we can do in this life is to protect the ones we love, to find those with great callings and protect what it is they are on Atabey to do. My entire family left me when I was young. They all died nameless deaths, in nameless places and for nameless people who simply offered them a high enough price for their sacrifice.

"And then the spirits brought me to the last storyteller on Atabey, and I knew that so long as I protected her, my death would not be in vain. I knew that everything my family believed in, everything they had fought for, everything they had lived and died for, would be realized by me. I've lived long enough to have defied death; to have loved someone truly, with all my being; to have created a family and seen a nation of storytellers be reborn. My life is complete. I'm not sorry for what we're planning to do or that it might cost your love his life, Nitàwesì. I'd rip to pieces anyone who tried to do that to me and Winu, but somewhere deep down inside, you know this might be the only way to free this world. And more than anything, you know your love enough to know he would sacrifice his own life in a heartbeat if it meant his child might grow up in a world without the Madjideye."

Nitàwesì started to cry, knowing that every word Bèl spoke was absolute truth.

Riordan exhaled. "So that's it, eh? We head fer the camp, rescue Shkitagen, and then ... what, we're just supposed to say goodbye to the three of yas?"

"Riordan, there's a great chance that none of us will get out of this alive," A'tugwewinu said, her voice so quiet she could barely be heard. "But there is also a chance that we will somehow manage to pull this off without any of us dying."

Riordan sighed. "We've defied death before." Xir stare turned serious. "Just don't leave me behind," xe croaked.

Yun-seo stared at the metal floor of the vehicle. "All right, then, let's go," they said at last, jumping back into the driver's seat. They tugged the lever and sparked the ignition. The engine sputtered valiantly to life.

Going west took weeks. They drove some distance north to avoid large crevices in the earth and had to navigate dizzying mountain ranges and pits that Yun-seo explained were the locations of lakes that had long since dried up. One morning, Bèl and A'tugwewinu excitedly returned to the vehicle with some dessert they'd found under some boulders. Though tensions were still high, they all enjoyed the precious, crunchy protein together. The days blended into each other, the monotony of drive, rest, drive, sleep, drive, eat wearing them all down.

Finally, an ominous glow appeared over the horizon—the lights from the Enforcer camp loomed.

CHAPTER XXXI

SHKITAGEN

"I'm sorry 'bout everythin'," Riordan confessed. "People and feelin's are hard fer me. Doesn't mean I have a right to be'n asshole, though."

"I know, it's fine," Yun-seo said. "We keep apologizing, but really, we shouldn't blame ourselves for what this world has made us into. I honestly don't have any regrets, not about any of it. More than anything, I'm grateful that you captured me and for anything of use I was able to tell you, especially if it helps take down the Madjideye."

Riordan sighed. "What an idiot I was, thinkin' ya were going to tell me some great secret that could destroy 'em from within. But ... I never thought beatin' 'em would mean losin' everyone I care about."

"Maybe not everyone." Yun-seo offered a sad smile. "Zhōng yang will still be there, and your kids will live on in your memory."

Riordan scratched the prickly hair on xir chin. "What about ya?"

"Oh. No one will miss me when I'm gone," Yun-seo breathed.

"I wouldn't be so sure 'bout that." Riordan nodded to Nitàwesì who, having overheard, blushed and quickly turned away.

Yun-seo sighed and brushed their hair from their eyes. "I honestly don't know what to do about that. I wish I was a sixth like you—being born complete would be great right now."

"Ha!" Riordan barked. "Ya know, there's a reason yer the way ya are. Besides, fer people who do fall in love and feel that attraction, sexual or romantic or whatever, the whole point is to learn from those people yer attracted to. There's nothin' wrong with it, just like there's nothin' wrong with me being born with all the teachin's I'll ever need already inside me. Just gotta live long enough to dig 'em out, ya know."

"It sounds beautiful when you put it that way."

"Just somethin' Winu told me once."

"Isn't it pointless, though? Tomorrow ... tomorrow might be the last time ... Am I supposed to learn something in one night?" Yun-seo ran their hands through their hair, mussing the straight black strands.

Riordan took a sip from xir cup. "Why don't ya go and find out?" Xe gestured to Nitàwesì. "I'm gonna babysit tonight." With that, xe wheeled away from the fire and headed back toward the vehicle.

Yun-seo looked at Nitàwesì. The healer glanced at their nails. The blush on their cheeks was illuminated by the soft glow of the flames.

"Do you, uh, want to go somewhere else to talk?" Yun-seo stuttered.

Nitàwesì nodded. They got up and joined Yun-seo, strolling away from the fire and the vehicle.

"So, after months on this journey, it's finally happening, eh?" Yun-seo said after a minute, trying to alleviate the tension.

Nitàwesì pressed their fingers to the warrior's lips. The two of them were far enough now that they wouldn't be seen or heard by anyone else.

"How about we do something other than talking?" Nitàwesì signed.

It was Yun-seo's turn to blush. "I've never done this ... consensually."

Nitàwesì pulled away. "Do you want to?"

Yun-seo inched closer. "Yes, absolutely, I really do. I'm just not sure what exactly …"

"How about this?" Nitàwesì signed, gesticulating slowly to make sure there was no miscommunication. "You say 'no' or 'stop,' and I'll do exactly that. I tap your skin twice, and that's my version of 'stop,' got it?" Yun-seo nodded, understanding every hand gesture. "The rest is simple: we do what feels good."

Yun-seo nodded again, a little breathless as Nitàwesì leaned forward and pressed their lips together. Yun-seo reached up and caressed the back of Nitàwesì's head, feeling the soft curls between their fingertips. They slid their other hand down the healer's side, their thumb brushing Nitàwesì's protruding belly. They sensed the life growing inside.

Nitàwesì pulled back and undid the clasps on Yun-seo's shirt, peeling away the layers to reveal the warrior's scarred chest.

"May I?" they signed.

Yun-seo nodded, wanting everything the fourth offered them.

Nitàwesì kissed the burn scar along Yun-seo's cheek, exhaled in their ear, sending a shiver through the third. Nitàwesì continued kissing downward, to the scars below each pectoral.

"Do you miss them?" they signed.

Yun-seo shrugged. "Honestly, not anymore. I'm kind of glad they're gone now. I just wish it had been my choice."

Nitàwesì nodded. "Help me with this?" they signed, then removed their shirt, revealing a bandage wrapped tightly around their breasts.

Yun-seo pulled at the wrapping as the fourth turned in slow circles. The last of the bandage came loose, and Yun-seo was greeted by the sight of Nitàwesì's small dusky nipples. Nitàwesì took Yun-seo's hands and placed them on the small mounds of their breasts.

Yun-seo brought their mouth down and kissed and sucked gently, just as Nitàwesì had done, marvelling as the fourth moaned. The two of them lay down and continued like this for while, hands roaming over each other as more layers of clothes were removed.

Yun-seo kissed their way down Nitàwesì's body until their mouth was close to what lay at the apex of the healer's thighs. Fingers tentatively touching, stroking. Nitàwesì gasped; their muffled moans spurred the third to continue.

Yun-seo reached for the wetness between Nitàwesì's thighs and the hardness there, then decided to go even further. They brought their hand to their mouth and wet their fingers before going back down.

"Wait, I have something," Nitàwesì signed. They reached for their clothes and grabbed a small bottle of liquid from a pants pocket.

Yun-seo stared, confused.

"Bèl gave it to me," Nitàwesì signed, embarrassed. Yun-seo chuckled and leaned forward, kissing them. "Let me." Nitàwesì coated their fingers, then approached Yun-seo.

The third gasped at the intrusion, at the warmth and the tingle they experienced. Their skin felt feverish to the touch, pebbled in gooseflesh. Electricity sparked between Yun-seo and Nitàwesì.

Eventually, Yun-seo felt a wave start to rise within. Nitàwesì peered into Yun-seo's deep black eyes.

"How do I—I mean how do we—the baby—" Yun-seo stammered.

Nitàwesì shushed them and lay on their side atop the discarded clothes spread out under them. Yun-seo followed suit, positioning themselves in front with their lower back up against the bump of Nitàwesì's belly.

Yun-seo felt Nitàwesì's lips against the back of their neck as the fourth entered them slowly—they held their breath the entire time. The two of them rocked together, Nitàwesì lightly running their fingers up and down Yun-seo's body, enticing them, teasing them.

Yun-seo gasped at the sensations rolling through their body, the ebbs and flows.

The tide overwhelmed Yun-seo—their body went taut, every muscle tensed, and they unleashed a wail from deep within their core. Sweat poured down their torso, and it felt like every cell in their body disappeared, then slowly floated back. They felt bliss.

After that, it took only a few moments for Nitàwesì, grinding their hips against Yun-seo's, to arrive at the same place. They rested their head on Yun-seo's shoulder and sighed contentedly.

"Thank you," Yun-seo breathed, embracing Nitàwesì.

"For what?"

"For showing me that this can feel good," Yun-seo signed.

Nitàwesì smiled. Yun-seo traced patterns onto their arm.

"Let's imagine we rescue Shkitagen tomorrow. Then the three of us can find a beautiful place to raise Ojiwan together and live in peace."

Nitàwesì sat up. "That is a dream my mind often goes to," they signed, smiling sadly.

"Do you think Shkitagen will like me?"

"He will love you so much." A tear rolled down Nitàwesì's cheek.

"What do you think he'll like about me?" Yun-seo held their breath.

"He'll love the way you smile, and how resilient you are. He will love your gift and the way your hands glow—all of it."

"And you? What do you like about me?"

Nitàwesì laughed through their tears. "I like that you had such a hard time with Ojiwan at first, but now you play with him. I like your commitment to righting the wrongs of your past. And I like that you understand my pain."

Yun-seo looked thoughtful.

"Did you understand all that?" Nitàwesì asked, their hands moving a little slower.

Yun-seo nodded. "I think I got the important bits." They paused. "I love your eyes."

Nitàwesì laughed. "That's what Shkitagen says too."

They lay back down together, limbs intertwined, and dragged their cloaks over their bodies to sleep.

■

Bèl was in position. She swept her hands over each of the weapons hidden throughout her clothing: the knives strapped to her thighs and ankles, some as small as her pinky and others, like her machete, thicker and longer than her forearm; the guns strapped around each shoulder and at her waist; and the guys that Riordan had graciously made for her carefully nestled in a pouch tied at her waist. She was a walking weapon. Her veins thrummed, her heartbeat was steady— she felt absolutely lethal.

She pressed her back against the cold concrete wall of the Enforcer camp. Felt fear seeping through the fortress as she inched closer to the side entrance she'd spied earlier. She slowed to a crawl, knowing that no matter how well she masked her body, the human eye could still pick up sudden movements. And if she was discovered before she'd even made it inside, this whole operation would be finished.

In her periphery, Bèl saw Yun-seo running toward the compound at full speed, swinging an old plastic tube whose end was lit to attract more attention.

Bèl overheard as one of the Enforcers stationed at the side entrance noticed this.

"Enforcer 345189, go see what that is," the first Enforcer stated to their partner. The second Enforcer started walking toward Yun-seo, who had already made a hasty retreat and was hiding behind a pile of twisted plastic filigree panels, where A'tugwewinu lay in ambush.

With only one guard remaining, Bèl charged the side entrance, machete in hand. The Enforcer had time only to gasp before the blade was slicing their throat through the gap between two pieces of armour.

Two down. Bèl quickly dragged the Enforcer's body into the shadows outside the compound and removed their armour. She winced at the human face beneath the mask: nineteen or twenty at most, their eyes blank, their face drained of colour.

Bèl did her best to outfit herself according to Yun-seo's specifications. By the time she was done, Yun-seo and A'tugwewinu were ready and waiting for her.

"Give me the body," Yun-seo commanded, a steel edge to their voice. Bèl hoisted the dead Enforcer under the arms and handed the body over to Yun-seo. The third shuffle-dragged it toward where the other Enforcer's body lay, leaving A'tugwewinu and Bèl alone.

"We need to hurry," A'tugwewinu said, her stolen Enforcer mask giving her voice a strange metallic echo. "Yun-seo said an entrance without any guards might raise just as much suspicion as finding a couple of dead guards."

"How long do they think we have?" Bèl asked.

"An hour if we're lucky. Apparently, supervisors make frequent rounds."

"What's your code?"

"I'm Enforcer 345189 from Unit 36," A'tugwewinu replied. "You?"

"Enforcer 78432, also from Unit 36."

The duo entered the compound, mimicking as best they could the motions and the marching patterns of the many Enforcers they had witnessed over the years. Their first objective was to locate the training area for new recruits. Though they didn't know exactly where it was, Yun-seo had described to them in great detail what it would look like.

A'tugwewinu tilted her head at an area off to the left—it seemed to match the description of living quarters given by Yun-seo. The storyteller flinched every time an Enforcer walked past. Though she hated wearing the armour, she was grateful for the protection and anonymity it provided.

"Calm down," Bèl whispered beside her. "Remember your training: breathe in your surroundings and become one with them." The warrior took deep, exaggerated breaths so that A'tugwewinu could try to match them. "I'll be with you the whole way."

"Enforcer 78432!" barked a robotic voice ahead of them.

The duo halted, quickly calling to mind every phrase and code Yun-seo had shared with them in the event they were stopped.

"I see you've completed your shift. Proceed to Unit 36 Command as instructed," the Enforcer ordered.

"Understood," Bèl said, attempting the robotic monotone she had heard so many Enforcers use.

The Enforcer nodded and walked past them. A'tugwewinu and Bèl breathed a sigh of relief and continued onward to what they hoped was their destination.

■

Yun-seo finished covering the Enforcers' bodies with the loose detritus they had gathered. It was enough to keep them hidden for at least a day, if they were lucky. And if everything went well, by then they should be long gone with their prize.

Yun-seo made their way back to the side entrance, which was still unguarded. So far, no alarms had been raised. They waited patiently for A'tugwewinu and Bèl to emerge, knowing full well that they might be waiting for hours and that their odds of getting away unscathed worsened by the minute.

Yun-seo retrieved the whistle Riordan had given them. The sound was too high pitched to be heard by human ears, but Riordan had outfitted each of them with a ring that fit inside their ears and would vibrate in response to the sound wave emitted by the whistle.

Yun-seo blew three short blasts through the tiny metal whistle, letting everyone know Yun-seo was ready to help with anything, from a distraction to a quick escape.

■

Riordan felt xir ear tingle. Xe tightened a screw on the guy xe was holding before placing it with the dozens already in xir pack. Soon, xe would wheel over to strategic points all along the compound's exterior and place the guys.

Xe blew xir whistle, one quick blast to let Yun-seo know xe'd got their message. Xe waited anxiously, knowing Bèl and A'tugwewinu would whistle only when they were safe and the mission was complete, or if they were in mortal danger.

■

After searching through eight dwellings, A'tugwewinu and Bèl still hadn't found any new recruits, nor even any information as to where they were being held.

"I have a bad idea," A'tugwewinu whispered.

"What?"

"Forgive me later if this doesn't work." The storyteller exhaled and marched over to an Enforcer in training clothes who was polishing a helmet. It was a shock to see an Enforcer without armour.

"Enforcer!" she shouted.

The Enforcer quickly stood at attention and saluted the two of them.

"We need to find a new recruit. Tell us where their habitation zone is!"

The Enforcer appeared confused. "We haven't had a new recruit in months," she stated.

"This recruit would have arrived months ago," A'tugwewinu clarified, hoping it would somehow be enough information.

The Enforcer thought about it. "We did have one recruit who failed the Almighty miserably."

Bèl stepped forward. "That's the one. We've been asked to retrieve him."

The Enforcer looked even more puzzled. "He's been in the brig for months—everyone knows that." She stared at the two of them for a second, but it was a second too long.

Bèl lunged forward, gripped the Enforcer's jaw and the back of her head, and spun her hands in opposite directions. Whatever shout had been building in the Enforcer's throat was cut off with a hard *snap*.

A'tugwewinu glanced around them. Somehow, they'd remained unseen. She pulled open the nearest door—a supply closet with boxes of vitamin mush, spare goggles, and boots neatly lining the shelves.

"In here," she whispered.

Bèl dragged the Enforcer's body into the supply closet and shut the door with a quiet click.

"Now," she said, dusting off her hands, "where do you think the brig is?"

They were surrounded by a maze of grey cube-shaped dwellings of varying size stacked on top of each other.

"Something's telling me to go this way." A'tugwewinu led the way as they headed toward the centre of the compound.

They knew as soon as they saw the oblong concrete dome that they had found the brig. Inside were cells, a single dim light hanging from the ceiling of each. The metal bars were wide enough to see through, but the cells so dark that it was difficult to tell which were occupied. Enforcers were positioned in front of each cell. It looked like the cell doors were controlled by some sort of keypad system.

Stationed at the edge of an overhang, the pair looked out over the smooth concrete floor below. A'tugwewinu sighed. "This isn't going to be easy."

"We're going to need a distraction," Bèl said. They weren't going to be able to fight or talk their way in themselves without being arrested. She reached beneath her armour for the whistle on a cord on her neck and quickly lifted her helmet. Bending down and covering her mouth as if to cough, she blew two long blasts—the signal requesting a distraction.

A minute later, an explosion echoed throughout the entire compound. It came from the main entrance.

Riordan had succeeded in placing xir guys.

In the ensuing flurry of action, all the Enforcers guarding the brig marched out toward the compound's main entrance—all save the one positioned in front of the last cell, at the end of the corridor.

Bèl surveyed the remaining Enforcer still guarding the cell. "That must be where they're holding our firekeeper." She and A'tugwewinu descended the steps into the brig.

The remaining Enforcer approached them as they reached the bottom. "Halt," they said. "State your business."

"Enforcer 78432 reporting from Unit 36 Commander, here to apprehend the failed recruit." Bèl stood straight and kept her voice level.

"Very well." The Enforcer waved for them both to follow, led the way back to the cell near the edge of the brig, and unlocked the door.

"I'm surprised Unit 36 Commander wants anything to do with this one," the Enforcer sneered.

Bèl and A'tugwewinu opened the door and stepped into the cell. The sight that met them was devastating.

A second was chained to the concrete wall behind him, his hands encased in gloves of thin mesh fabric. His chest was bare and covered in stab wounds, scars, and burns. His hair was long and matted, chunks of it missing, with still-bleeding scabs on his scalp. His facial features were barely discernible under all the swelling—both eyes were bruised, his nose was clearly broken, and a gash extended from his neck to his temple.

There was no way to know from sight alone whether this person was Shkitagen.

A'tugwewinu let out a sharp exhale. She moved her right hand to her waist, a coded gesture that told Bèl to be ready.

The prisoner's breath rasped. He glared at them with the eye that was not swollen.

"Ànìn ejinikàzoyan?" A'tugwewinu asked him. The prisoner inhaled at the words. Behind them, Bèl rushed the Enforcer, but the latter was ready for an attack. The Enforcer reached for the gun at their belt and pulled the trigger just as Bèl's machete found the narrow space between the bottom of their helmet and the top of their neck guard. The Enforcer collapsed to the floor, blood spewing from their throat.

A'tugwewinu turned to Bèl, who grunted in pain. She placed her hand on her side and then lifted it to her face. Her palm was covered in blood. A'tugwewinu paled at the sight.

"Ànìn ejinikàzoyan?" she screamed at the prisoner. She removed her helmet so he could see her face.

The prisoner had initially recoiled at the words. Now he gasped, seeing the features of the person before him. "Shkitagen. Pasakamate nidonjabà," he stated hoarsely.

A'tugwewinu breathed a sigh of relief. She went over to the dead Enforcer and retrieved the keys on their belt, then returned to Shkitagen and unlocked his restraints.

"You look like someone I know," Shkitagen muttered as he ripped the gloves off his hands. He snapped his fingers, watched as flames sparked to life on them.

A'tugwewinu nodded. "Nitàwesì sends their regards. We're cousins. Can you walk?"

Shkitagen's eyes teared at his love's name. He nodded.

A'tugwewinu turned to Bèl. "How bad is it?"

Bèl hissed. The pain was fire hot and slowly spreading throughout her body. "The bullet went through. There's no way I can get out of here, not like this."

"I can cauterize the wound," Shkitagen said.

Bèl nodded. "Do it."

Shkitagen hummed a quick prayer. A'tugwewinu and Bèl watched as his hand ignited. He approached the warrior and lifted her shirt. A fresh glob of blood spat out onto the cell floor.

"Here." A'tugwewinu handed Bèl one of the gift-cancelling gloves to bite down on.

Shkitagen slapped his hand over the wound, searing the flesh. Bèl screamed in muffled agony. The stench of burning flesh reached the firekeeper's nostrils.

"That won't hold long," he stated. His hand steamed, cooling as he removed it from Bèl's side. Shkitagen looked at his two rescuers. "So, how are we doing this?"

"We need to get you to the side entrance," A'tugwewinu replied, putting her helmet back on, while Bèl wrapped her side with scraps A'tugwewinu had torn from the dead Enforcer's clothes.

"Is there any way you could fit into that Enforcer's armour?" Bèl asked. But even as she spoke, she knew it was ludicrous. The dead Enforcer was shorter than A'tugwewinu and nearly as small; meanwhile, Shkitagen was similar to Bèl in size and height.

"An Enforcer walking around in a barely fitting uniform will raise more suspicion than a prisoner being led to his death," Shkitagen answered.

"Mi-iw, so that's our story?" A'tugwewinu said.

"Eh-heh. Tell them you're going to shoot me in the field out back. They do it all the time."

"Off we go, then," Bèl grunted. She tied Shkitagen's hands behind his back and added the gloves to complete the illusion, but left everything loose so that he could remove his binds to fight at a moment's notice.

A'tugwewinu and Bèl each placed a firm hand around one of Shkitagen's upper arms and let him direct them to the fastest route back to the side entrance. Bèl sweated the entire time, the pain in her side not lessening in the slightest. She swore under her breath with every Enforcer who approached them. *Shouldn't they be panicking more?* she wondered—until she realized something awful. Since the initial explosion, things had been silent for some time now.

Something had gone wrong.

They exited through the unguarded side entrance into a dark field. After they'd walked far enough away from the compound that they wouldn't be spotted, A'tugwewinu ripped off her helmet and stripped off the offending armour before rushing over to help Bèl do the same. The warrior swore with every motion—her wound had reopened.

A'tugwewinu pulled out her whistle and blew one long blast followed by two short ones, signalling that they were ready for pickup, with one wounded.

She waited for the sound of a gently purring engine, but heard nothing.

■

Yun-seo was crying, their forearms covered in blood. More of it flowed between and over their fingers as they tried desperately to hold Riordan's guts inside xir body.

"Come on, come on, *come on,*" they cried, sobbing as they attempted to call upon their gift in a valiant effort to try and fix this.

Everything had been going so well until Riordan had been caught with one of xir guys as the flood of Enforcers rushed the main entrance. They made quick work of Riordan, slicing xir open and mocking xir. Then two of them dragged the inventor away from the compound and over to a series of posts, ready to string xir up as a warning to anyone else who might dare to attack their camp.

Yun-seo was ready for them, though, having realized when the expected series of explosions failed to come that things hadn't gone as planned. Using a combination of their fire gift and the warrior training Bèl had drilled into them, they quickly took care of the two Enforcers. Then they hurried over to Riordan, whose ivory pallor had turned even paler.

Yun-seo knew the Enforcers would be missed soon; someone would soon come to check up on them. They knew, too, that there was no way they could possibly fix Riordan's injury with their own gift—they weren't even sure Nitàwesì would be capable of repairing this.

There was only one thing left to do. Yun-seo exhaled and let their mind travel to the deep well within, to their core, to the place Nitàwesì and A'tugwewinu had trained them to find.

The well appeared to them. Around it stood countless warriors clad in armours of old.

"Ancestors," Yun-seo whispered, "all I have to offer you is this." They grasped the knife at their belt and sliced their forearm in several places, until a small river of blood had soaked the soil where they knelt before their sibling.

"Please accept my blood and help me," they pleaded. They felt it then, a sensation deep within, an otherworldly warmth as a portal of golden light emanated from deep inside the well. The light grew brighter and brighter, until it filled Yun-seo entirely. They gasped, the light erupting from their eyes and mouth—great beams of it spilled out of them and onto Riordan's body.

Instinctively, Yun-seo knew exactly what to do. Their ancestors continued to spill from their mouth, growing in size until they were like giants standing next to Yun-seo. The third raised their hands over Riordan's body and watched as the inventor filled with light.

Blood continued to pour from Yun-seo's arm. They arched it over Riordan's body so the blood flowed in. Yun-seo cried out. It felt as if their own body was suddenly heavier. The weight too much for them to bear, they dropped to all fours. The spirits encircled Riordan's body, and gradually Yun-seo felt lighter. Warmth and cold warred within their body like waves crashing into one another. Pressure pulled at their skin as if gravity was both crushing them down and also trying to untether them from the earth. It left them feeling nauseated. Though they felt an urge to push back against the onslaught of feelings, they ignored it. A'tugwewinu and Nitàwesì had instructed them that every ask from the spirit world was different; every trade had different terms of sacrifice. They needed to simply flow with the pain, to try and stay as calm as possible during the exchange.

Yun-seo watched as Riordan's wounds closed little by little, muscles and tissue mending right in front of them, organs returning to their rightful places.

Yun-seo let loose tears of joy. They whispered gratitude to the spirits around them, reciting the words over and over again like a mantra: "Kichi miigwech, giibi, kichi miigwech, giibi, kichi miigwech, giibi!"

Then, as if the earth itself sighed, the light pulled back inside of Yun-seo with a *snap*. They inhaled sharply, gasping as if they'd almost drowned.

Riordan's chest rose and fell, a slow rhythm settling in as colour returned to xir cheeks. Yun-seo held the sixth's hand and brought it to their face. "Oh, thank Kichi Manido," they muttered through their tears.

They felt it then—a ringing in their ear. They sat up, alert. Counted the blasts.

Someone else was in trouble, and they needed to get away, now. Yun-seo swore—they were far away from where they were supposed to be. They swallowed, knowing they had no choice: A'tugwewinu and Bèl would have to wait. Hoisting Riordan onto their back, Yun-seo was thankful in that moment for having been born a third. Had they been born any other gender, they would not have been able to carry someone almost twice their size.

Riordan in place, Yun-seo began the slow, arduous march back to the vehicle, wincing with every step. The dizziness and nausea that came of having used so much of their gift were taking their toll. Yun-seo's vision blurred at the edges.

■

"We need to keep going on foot!" Shkitagen said urgently while applying pressure to Bèl's wound. Bèl lay on the ground, trembling, passed out from the pain.

A'tugwewinu shook her head. Her own hands were shaking, and her features had started shifting—she felt anxiety beginning to overtake her. "No! This is where we're supposed to rendezvous. They're coming for us, I know they are!"

The silence was eerie. Then: a familiar hum in the distance.

A'tugwewinu watched as the vehicle slowly emerged through the cover of night, its lights off so as to not arouse suspicion. It slowed to a stop, and Yun-seo's distraught and blood-spattered face came into view as they threw open the door and jumped out.

"What happened?" A'tugwewinu cried.

Yun-seo ran toward them, breathless. "Riordan almost died. I fixed xir, but I'm at my limit—I won't stay conscious much longer."

A'tugwewinu nodded. "Okay. Help me get Bèl into the back, and I'll drive us over to Nitàwesì. They'll fix her. Everything's going to be okay."

Shkitagen hopped into the back of the vehicle, keeping his hand on Bèl's wound while moving carefully around the other unconscious body there. Yun-seo got in next to him, covered in sweat, eyes feverish.

The third placed a bloody hand on Shkitagen's cheek. "I'm Yun-seo. Nitàwesì said you'd like me. I hope you ... like ... me ..." Their hand slipped from the firekeeper's cheek—leaving behind a red smear— and dropped to their side as they lost consciousness.

The firekeeper was confused for a moment, but focused on trying to keep his rescuer alive.

A'tugwewinu got in the driver's seat and slammed her foot down on the pedal, like Yun-seo had shown her. They drove away from the compound.

CHAPTER XXXII

REUNION

Nitàwesì held Ojiwan and rubbed his back as they hummed under their breath, attempting to soothe the toddler and themselves at the same time.

Their family had been gone for hours now. They were too far away to hear anything—strategically placed far enough away from the compound that they could get away on foot with Ojiwan if necessary, but close enough to rendezvous with their family, providing they made it out alive.

Nitàwesì prayed to the sky, having put down the last of the asema from A'tugwewinu's cigarette pack as offering. In the distance, the fourth heard the hum of an engine. They quickly hid behind a small outcropping of rocks.

The vehicle slowed to a stop. The healer waited with bated breath.

"Nitàwesì!"

Shkitagen. A voice they had sometimes doubted they would ever hear again, had dreamed about, had forced themselves to remember.

Nitàwesì had fantasized about this moment, when the two of them would finally be reunited, but not until this very second did the fourth realize that a small subconscious part of them hadn't thought it would actually happen. That part had feared the worst, that Shkitagen had been killed or brainwashed into becoming an Enforcer. Nitàwesì had never consciously entertained these thoughts, but all the same, they cried out at the sound of his voice, and the realization that Shkitagen was alive lifted a weight from their heart.

Nitàwesì dashed out from their hiding place and ran toward his voice—toward Shkitagen, who stood there, his jaw slack and his eyes filled with disbelief. Stopping only a foot away from the firekeeper, Nitàwesì gently placed Ojiwan on the ground. They felt a pinch in their chest upon seeing the horrid state of their lover. Ojiwan looked up at the two of them, curious.

Shkitagen raised a shaking hand to Nitàwesì's lips and moved his fingertips down until they rested above Nitàwesì's heart. He put his palm against it, felt it beating.

"You found me," he whispered.

Nitàwesì swallowed, their tears flowing freely. They reached out and held Shkitagen's chin in their palm, brought him forward and kissed him fiercely. They pushed aside their fears and doubts, the pain of watching him be taken by hunters, the anxiety of being left alone. They embraced him fully.

Shkitagen gripped Nitàwesì around the waist and brought their body flush with his. He gasped suddenly at the unexpected warmth emanating from Nitàwesì's protruding stomach. He pulled back and stared.

"Are you …?" Shkitagen asked, afraid to finish his sentence.

Nitàwesì nodded. "Around six or seven months," they signed, wiping away their tears.

Shkitagen collapsed to his knees and rested his head on Nitàwesì's stomach. He cried while muttering prayers of gratitude, speaking soft words of love to the new life inside his lover.

Nitàwesì stroked his head, noting the wounds and scars now decorating his body. He was alive, though, and that was all they had prayed for.

"What about Nodin?" they asked.

Shkitagen simply shook his head.

A'tugwewinu approached the two of them, her face pale, her hands shaking. "It's Bèl."

Nitàwesì nodded. Shkitagen stood up and wiped his eyes as Nitàwesì went over and opened the rear door of the vehicle. They were struck by panic the instant they looked inside.

Yun-seo was either unconscious or asleep, Nitàwesì wasn't sure. The warrior was gaunt, covered in sweat. They had completely exhausted their gift, Nitàwesì realized, but they would pull through.

"Get Yun-seo out of here and lay them down next to a fire," Nitàwesì signed to A'tugwewinu. "Try and feed them something if you can."

"Who are they to you?" Shkitagen signed, watching as A'tugwewinu struggled to lift the depleted third from the vehicle.

Nitàwesì placed a kiss on Yun-seo's forehead. "My lover," they replied.

Shkitagen smiled. "I thought I was going to die alone in that cell," he said gravely. "Then I'm rescued by my cousin-in-law and her life's love, and I arrive here to find you pregnant and with a newly adopted child and a lover. Kichi Manido has been too good to both of us." His voice cracked—he felt gratitude to the spirits for blessing him so.

"You always wanted a big family." Nitàwesì smiled.

Shkitagen shook his head, briefly pondering how dramatically—and suddenly—his fate had changed. Both then turned their attention to the unconscious Bèl, still lying in the rear of the vehicle.

"I cauterized the wound twice," he explained, pointing to Bèl's side, "but she's lost a lot of blood. I'm pretty sure the bullet ruptured something."

"There's some internal bleeding," Nitàwesì signed, investigating the obvious bruising around the wound. "I'm going to open her back up and go in."

"What about Riordan?" A'tugwewinu asked from behind them.

"Leave xir there for now. It looks like Yun-seo saved xir life, but I need to take a look at that leg. Xe might lose it." Nitàwesì motioned to Riordan's left leg—xir knee was shattered and mangled, xir wheeled footwear in pieces at xir feet. The leg itself was twisted at an obscene angle. The joint was clearly severed, but xir injuries weren't as life threatening as Bèl's—xe would have to wait.

Many hours later, Nitàwesì had patched up Bèl from the inside and successfully amputated Riordan's left leg from the knee down. Yun-seo was still unconscious, A'tugwewinu was exhausted, and Nitàwesì had reached their limit.

A'tugwewinu opened a can of food and passed it around. Nitàwesì and Shkitagen quickly swallowed the salty brown and orange chunks covered in a thick sauce, knowing it was for sustenance and not satisfaction. Then the three of them lay down next to the fire and slipped into a deep, dreamless sleep.

They changed their location repeatedly over the next few days, staying within the general vicinity of the rendezvous spot while making sure they could keep a clear eye on the Enforcer compound at all times.

Yun-seo was the last person to regain consciousness. They woke up alone in the flatbed at the back of the vehicle, hearing sounds of conversation and laughter outside. It comforted them. Somehow, miraculously, they must have all made it through. They pulled on an extra layer of clothing to shield themselves from the cold and then joined their family outside, where they were all seated around a roaring fire.

Ojiwan was the first to notice them and waddled over. Yun-seo picked him up and held him. They looked at Nitàwesì, who smiled proudly at the sight.

Sitting next to them was Shkitagen. His wounds had mostly healed, though the trauma of his many months in captivity was evident in the faraway look in his eyes. He'd likely be working through that for some time—years, potentially.

But despite his suffering, he offered Yun-seo a small smile.

Riordan waved happily. Xe grabbed a crutch made of scrounged metals and wood bound together by wire and hopped over.

Yun-seo looked down at xir rolled-up pant leg tied at the knee. "Your leg! What happened? I thought the spirits—"

Riordan shrugged. "I'm already buildin' a taller wheel for this leg. It's fine, really. Ya saved my life." Xe paused. "I felt it, ya know. The light …" Xe trailed off, as if xe, too, couldn't believe what had happened. "I guess now ya'll have to let me repay ya," xe stated.

Yun-seo tilted their head back and guffawed at the absurdity of this little game the two of them had been playing. They went over and sat down with the rest of their family, who explained what they had missed over the past few days.

"Which brings us to the portal," A'tugwewinu finished, some time later.

Nitàwesì clenched the spoon in their hand until their knuckles turned white. "He's barely healed! All of us are barely healed!" they signed furiously.

"The longer we stay here, the greater risk we'll be discovered," Bèl cautioned.

"Then let's leave and come back when we're all in better condition," Nitàwesì argued.

A'tugwewinu shook her head. "We're running out of time. The darkest day of the year is fast approaching—that's when the veil between worlds will be at its thinnest. We need to open the portal then."

Nitàwesì hung their head. Shkitagen placed his hand atop theirs.

"I'm confused," he said. "You've told me bits and pieces, but explain this to me from the beginning."

A'tugwewinu took a deep breath. "Nitàwesì found us in Zhōng yang and told us you'd been taken by Enforcers. During our search for you, Nokomis came to me in a dream and told me to fast and ask the spirits where you'd been taken. I received that information, but also so much more. The spirits showed Bèl and me everything—how this world came to be and what we have to do to free our people from the Madjideye."

"Enh," the firekeeper interrupted. "I know that story. It's passed down through the firekeepers' society in Pasakamate. One of the gifts passed to all firekeepers is the connection to hellfire—basically, opening a portal within yourself to release destruction. There is a place of transition before the hellfire, where a half-place is found. It may be possible to use this half-place to pull the Madjideye back through to wherever they were before they entered our world. However, I won't be able to open the portal by myself. There must be two of us to do it."

"Two what?" Bèl asked.

"Firekeepers. They need to carry the ability and also be able to call upon the spirits," Shkitagen elaborated.

Silence echoed through the clearing. A'tugwewinu looked around at the rest of her family, dejected.

"Not all is lost, though," Shkitagen said. He reached out and grasped Yun-seo's hand, a small flame at the tip of his index finger. Yun-seo expected to feel heat, expected the flame to burn them. Instead, the small flame jumped from Shkitagen's fingertip to Yun-seo's.

"I learned a lot during my capture. It seems Enforcers are recruited from all corners of this continent, and people from all different places. But the Elites, those who use gifts, most of them are first peoples. Not all, but I recognize a firekeeper when I see one." He stared into the dark eyes of the warrior seated next to him.

"So, if they had never caught me, I would be like you?" Yun-seo said hesitantly.

"Yes and no," Shkitagen responded. "From what everyone here tells me, there is more to your gift than just fire. The fire may indeed come from the ishkode, the fire spirit of the first peoples, but your healing is a gift from another nation. Had you been raised in a first peoples' village, I believe you would have received firekeeper training. Someone would have taught you the prayers and songs so that you wouldn't need to trade pieces of your spirit every time you use your fire."

Yun-seo took a moment to process this. "I still don't have all my memories back, but ... I think my father could do this. He was from Omamiwinini. That means the armoured warriors are a gift from my mother." They stared longingly at the little flame dancing at their fingertip.

"Unfortunately, I don't have time to teach you everything," Shkitagen said. "I spent three decades learning what I know. But I should be able to teach you enough that you can help me open the portal and keep it open long enough for the Madjideye to be pulled through."

"What about sacrifice?" Nitàwesì asked. Their hands trembled.

"From what the elders tell me, no firekeeper has opened this portal in generations," Shkitagen explained. "But we're taught this ceremony— all of us. The prayers should open the portal, and from what I understand, at that point the Madjideye should simply go back to where they came from, as should any entity that was never meant to be in this realm. It's a ceremony to bring back balance—the universe should side with us and right this wrong. The challenge is concentrating long enough to stay in the half-place and not let the hellfire consume you."

Riordan heaved out a sigh. "So then, I jus' gotta make sure no one stops yas from opening that portal, eh?"

Shkitagen nodded. "Once the portal opens, the spirits possessing the Enforcers should depart their bodies and go through."

"What will happen to the Enforcers?" Bèl asked.

"Hopefully they'll return to their senses, but ..." Shkitagen trailed off and shrugged. "The stories speak of spirits filling the sky like rain and descending into the portal. If we do this right, we should rid this entire world of the Madjideye."

He glanced around, noting the confused and befuddled faces of his newfound family. The firekeeper sighed. He decided to share the story as it had been passed down to him.

"All right," he said, "let me start at the beginning."

CHAPTER XXXIII

PORTAL

It seemed like only yesterday that Nitàwesì had waved goodbye to their family and wished them luck in retrieving their lover. Now here they stood again, watching as the group of them packed up the vehicle with everything they needed to return to the first Enforcer compound that the Madjideye had erected on this continent.

A'tugwewinu approached her cousin. "Can we talk?" she asked.

Nitàwesì nodded.

"There are currently twenty-seven storytellers alive in the world. They were either made by me, or they picked up the calling from those I made while imprisoned. None of them carry the ability to create marks, but their memorizing works just as well. I'm worried, though, that it won't be enough."

Nitàwesì looked at her. "What are you trying to say?"

A'tugwewinu looked them in the eye. "I want you to memorize the creation story, the first story we share with little ones to give them marks. Maybe one day the marked ones will be reborn again. You

could carry forth the ceremony—you could help birth a new generation of storytellers."

Nitàwesì placed a hand on their belly. Fear bubbled in their chest.
They wanted to protest, to tell their cousin to have hope that everything would go according to plan, and they would see each other again
soon. But the look in A'tugwewinu's eyes gave them pause.

They looked up. "I'll do it," they signed.

A'tugwewinu leaned forward and brought their foreheads together.
She inhaled slowly, glimpsing Nokomis in the distance. The tattooed
markings that covered his body were evident, even through the
blue shimmer of his incorporeal form. Nokomis nodded. Resolved,
A'tugwewinu exhaled and pressed the symbol above her left breast.
She felt the familiar, comforting snap as her mind emptied. Then, as
if hearing it for the first time and the thousandth simultaneously, the
storyteller's mouth opened, and word after word tumbled out.

Four times, A'tugwewinu repeated the story. With each retelling,
Nitàwesì grew more and more attentive, almost as if in a trance.

Finally, A'tugwewinu's eyes shifted back from ghostly white to soft
brown. She sighed.

"Did you memorize it all?" Bèl asked, having quietly approached
the two of them halfway through the second rendition.

Nitàwesì nodded. There was determination in their stare. "Every
word," they promised.

A'tugwewinu reached forward again and took her cousin in her
arms. She inhaled their scent—metallic, like blood, but also warm
and somehow soothing. She smiled through tears. The storytellers
would live on. She prayed that someone somewhere would hear this
story and that one day the marked ones would be reborn.

"Promise me you'll come back," Nitàwesì ordered. Shkitagen smiled and brushed their cheekbone with his thumb. He nodded. "And promise me you'll bring Yun-seo back with you."

Shkitagen chuckled. "We'll keep each other safe. Besides, I've seen Riordan's arsenal—those Enforcers won't know what to do." He grabbed Yun-seo, who was standing awkwardly to one side, and brought them close.

Shkitagen gave Nitàwesì a fierce kiss—it was a promise to raise their child together, to listen to stories, to never let Nitàwesì get cold or hungry. And most of all, to return.

Then Nitàwesì pulled Yun-seo in, and the three of them hugged. Nitàwesì leaned back and kissed Yun-seo, who blushed.

"Yun-seo," Shkitagen said, placing his arm firmly around the third's shoulders. Yun-seo stared up at him. "Nitàwesì was right: I do like you."

The ball of concealed light in the sky, barely visible behind the haze of pollution, began to set. As it did, the group of them, this found family, piled into the stolen Enforcer vehicle. The landscape darkened. It was time.

Nitàwesì drove at full speed toward the Enforcer compound. Once there, they drove around to the back wall, which looked to be the least guarded of the four, and slammed on the brakes. Immediately, everyone save Nitàwesì and Ojiwan piled out of the rear doors. As soon as they had all exited the vehicle, Riordan slammed the doors shut, and the healer sped off into the night. They would hide in the shadows some distance away, waiting to pick up their family—or what was left of them—once their task was complete.

"'Stoodis!" A'tugwewinu roared.

Riordan sped away, still adjusting to xir new set of wheels. Xe felt pain snaking its way up xir thigh at the unfamiliar pressure. Xe placed xir guys in a semicircle around the perimeter of the back wall, then went ahead and placed pressure-sensitive guys in the ground around those. Finally, xe positioned xirself in front of xir family, holding the largest multi-barrel gun xe had ever built. Xe lay down in a sharp-shooter position and used a heavy metal sheet xe'd salvaged from a debris pile to shield the majority of xir body. Xe raised xir hand and gave a thumbs-up—xe was ready.

Shkitagen ran his palms across the cold concrete wall, his skin crawling at the contact. His heart was beating quickly, telling him to run the other way, to get as far away as possible from this place where he'd been held. Where he'd been tortured.

Yun-seo approached him from behind. "It helps if you think of happier times," they said, "from before."

"Does that work for you?"

They shook their head. "They got me young. I don't have many happy memories to remember."

"Well, I look forward to making some with you and our lover in the future." Shkitagen smiled.

Yun-seo nodded. "You know, you can always talk to me. About anything, especially what happened while they had you."

Shkitagen looked them up and down. "You were an Enforcer." The third nodded. "I have a hard time imagining you like that. But I remember seeing all those Enforcers without their armour, and all the things they did to me with their human faces and human voices. If it hadn't been for my training, I wouldn't have been able to see the Madjideye spirits lurking behind their eyes or to resist their attempts to break my spirit." He shuddered. "I don't know how you were freed from their grasp."

Yun-seo hesitated. "Sometimes I wonder if I am free. Maybe not. Maybe this is all a dream, and I'm still the enemy."

Shkitagen stroked the side of Yun-seo's face. "I see no Madjideye in you. I see scars and fear, but more than anything, I see a protector. I see someone who would do anything for those they love. I see bravery in waking every day, in surviving. I see you, Yun-seo, and you are not the enemy."

Yun-seo offered a shaky, watery smile and wrapped their arms around the taller second. They held each other as long as they could.

A'tugwewinu and Bèl approached, carrying more of the giant metal sheets Riordan had retrofitted. They were modelled after the Enforcer vehicles' bulletproof exteriors and would hopefully keep Shkitagen and Yun-seo safe from bullets as they worked to keep the portal open.

Bèl finished planting the curved metal plates into the ground. She looked around, rechecking to make sure the coast was clear, that they hadn't been discovered. "Ready?"

Shkitagen and Yun-seo nodded. The two of them crouched with their shoulders and thighs pressed to the compound wall on one side; the other side was shielded by the metal plates.

"No matter what happens, we keep praying," Shkitagen said. "Once the portal opens, the Madjideye should be drawn to it. Hopefully they'll go through."

"Hopefully?" Bèl asked.

"There's always a chance that they might try and hold on to this world, that they might need a bit of convincing."

"Let us take care of that," A'tugwewinu stated.

Shkitagen nodded. "Just make sure you don't go through yourself," he warned.

Then, suddenly, came the sound of a gun firing, followed a second later by the sharp *ping* of a bullet ricocheting off the plate.

"They've seen us!" Riordan screamed from xir vantage point far ahead.

A'tugwewinu and Bèl scurried into position, hiding quickly behind some piles of garbage several feet away from the two firekeepers.

Shkitagen looked at Yun-seo, took a final breath, and opened his mouth. Prayers spilled forth. Words in ancient tongues filled his veins with fire as bright orange lines of heat snaked their way across his dark skin. "With me now!" he ordered.

Yun-seo closed their eyes. The words they had spent days practising now danced on their tongue.

"Kichi Manido nòndam wiin ayamìye!" the two shouted in unison.

Yun-seo felt energy rush through their entire being as flames licked their bloodstream. They peered at Shkitagen. His chest heaved, and he offered a sly smirk—the joy of feeling the fire respond to his prayers.

Shkitagen and Yun-seo faced each other and crouched down, their knees resting on the coarse, cold soil. They were close enough to the wall of the compound that they could lean on it. Shkitagen placed his palms flat on the ground, fingers splayed out, and Yun-seo slid their own fingers in between, their palms also flat on the ground. Underneath their hands, a crack formed and spread to the wall next to them. It wove a scraggly, misshapen circle several feet behind Yun-seo. Shkitagen had a clear view of his new apprentice and of the portal they were about to create. The circle was massive, easily large enough to ensnare a few Enforcer vehicles. They continued the prayer until, together, they reached the end of the first part of the ceremony.

The earth groaned and heaved, the ground beneath them starting to tremble. With a *pop* and a rush of wind, a portal materialized in the wall of the compound: viscous, dripping black liquid, with tendrils in the shapes of arms and hands, slick and untrustworthy, creeping on the surface. The portal tremored slightly. Strange sounds came from within, like wind whooshing through trees or thousands of people whispering all at once.

Yun-seo craned their neck around and looked at the portal behind them, watching it with both wonder and apprehension. They waited, but saw no Madjideye going through.

From their position, A'tugwewinu and Bèl likewise watched as, unfortunately, nothing happened.

A'tugwewinu laughed suddenly—a desperate, shrill sound. "Well, here we are," she said. "Right where we always knew we would be." Her expression crumbled. "What if we get separated?"

Bèl took A'tugwewinu's face in her hands. "Wherever we go to next, I will find you. My blood speaks only your name, my mind knows only your face, my spirit knows only your voice. On the lives of my ancestors and all the spirits who guide me in this life, I swear, I will always find you, Winu."

A'tugwewinu nodded firmly. "Together for the remainder of all our lifetimes. Don't let go of my hand." She brought their foreheads together, and they kissed. It was not a farewell, but a promise—to defy death, to upend the entire universe, if need be. To see each other once again, on whatever plane awaited them.

They stepped out from their hiding place. Together, they moved in front of the portal.

A'tugwewinu removed her cloak, her ripped pants, and her thin shirt, baring her marks to the Enforcers now appearing by the dozens and marching briskly toward them in military formation from around the sides of the compound, descending upon the family with violent intent.

"The last storyteller of Andwànikàdjigan stands before you!" A'tugwewinu screamed. "Watch as we bring an end to the Madjideye!"

Nearby, Yun-seo gasped. "Winu, don't do this!"

They rose slightly, but Shkitagen shot out his hands and grasped Yun-seo's wrists, slamming their palms back to the earth.

"You can't move! The portal has to close on its own!" Shkitagen's shouts were barely audible over the roar of the explosions in the distance as Enforcers stepped on the guys Riordan had buried in the ground, ready to be activated by pressure. It was chaos—bullets ricocheted off the metal plates protecting the two firekeepers on one side and the compound wall on the other. The portal's whispers rose in volume, sounding menacing now. Across from Shkitagen, Yun-seo wailed.

All around them, the Enforcers halted in their approach. Some heaved and swayed in place while others removed their helmets and seemed to stare at nothing. They foamed at the mouth, appearing every bit the mind-controlled drones they had been turned into.

Far back in the distance, Riordan peered at them, confused. Why had the assault stopped so suddenly? Was the portal working? Xe could only just make out xir siblings and was too far away to hear them.

A'tugwewinu looked at Bèl. The two began to speak at the same time.

"A'tugwewinu of the Andwànikàdjigan Anishinabeg offers her life in exchange for the balance of this world!"

"Bèl of the Guazabara Taino offers her life in exchange for the balance of this world!"

The earth shook at this pledge. Tendrils of smoke and spirit reached out from the portal, snaking and coiling around their limbs, enveloping both warrior and storyteller and pulling them through. It felt as though the air itself took a deep breath, then sighed.

Then the Enforcers moved in unison. Weapons raised and arms outstretched with gifts of fire in their palms, they retaliated with renewed vigour. Bullets struck the ground near where Riordan lay prone. Xir bewilderment at the Enforcers' strange behaviour forgotten, xe focused again on xir task to protect xir siblings at any cost.

Firing bullet after bullet and detonating xir guys all around, xe mowed down dozens of Enforcers in minutes. In the cacophony of artillery and explosions, xe didn't care whether the Enforcers were dead or wounded—xir job was to keep them away from the portal.

Xe glanced back once more, just in time to see A'tugwewinu and Bèl vanish through the portal. Something shattered inside Riordan's mind. Xe screamed. A white rage filled xir every pore. From around both sides of the compound, more Enforcers approached, guns raised, already firing at the inventor and the two firekeepers. An Elite Enforcer unit sprinted toward the portal, their hands aflame, some shooting bursts of light at the remaining three rebels. Riordan cried out, tears clouding xir vision. Xe felt only fury and vengeance with every bullet xe fired.

Shkitagen swore.

Yun-seo's chest was heaving from the physical toll of keeping the portal open. "What happened?" they asked.

Shkitagen shook his head. "Keep praying—we can't stop until the Madjideye go through."

"But what about Bèl and Winu?" Yun-seo shouted above the chaos. The portal groaned and creaked, the eerie, otherworldly sounds coming from it making Yun-seo's hair stand on end.

"You heard them," Shkitagen said, distraught. "This must have been their plan all along. They're not coming back."

"But I've seen miracles happen for less!" Yun-seo cried.

Shkitagen noticed the third's shirt was starting to singe as flames spread from their veins through their skin.

"The fire is consuming you!" he cried. "We have to keep the prayer going or we'll lose you too!"

With a cry, Yun-seo restarted the prayer. Shkitagen joined in. Both shouted as loudly as they could, empowering their words with their shock and fear.

■

A'tugwewinu squinted, shielding her eyes from the intense light surrounding them. From the physical plane of existence, the portal had seemed ominous—an eerie opaque liquid suspended in the air like a chasm in reality. Once they were pulled through, however, there was no sign of the tendrils and arms that had ensnared them, of the darkness. Only bright white light and emptiness in every direction. The light hurt; they had never experienced anything so luminous in their own world. Nonetheless, it was beautiful.

It was eerily silent. The lack of noise was startling, and the air was stagnant and thick.

"Have you ever heard any stories about this place?" Bèl asked. She gripped A'tugwewinu's hand even tighter. The two refused to let go of each other, afraid they would be separated.

"I've been told that death is different for everyone. But many people speak of a bright light toward the end. Was it like this for you?" A'tugwewinu asked.

Bèl shook her head. "It was darkness and whispers, and much more painful."

"Maybe you weren't really dead, then."

"So ... where do we go now?"

They looked around themselves, searching for what, they did not know, and finding only endless white light in every direction.

And then, before them, a figure appeared.

"Nokomis!" A'tugwewinu exclaimed when the spirit fully materialized.

A smile appeared on Nokomis's weathered face. He reached out and ruffled the short hair on A'tugwewinu's scalp.

"The warriors await us," he said.

A'tugwewinu and Bèl looked ahead, confused. There was a rumbling far off in the distance—the spirits were coming closer, as if riding the wind.

Warriors of old, the nij-manidowag, the balance bringers, appeared all around them. Giants with rippling muscles, covered in war paint, wearing breastplates made of bones and wielding gleaming spears, they approached. Hundreds of them materialized from every angle, emerging as if through fog. Some had long braided hair; others had ceremonial scars and tattoos that they'd earned through their many victories. The ayahkwewak were present—all first peoples to this continent, their glowing skin every shade a human's skin could be. They wore the regalia of hundreds of different nations and smiled eagerly at their imminent feast of flesh, blood, and bone.

A'tugwewinu looked down as armour made of bone and metal materialized over her body. Adorning the armour were beads of every colour, prayers for strength and bravery woven into each individual fibre of the armour. Beside her, Bèl glowed, her weapons taking on a spiritual essence; the treaties she had made with each of them shone as they wove around her skin, her limbs, and turned the warrior into the weapon she was always meant to be.

With feral grins, the two turned and faced the portal that had appeared behind them. Where before there was only light, now there was a clear window into the realm the lovers had just left behind. None of their family on the other side could see through to this world, but A'tugwewinu and Bèl could see them as clearly as if they were looking through glass. They watched as the Enforcers approached their family at a glacial pace. It seemed that time flowed differently between the realms.

Nokomis shouted a prayer, slapped his palms together, then slowly pulled his fingertips apart as if he were stretching twine between them. A small tornado appeared between his palms. It swirled and growled and grew larger and larger as it approached the portal.

■

Yun-seo had felt a tremor ripple through the air the instant Bèl and A'tugwewinu went through the portal—a heaviness and a sudden humid warmth. Perhaps the temperature change was due to the fire spreading to their forearms. They panted; they were dripping with sweat, doing everything they could to keep their focus trained on the portal. To keep it open at all costs.

They heard explosions in the distance and looked up to see streams of Enforcers attempting to infiltrate Riordan's circle. Yun-seo flinched as a bullet ricocheted off the plate in front of them. They shivered and shimmied closer to the compound's wall.

"Don't break focus!" Shkitagen yelled. Yun-seo noticed that the portal had shrunk slightly on their side. They breathed deeply and continued their prayer, speaking it loud enough for Shkitagen to hear. The second joined in.

Shkitagen's arms shook from the strain—the fire had spread to his torso and was burning away his shirt. He could tell that although Yun-seo was doing everything in their power to help maintain the portal, they were fading fast. *It's been too long already*, Shkitagen thought. He heard a grunt and a roar—two Enforcers had broken through Riordan's perimeter. Xe was engaging both with only xir fists, having run out of bullets.

Shkitagen watched in horror as the sixth was overtaken. Xe valiantly returned every hit xe got, but was losing nonetheless. Shkitagen turned back to Yun-seo—the third's eyes had rolled back in their head, and their shoulders were slumped forward.

"Yun-seo!" Yun-seo's head snapped back. They looked him in the eyes. "Hold on! Don't let the hellfire take you!" Shkitagen screamed, but it was too late—Yun-seo's deep-brown eyes were suddenly aflame. The fire had spread through their entire body and was consuming them from within.

Riordan let out a roar as xe snapped the neck of an Enforcer. Shkitagen watched a dozen more make their approach, firing at Riordan, who managed to quickly pull up xir shield in front of xir. One of xir arms hung limp at xir side.

We're finished, Shkitagen thought.

The portal shook, and a torrent of wind burst forth. It knocked Yun-seo and Shkitagen to their bellies, but their palms remained glued to the ground, never moving from the positions that maintained the portal. The wind tunnel spread out with a deafening howl, blowing away everything in its path. Moments later, it reversed.

"Hold on!" Shkitagen screamed futilely beneath the deafening wail.

A thousand screams fractured the air; squeals both terrifying and inhuman echoed from inside the compound's walls.

The compound wall disintegrated before Shkitagen—the concrete dissolved, turning to dust. Thousands of spirits in shapes that were equal parts grotesque and beautiful materialized in the sky above: the Madjideye's pale-grey spirits were elongated, their arms outstretched, their spindly, crooked fingers with nails like needles clasped in prayer. In their faces were row upon row of venomous teeth so bright they split the darkness. Their seductive smiles warped and twisted as their bones cracked and bent, contorting their spirits into inhuman shapes.

They sneered, as if even in their last moments, they believed all of humanity was beneath them. Mangled and split by the pull of the vortex, they were an army of ghosts bellowing, braying for mercy.

Shkitagen spat, watching as the Madjideye were pulled through the portal against their will. Then, as violently as it had emerged, the tornado retreated back into the portal with a loud *pop*, like an implosion. It launched Shkitagen back a dozen feet.

It took a few moments for him to come to his senses. His vision was blurry, and his ears were ringing. Eventually, the ringing cleared and was replaced by deafening silence.

He sat up and looked around in horror. Where the portal had been, there was now empty space. The fortress—a seemingly indestructible symbol of their oppression—had been reduced to ash at their feet. The field around them was empty, save the numerous bodies of the Enforcers Riordan had killed.

"Where are they?" Riordan screamed at the top of xir lungs. Xe wheeled over to where the portal had been, cradling xir wounded arm. Yun-seo stood up shakily and looked around, also searching. There was no sign of Bèl or A'tugwewinu.

"Let me go! Let me get 'em back!" Riordan collapsed to xir knees and started to sob. Xe pounded the earth with xir fists. "No, no, no!"

■

A'tugwewinu watched the portal close in front of her. The last thing she saw from the world outside, their world, was Riordan screaming, reaching for the shrinking opening while Shkitagen and Yun-seo held xir back. It was a painful sight. A'tugwewinu watched until the last possible second, until the portal shrank to the size of a tiny speck, then vanished completely.

All around them, warriors of old battled the pale-grey Madjideye, whose razor-sharp claws were outstretched, ready to attack. Venom dripped from their lips.

Bèl pulled A'tugwewinu forward. Weapons raised, hand in hand, they charged.

It could have taken years or mere minutes—time no longer existed for them—but eventually, the Madjideye were decimated. Only the nij-manidowag, the ayahkwewak, the in-betweens, the keepers of balance, remained, victorious.

Nokomis approached Bèl and A'tugwewinu. "Shall we go on, then?"

"Go where?" A'tugwewinu asked, surveying the field of battle. Any remaining Madjideye were being feasted upon by the droves of warriors.

"To the next place, where your families and all those who came before await your arrival."

A'tugwewinu and Bèl nodded in unison.

"Together," Bèl whispered.

"Together," A'tugwewinu whispered back.

CHAPTER XXXIV

TWELVE YEARS LATER

"Kwenàdjiwi! Have you seen your siblings?" Yun-seo called.

"Ojiwan is getting Animke ready by the school, and Nmama has Nibwàkà and Makwa," Kwenàdjiwi answered. Their hands shook slightly.

Yun-seo went over to them and helped fasten the buttons on the wrists of their ribbon shirt, which Shkitagen had lovingly sewn for their second-oldest child's rite of passage ceremony.

"What if it doesn't work?" Kwenàdjiwi asked.

Yun-seo sighed. "Then it doesn't work. But know that we won't love you any less. You'll still be our baby."

"Hey! I'm about to be grown," the seventh exclaimed.

"Yes, yes, let me enjoy your being my baby for just a few more hours," Yun-seo giggled.

Yun-seo returned to the family's main room just as Shkitagen was putting the last of the food on the table. Nitàwesì sat in a rocking chair Riordan had made for them, nursing the several-months-old

Makwa in their arms. The child had Yun-seo's eyes, Nitàwesì's curls, and Shkitagen's broad nose and strong chin. Nibwàkà played at their feet—their fourth day count was coming soon.

Yun-seo had dreamed of a home like this. After years of journeying, they had finally found this place up in the mountains, safe from both hunters and rising waters. Between the knowledge Yun-seo had gleaned from the Enforcers' books, Shkitagen's teachings from the elders, and Riordan's innate tech ability, the group had figured out how to build homes for themselves with materials they collected during their journey. It had taken months to ferry everything up and down the mountain, but now they had homes for even the new families who joined them. Some were Anishinabeg, and others were from different nations. Most carried gifts. Together, they were rebuilding their world, sharing stories, and healing.

"Isn't Riordan supposed to be here by now?" Shkitagen asked.

Yun-seo shrugged. "Xe's probably at one of xir orphanages."

The inventor was often away, travelling between Zhōng yang and a few other dilapidated cities in xir reformatted Enforcer vehicle. Xe kept busy building orphanages, assembling groups of children, and creating new families.

Ojiwan walked in holding Animke's hand. "We saw Auntiuncle Riri's car driving up the road," he stated nonchalantly. The second's voice had deepened, and his hands were covered in ash and various medicines. He reached over and brushed his thumb over a small scratch on Animke's cheek with a whispered prayer. The scar disappeared.

"Kwenà!" Shkitagen called. "Are you ready?"

The seventh entered shyly. Their hair was braided, and the ribbons on their regalia gleamed in the dim light.

"You look perfect," Nitàwesì signed to the first child to have come from their body. The healer was filled with pride at the sight of their second-oldest child now ready for their coming-of-age ceremony. It brought tears to their eyes.

"First we feast to celebrate and honour you," Nitàwesì signed. "Today you join the community, no longer a child, but recognized as an adult."

Riordan arrived at last and immediately started regaling the children with tales of xir adventures, the latest news from the cities, and how xir newest children were doing.

Once everyone had eaten their fill, the moment arrived.

Everyone sat in the main room, Yun-seo and Shkitagen holding the younger children. Riordan handed Animke some new tech—a disk with knobs that could keep track of measurements—and watched gleefully as the fifth marvelled at the gadget.

Nitàwesì cleared their throat. Everyone focused their attention on the healer.

"When Ah-ki' was young, she had a family: Tibik-kizis was her grandmother, and Kizis was her grandfather. The Creator of this family was Kichi Manido, who placed the four directions on Ah-ki', and each direction was sacred. Then Kichi Manido filled Ah-ki' with water and sent the singers and the flyers to Ah-ki' to fill the sky, then the swimmers to fill the water, and it was a beautiful place ..."

Nitàwesì told the story in detail—to this day, they remembered every word they had memorized over a decade ago, after first hearing it from their cousin. They embellished here and there, their fingers twisting and dotting the air in front of them. The other members of their family sat and watched, enraptured.

Nitàwesì finished with a flourish of their hands. Everyone waited.

"Look!" Kwenàdjiwi exclaimed. The seventh pulled down their ribbon shirt to reveal small scratches appearing on their skin, right above their heart.

The dwelling erupted with cheers. The marked ones had been reborn.

Tears formed in Riordan's eyes. *If only ya could see yer legacy passed on, Winu.* Xir happiness was bittersweet.

"What's that?" Kwenàdjiwi asked, nodding at the open front door.

In the entryway hovered two blue figures—the spirits gradually took shape, until finally their identities became clear. Before their assembled family stood the lover matriarchs who had sacrificed their lives to liberate the world. The spirit of A'tugwewinu smiled at Kwenàdjiwi, the new storyteller. Clutching her lover's hand, Bèl saluted her family.

Standing among xir astonished family, Riordan was speechless, paralyzed by the onslaught of emotions inside xir. For years xe had been dreaming about xir siblings, reliving on a loop the moments they had shared together, as if it was the only way to keep their memory alive. Now, here they stood before xir—it was too much. Riordan let out a sob in a rush of relief. No one was truly ever gone, and here was the proof.

Then, just as easily as they had appeared, the two matriarchs dissipated, returning to their realm.

Shkitagen stood up and went to his child. "Remember, Kwenà, the spirits will always be there for you. Your ancestors will guide you."

"Those were my ancestors?" the new storyteller asked.

"Yes, but not just any. Those were your direct family line. One day, Auntiuncle Riordan will tell you stories of the fierce warrior and the last storyteller, who fell in love with one another and freed our world from the Madjideye."

"And I will carry marks from that story?" Kwenàdjiwi asked.

"From now on, every story you're told with intent, you will carry," Yun-seo stated.

Suddenly, the toddler in Yun-seo's arms started shouting, motioning to the door.

The family walked outside together with a renewed sense of hope. Riordan held on to Shkitagen for support. The second wrapped his arm around the inventor, gently rubbing xir arm to soothe xir warring emotions.

Shkitagen smiled reassuringly to his lovers, a gesture that they returned. The group of them, their growing family, stood outside, in front of their home, feeling content—with their family, their village, and the beauty of a world without the Madjideye.

Above them, the haze of pollution slowly parted, allowing a single ray of sunshine to peek through. It illuminated the earth and the village with light that had not been seen in generations.

Gizhitaa mi

The End

LEXICON

ALGONQUIN/ANISHINABEMOWIN WORDS

Ahkigowin aki / Ah-ki' *(ah-key)*: Grandmother of the earth or Mother Earth

amisk *(ah-misk)*: beaver

andwànikàdjigan *(uhn-dwah-nih-kah-djih-guhn)*: to record; to set down in writing or the like for the purpose of preserving evidence

animke *(ah-ni-mi-kee)*: lightning

Ànìn ejinikàzoyan? *(ah-neen eh-jee-nee-kah-zoh-yan)*: What's your name?

eh-heh / enh: yes; agreed; okay

enàbigis *(en-ah-bah-gis)*: please

gizhitaa mi *(gih-jee-tah mee)*: we are done

ishkode *(ish-koh-day)*: fire

Kichi Manido *(key-chii man-ii-doh)*: Great Spirit / Creator

Kichi Manido nòndam wiin ayamìye *(Kee-jay man-ee-doe non-dam ween ah-yah-mee-yay)*: Creator, hear our prayers

Kìjìgong Ikwe *(key-shee-gong eh-kway)*: In-the-Sky Woman

kizis *(gee-zus)*: sun

kwenàdjiwi *(kwe-nah-je-wi)*: beautiful

kwey *(k-way)*: hello

Madjideye *(ma-jeh-day)*: evil-natured

màgòdiz *(mah-goh-dihz)*: a rebel; a person who refuses allegiance to, resists, or rises in arms against the government or ruler of their country

makwa *(mah-kwah)*: bear

mashkiki *(mash-key-key)*: medicine

miigwech / chi miigwech or kichi miigwech *(mee-gwetch)*: thank you / thanks a lot

mi-iw *(meh-ew)*: okay

mikinàk *(mik-kin-nahk)*: turtle

nibwàkà *(nih-bwah-kah)*: virtuous: conforming to moral and ethical principles; morally excellent; upright; to lead a virtuous life

nìdòkàzowin *(nee-doe-kah-zoh-win)*: help me

nidonjabà *(nee-don-ja-bah)*: I am from

nikineshkà *(nih-kih-naysh-kah)*: nightmare

nitàwesì *(nit-ah-weh-see)*: being mute

nokomis/kokomis *(no-kuh-miss)*: my grandmother / your grand-mother

odey *(oh-day)*: heart

ojiwan *(oh-she-wan)*: fishtail or snowshoe

oshis *(oh-shis)*: grandchild

pasakamate *(pa-sa-ka-ma-teh)*: fire goes underground

pejik *(peh-jik)*: one

shkitagen *(sha-kih-tah-gun)*: chaga, a type of mushroom that grows on birch trees in the north

tibik-kizis *(tih-bihk gee-zus)*: moon

wajashk *(wuh-zhuh-shk)*: muskrat

PLAINS CREE WORDS

ayahkwew *(ah-ya-kwey)*, plural **ayahkwewak** *(ah-yah-kwey-wuk)*: two-spirit, gender-fluid person; someone who is at the service of their community

MI'KMAQ/L'NU WORDS

A'tugwewinu *(ah-duh-gwey-wee-nu)*: storyteller

TAINO WORDS

ita' *(ee-tah)*: don't know

akani *(ah-kah-ni)*: enemy

aracoel *(are-ah-coh-el)*: grandmother

Atabey *(ah-tah-bay)*: Mother Earth

guaili *(gwa-ee-lee)*: boy or small infant child

guatu *(gwa-too)*: fire

guazabara *(gwa-zah-bara)*: war or warrior

nanichi *(nan-ee-chi)*: my heart or my love

naguakio *(nah-gwa-ki-o)*: transgender woman / transfeminine
person; literal translation is "life-bearer spirit" and "bird beak"

OTHER WORDS

Bèl, from "belle" *(bell)*: beautiful (French)

Cassiopeia *(kas-ee-uh-pee-ah)*: a constellation named after a
mythological figure (Greek)

Mohammed *(moe-ham-med)*: worthy of praise (Arabic)

Riordan *(ree-ore-dun)*: royal poet (Irish)

Sachit *(sah-chit)*: wise consciousness (Hindi)

Yun-seo *(yoon-su)*: "soft, sleek" and "felicitous omen, auspicious"
(literal translation, Sino-Korean)

Zhōng yang *(jong-yang)*: centre, the middle (Chinese)

KICHI MIIGWECH
KAKINA KINAGEGO

ACKNOWLEDGMENTS

I started writing this story in bits and pieces, with the guidance of many two-spirit elders, knowledge keepers, and ceremony carriers— Sharp Dopler, Theo Paradis, Blu Waters, Beverly Littlethunder, Jack Saddleback, Richard Jenkins, Ed Lavallee, Ma Nee Chacaby, Charlotte Nolin, Majorie Beaucage, Leigh Thomas, Barbara Bruce, Alex Wilson, Albert McLeod, and Myra Laramee—as well as Indigenous elders who carry stories and teachings about two spirit—Jo-Ann Saddleback, Leonard Saddleback, and Jerry Saddleback. I sincerely want to say kichi miigwech, the highest form of gratitude, to all those named above and those not named, who came before to empower me as a two-spirit person and also so I could incorporate two spirit into writing and help empower others in their journeys. As two spirit and as a storyteller, I began to weave two-spirit roles and responsibilities into a postapocalyptic novel, utilizing the sci-fi subgenre with the understanding that, for the Indigenous peoples of Turtle Island, our apocalypse happened hundreds of years ago, when our carefully curated way of life that resided in balance and treaty making with all our relatives, human and non-human, was so devastatingly disrupted.

This novel is my love letter to all two-spirit, gender-diverse, transgender, nonbinary, queer, disAbled, neurodivergent, Black, Brown, Indigenous, mixed-race folks and People of Colour who have been ignored, who have been silenced, who have never seen themselves in the solutions, who have been secondary characters or expendable characters. We are the future, we are the balance bringers, we are the

in-betweens, and without us, this world will never know peace, healing, or harmony. After all, liberation is a true, unconditional love for
the people, and this book, although fiction (to some), is my manifesto.
I give you my dreams, that they may be utilized on our path toward
liberation. I give you my dreams because I have hope for our collective
future and that of the next seven generations.

I wish to thank my life's love, my wedded spouse, my greatest
companion, Pilar Roqueni Calderón, for the inspiration to follow my
calling as storyteller and weaver of words, and for all the encourage-
ments and edits. Without you, this novel would not be a reality. Kichi
miigwech nichimoos.

I also want to thank my family: Boyd Whiskeyjack, Quetzala Carson,
Jazzmin Foster, Peter Quedent, Jeremie Castilloux, Armando Garcia,
Tiffany Dumont, Morgan Commanda, Nam-Thu Tran, Abuela Beatriz
Villegas, and Mayahuel Aranda. You have given me life and love in a
world that is so painful.

To the folks in my peer review council, who ensured that the
characters who reflect identities which I do not carry are adequately
represented: Young So, Shay Lewis, Alyssa Demers, and Cleopatra
Tatabele. Chi miigwech for the labour of ensuring that this book hon-
ours your identities and communities.

To my Anishinabemowin and Nehiyawmowin language editors,
Darlene Auger and Kokum Makwa, chi miigwech for ensuring the
authenticity of the language in this novel.

To the Edmonton Arts Council, for giving me a grant that ensured
all peer reviewers and language editors received adequate pay for their
services and that empowered me to write this book in a good way.

To the epic crew of *Love After the End* (for which I wrote the short
story "Andwànikàdjigan," which comprises the first three chapters
of A'tugwewinu and Bèl's story), especially Joshua Whitehead, chi

miigwech for answering all my questions and nurturing my entry into the novel-writing world. I could not have asked for a better two-spirit and Indigiqueer literary family.

To the team at Arsenal Pulp Press, Brian, Jazmin, and Catharine: for a few years, I was afraid that no one would ever publish this book, that perhaps it was too radical, but you never hesitated and welcomed me into the publishing world with open arms, and for that I thank you all.

To my editor, Andrew Wilmot, who took my manuscript and went through every twist and bend of my overactive verbiage and finessed the words of Màgòdiz so that this story could soar: I have so much gratitude.

To Moe Butterfly, you took my characters and infused them with spirit. You are a true visionary, and I cannot thank you enough for the incredible work you have done with the cover art of this novel. Chi miigwech.

To all the incredible gender-diverse, queer, and Indigenous writers, storytellers, and authors who have supported my writing over the years: Matthew Stepanic, Waubegeshig Rice, the Three Hares Collective, the Banff Centre for Arts and Creativity, and everyone at the Write Over Here Residency. Chi miigwech for your continued encouragement and guidance.

Finally, to all those who came before us, all the two-spirit, queer, gender-diverse ancestors and trancestors who paved the way, who sacrificed their lives, comfort, and stability to ensure a better future for those of us alive today, and to all the land defenders, water protectors, social justice activists, and warriors who today are fighting for liberation, for a better tomorrow, I say kichi miigwech.

Photo credit: Cole Richards

Gabe Calderón (they/them) is a two spirit, trans nonbinary, and queer white settler with Indigenous ancestry. They originate from Omawinini Anishinabeg aki (Ottawa) and currently thrive in Treaty 6-Amiskwacîwâskahikan (Edmonton). Gabe shared the Lambda Literary Award for LGBTQ+ Anthologies in 2021 as a contributor to the Indigiqueer anthology *Love After the End*. *Màgòdiz* is their first novel.